The Author

D0250844

MARGARET LAURENCE was born in Neepawa, Mani-
toba, in 1926. Upon graduation from Winnipeg's United
College in 1947, she took a job as a reporter for the *Winnipeg Citizen*.

From 1950 until 1957 Laurence lived in Africa, the first
two years in Somalia, the next five in Ghana, where her
husband, a civil engineer, was working. She translated
Somali poetry and prose during this time, and began her
career as a fiction writer with stories set in Africa.

When Laurence returned to Canada in 1957, she settled
in Vancouver, where she devoted herself to fiction with a
Ghanaian setting: in her first novel, *This Side Jordan*, and
in her first collection of short fiction, *The Tomorrow-
Tamer*. Her two years in Somalia were the subject of her
memoir, *The Prophet's Camel Bell*.

Separating from her husband in 1962, Laurence moved
to England, which became her home for a decade, the
time she devoted to the creation of five books about the
fictional town of Manawaka, patterned after her birth-
place, and its people: *The Stone Angel*, *A Jest of God*,
The Fire-Dwellers, *A Bird in the House*, and *The Diviners*.

Laurence settled in Lakefield, Ontario, in 1974. She
complemented her fiction with essays, book reviews, and
four children's books. Her many honours include two
Governor General's Awards for Fiction and more than a
dozen honorary degrees.

Margaret Laurence died in Lakefield, Ontario, in 1987.

MARGARET LAURENCE

The Prophet's Camel Bell

With an Afterword by Clara Thomas

M&S

This book was first published in 1963 by McClelland & Stewart.
New Canadian Library edition 1988

National Library of Canada Cataloguing in Publication

Laurence, Margaret, 1926–1987
The Prophet's camel bell

(New Canadian library)
ISBN 0-7710-4706-1

1. Somalis. 2. Somalia – Description and travel.
3. Djibouti – Description and travel. I. Title.
II. Series.

DT406.L38 1988   916.7'7   C88-094195-2

We acknowledge the financial support of the Government of Canada
through the Book Publishing Industry Development Program and that of
the Government of Ontario through the Ontario Media Development
Corporation's Ontario Book Initiative. We further acknowledge the
support of the Canada Council for the Arts and the Ontario Arts Council
for our publishing program.

Photographs by C.J. Martin and by the author
Map by William Bromage

Printed and bound in Canada

McClelland & Stewart Ltd.
The Canadian Publishers
481 University Avenue
Toronto, Ontario
M5G2E9
www.mcclelland.com/NCL

4   5   6   7   8   07   06   05   04   03

For Jack
who shares these memories

God be thy guide from camp to camp,
God be thy shade from well to well.
God grant beneath the desert stars
Thou hearest the Prophet's camel bell.

JAMES ELROY FLECKER
'The Gates of Damascus'

Contents

This map was specially drawn to show the area of the Haud in Somaliland where Margaret Laurence and her husband lived and which she describes in this book.

CHAPTER ONE

Innocent Voyage

MAY THEY not just possibly be true, the tales of creatures as splendidly strange as minotaurs or mermaids? Will there be elephants old as forests, white peacocks with crests of azure, jewel-eyed birds as gaudy as the painted birds in the tombs of pharaohs, apes like jesters, great cats dark and secretive as Bast, men who change into leopards at the flick of a claw?

Nothing can equal in hope and apprehension the first voyage east of Suez, yourself eager for all manner of oddities, pretending to disbelieve in marvels lest you appear naïve but anticipating them just the same, prepared for anything, prepared for nothing, burdened with baggage – most of it useless, unburdened by knowledge, assuming all will go well because it is you and not someone else going to the far place (harm comes only to others), bland as eggplant and as innocent of the hard earth as a fledgling sparrow.

There you go, rejoicing, as so you should, for anything might happen and you are carrying with you your notebook and camera so you may catch vast and elusive life in a word and a snapshot. There you go, anxious, as you may well be, for anything might happen and so you furtively reassure yourself with pages from the first-aid book in which it says the best thing to do for snakebite is to keep the patient quiet until the doctor arrives – luckily, you do not notice that it does not tell you what to do if there is no doctor within a hundred miles.

And in your excitement at the trip, the last thing in the world that would occur to you is that the strangest glimpses you may have of any creature in the distant lands will be those you catch of yourself.

Our voyage began some years ago. When can a voyage be said to have ended? When you reach the place you were bound for, presumably. But sometimes your destination turns out to be quite other than you expected.

We could not have found a better-named ship than the *Tigre* to carry us away from a sleet-sodden English December and into the warm waters of the Mediterranean and the Red Sea. She was a Norwegian passenger-cargo vessel, and we had crossed the bilious channel and were waiting for her at Rotterdam. She was delayed, and we, almost penniless, walked the slippery streets of the chilly port, turning up our coat collars against the blowing snow and searching near the docks for a sailors' café where we could afford to eat. We found it in *Die Drie Steden*, but we also found that English was spoken only in the more expensive restaurants, and we did not have a word of Dutch. Fortunately, *wiener schnitzel*, that fine old Netherlands dish, was listed on the menu, but we had no luck with dessert. Finally, the impatient waitress beckoned us to the front of the café, past rows of weathered old pipe-sucking mariners who peered and chortled, and we were faced with a glassed-in cabinet containing a selection of pastries.

"Go ahead," Jack said. "Pick one."

"*Slagroomwafel,*" the waitress said, as I pointed blindly.

It was a waffle with whipped cream. For seven days, out of pure necessity, we ate nothing but *wiener schnitzel* and *slagroomwafel*.

We had plenty of time, during that week of waiting, to wonder where we were going, and why, and what it would be like when we got there. An advertisement in a London newspaper had started the venture.

'H.M. Colonial Service. Somaliland Protectorate. A vacancy has occurred for a civil engineer to take charge, under the direction of the Director of Public Works, of the construction of approximately 30 earth dams over an area of 6,500 miles. The average maximum capacity of each dam will be 10 million gallons. The Engineer will be required to carry out all reconnaissance and detailed survey, to do all calculations and designs, to be responsible for expenditure and the supervision of staff and plant . . .'

Jack applied for the job and got it. It was no sudden whim on his part. As an engineer, he had felt a certain lack in any job he had in Canada or in England. We lived in an increasingly organized world, a world in which the most essential roads and bridges had already been built. He felt a need to work for once on a job that plainly needed doing – not a paved road to replace a gravel one, but a road where none had been before, a job whose value could not be questioned, a job in which the results of an individual's work could be clearly perceived, as they rarely could in Europe or America. It may have been a desire to simplify, to return to the pioneer's uncomplicated struggle. Or it may have been the feeling, strong in all our generation, that life was very short and uncertain, and a man had better do what he could, while he could. Perhaps these feelings were good and sufficient reasons for going to Africa; perhaps they were not. But they could not be shrugged off or ignored indefinitely.

After Jack signed the contract, the Colonial Office informed us regretfully that no accommodation for married couples seemed to be available in Somaliland at the moment, but perhaps Mr. Laurence's wife would be able to join him in six or eight months. This arrangement did not suit us at all, so Jack explained carefully that his wife, being a hardy Canadian girl, was quite accustomed to life in a tent. In fact, I had never camped out in my life, but fortunately the Colonial Office was convinced by the striking description Jack gave of me as an accomplished woodswoman, a kind of female Daniel Boone, and I was permitted to go.

We had to consult an atlas to discover exactly where we were going. This ignorance was not unusual, we later found. Once we saw a gloomy note in the Protectorate News Sheet commenting on the delays in mail owing to letters having been mis-sorted by the Post Office in England, and explaining that "this arises, no doubt, from the fact that very few people outside this country seem to know where it is."

What do you take to such an out-of-the-way place, when you have no idea what life will be like there? Tents or topees, evening dress or bush boots, quinine or codeine, candles or sandals? The Colonial Office provided us with a pamphlet designed to set at rest the minds of persons like ourselves. It was firm and clear in its advice. We must take a year's supply of tinned goods and a portable bath. Fortunately, we were also given the name and address of an administrative officer from Somaliland who was on leave in London. He roared with laughter.

"Pay no attention," he told us. "Those pamphlets are always half a century out of date."

The booklet also warned us against "woolly bears," a ferocious cloth-eating insect. In Somaliland we never once encountered a woolly bear, nor did we ever meet anyone who had heard of them. What a wily pamphleteer, focusing our attention on mythical beasts – had he warned us of the actual difficulties, we might never have gone and so would have been the poorer all our lives.

Even the history we ferreted out from libraries had a limited meaning for us, despite its power to stir the imagination with past glory or disgrace, the tramplings of time over one corner of the earth. We were going to the same country where Sir Richard Burton had gone so long before, when he believed his footsteps were the first that really counted for anything in East Africa and when, disguised as the merchant Haji Abdullah, he preached in his superior Arabic at the Zeilah mosque, and was commended by the local elders, none of whom knew the Qoran as well as he.

But he had come late in the roster of explorers. That desert land was known to the ancient world as Regio Cinnamomifera, when ships from the Far East went there with cinnamon which they exchanged for frankincense and myrrh, greatly valued in those days and sometimes purchased by well-to-do Magi to bestow as gifts. There the forty saints from the Jadramaut landed, proclaiming the Word – *There is no God but God, and Mohamed is His Prophet*. It was a land of warriors, too, brave cruel men like Mohamed Granye, the Left-handed, the Somali king who in the sixteenth century very nearly conquered all of Ethiopia, until at last he fell to the intruding Portuguese, indomitably armoured, who had come to rescue the Coptic Christian emperor in the belief that he was the fabled Prester John, white knight in the black continent, and who were most perturbed when they discovered he was not.

For many men and women, princes and commoners from the distant forests and from the river lands as far away as the Niger, Somaliland was the end of a bitter journey and the beginning of a lifetime of bondage, for there the Arab slave routes had emerged at the sea, and from there the dhow-loads of slaves had once been shipped across the Gulf of Aden to be sold in the flesh markets of Arabia. In that same land, early this century, Mohamed Abdullah Hassan, the so-called Mad Mullah of Somaliland, had fought the British for years and was defeated only when at last his forts were bombed.

We read of these events, and pondered them. But they could not tell us what we would find there now.

At last the *Tigre* steamed into Rotterdam. About time, too. We were disgruntled and irritable after a week of having been snubbed by hotel clerks who had rapidly discovered our penury. We tramped on board dully, expecting nothing. To our amazement, we found we were the only passengers, and there, spread out before us, was our accommodation – the owner's suite, an unbelievably spacious three rooms, full of polished brass and green plush and shiny mahogany, and best of all, paid for by the Crown Agents. When we had recovered from the initial shock, we set ourselves to adjust to our altered status.

"We mustn't act surprised," Jack said with a grin, as he sprawled luxuriously on the Edwardian velour sofa. "The idea is that we take it all completely for granted."

But I could not get over the wonder of it, especially the fact that we had our own bathroom. In our year in London, we had lived in a bed-sittingroom and shared a bathroom with so many others that the nightly bath schedule was like a railway timetable.

The *Tigre* was our home for a month, and we developed a high regard for Norwegians. As passengers, we must have been a nuisance to them, but they never resorted to mere cold politeness. They were warmly friendly, and gave us the run of the ship. We were invited up to the bridge, and allowed to peer through the Captain's binoculars. We chatted with Johan, the wireless operator, about modern American writers, feeling ashamed that we knew nothing of modern Norwegian writers. Hemingway was his favourite – there was a writer a man could understand.

At night sometimes we went up to the bridge and talked with the second mate while he was on watch. He was a burly, laughing man, who had sailed in the West Indies a great deal. Once he did not see his wife for ten years, he told us. In Montreal, on one occasion, he and a companion smuggled two girls aboard. The men had adjoining cabins, and suddenly through the wall had come an enquiring voice.

"Marie, are you doing any wrong in there?"

"No, Germaine," was the virtuous reply, "I'm not."

"Well, then," called Germaine, "pray forgiveness for me."

These French-Canadian girls, the second mate said. His laughter went booming out over the dark sea.

We were on the *Tigre* for Christmas. The Norwegians celebrated mainly on Christmas Eve, when there was a mammoth dinner and gifts all around. Jack was given a bottle of Scotch, while I received a little marzipan pig with a verse attached to it.

To our little sporty guest,
A happy sailors' julefest!

That evening we sang carols in Norwegian, with the aid of *aqua vite* and songbooks, although the only word Jack and I could understand was "halleluja." Johan, who had discovered that Jack's people came from the Shetland Islands, originally settled by Norsemen, leaped to his feet and proposed a toast.

"To our ancestors and yours – THE VIKINGS!"

"*Skol!*" shouted everyone. It was a fine Christmas.

At Genoa the ship stopped for several days, and we walked on the hills and saw the harsh port town softened by distance, the pink and yellow walls looking clean and pastel although in fact they were dirty and garish, the harbour with the big rusty freighters packed in prow to stern, and the tugboats skimming around like frantic water-beetles. At the Staglieno cemetery, where marble angels loomed like spirits of vengeance among the green-black cypress trees and where the poor rented graves for seven years, we met two Englishmen who said they wondered if they had not been foolish after all to visit sunny Italy in mid-winter. The day was piercingly cold and we were needled by a sharp unceasing wind. We walked along with them to find a place where we could get shelter and a warm drink. The Englishmen had surely read somewhere how the English are expected to behave in foreign lands, for they were loyally true. They ordered tea.

"But first –" one of them said anxiously to the proprietor, "tell me, please – can you really make it properly?"

The Mediterranean, that time of year, was truly the wine-dark sea. High up on the *Tigre*, whipped by the icy winds, we watched the wild hills of Sicily pass by. At night we saw a far-off red glow in the black sky, Mount Etna in eruption. And sometimes in the darkness we saw a phosphorescence, plankton perhaps, frothing up suddenly in the waves and seeming to run along the surface of the water like sheet lightning. I wrote in my notebook – "for the first time, I can believe we are in southern waters."

Port Said, and my first view of the mysterious East was a Coca-Cola sign in Arabic. But the dhows were there, too, with their curved prows and triangular sails, shabby little fishing dhows with the nets slung to dry between the masts, and big trading dhows from the ports of the Red Sea and as far away as the Persian Gulf, coming here with their cargoes of dates and millet or marvellously patterned carpets woven in Basra or Sheraz, perhaps, by weavers who learned their craft as children and were said to go blind young over their looms.

We went ashore and walked the crowded and intricate streets where stained mud buildings stood side by side with slick stuccoed apartment blocks in florid pinks and greens. Rows of ragged palms fringed the roads where horse-drawn carriages unbelievably rattled along like old engravings come to life. And the people – merchants waddling slow and easy in long striped robes and maroon fezzes, nimble limping beggars who trailed the tourists, girl children with precociously knowing eyes, self-styled guides who hovered around us like the city's flies, wizened and hunched labourers wearing only a twist of rag around skinny hips, boys in flapping cotton pyjamas, business men in draped suits and shiny tan shoes, police in sand-coloured breaches and black jack-boots, thin stooped Egyptian women all in black and wearing the thick veil of *purdah*, westernized Egyptian girls with long black hair and short white skirts and high rhinestoned heels, the conjuring gully-gully men who would clench an empty fist and then open it and presto – there was a live chick.

Bustling up to us came a plump and jazzy character, gabardine-suited, looking like a smaller edition of King Farouk in sunglasses and Panama hat. Port Said was a city of thieves, he informed us. He personally would see to it that we were protected from these undesirables. He called himself Billy the Kid, and told us he could get us anything we wanted for a reasonable price – binoculars, cameras, watches. We thanked him, but declined. He pattered along beside us for a while, and finally departed for greener pastures, singing "Rum And Coca-Cola." We heard, echoing back to us, a voice jaunty as a sparrow.

"Working for the Yankee dollah!"

In the course of the afternoon, we shed many of his kind. We were a little pleased with ourselves. To avoid the clutches of the sharks and sharpers – that is not such an easy thing. We wandered through bazaars hung with cotton carpets horribly embellished with scarlet pyramids, blue camels, tigers yellow as egg-yolk. We looked at crocodile handbags, some plainly imitation and some possibly genuine, and all manner of cheap jewellery and souvenirs. Then, in a back-street shop apparently unvisited by tourists, we saw inlaid cigarette boxes. The inlay was ivory, the man told us. We were not deceived. We knew it was not ivory but bone. We liked the patterns, however, so we dickered over price and finally bought. We carried that cigarette box around with us for years, and ultimately in its old age it became a crayon box for our children. When it was left outside in the rain, not long ago, a small illusion was shattered. The inlay was not even bone – it was lacquered paper.

Who would ever suspect that the air would be so cold going through the Suez Canal? We put on all the sweaters we owned, wrapped ourselves in coats, and from the *Tigre* decks we watched the nearby shore where camels were squashing stoically through the beige sand. The water was a deep blue, so strong a colour it looked as though it had been dyed, and the sky, filled with particles of dust, was an astonishing violet. Villages of square clay houses slipped past us, and tattered children, and black cattle, and women in *purdah*.

The bleak stretches of the Sinai desert, then, and the distant peak of Mount Sinai where Moses received the stone tablets of the Law. And I recalled what I had chanced to read only a short time before.

Jack had foresightedly brought *War and Peace*, and in Rotterdam he had settled down to read it. But I had gone ill-provided with reading material and had paced the hotel room until I discovered in a dressing-table drawer the ubiquitous Gideons Bible and read for the first time in my life the five books of Moses. Of all the books which I might have chosen to read just then, few would have been more to the point, for the Children of Israel were people of the desert, as the Somalis were, and fragments from those books were to return to me again and again. *And there was no water for the people to*

drink – and the people thirsted. Or, when we were to wonder
how the tribesmen could possibly live and maintain hope
through the season of drought – *In the wilderness, where
thou hast seen how that the Lord thy God bare thee, as a man
doth bear his son, in all the way that ye went*. Or the verse
that remained with me most of all, when at last and for the
first time I was myself a stranger in a strange land, and was
sometimes given hostile words and was also given, once, food
and shelter in a time of actual need, by tribesmen who had
little enough for themselves – *Thou shalt not oppress a
stranger, for ye know the heart of a stranger, seeing ye were
strangers in the land of Egypt*.

Aden at night. The shore lights seemed frail and wavering in
the black vastness of sky and water. This was the parting of
the ways, for here we would leave the familiar, the clean and
well-ventilated world of the *Tigre*, and move into something
entirely different. From now on, we were committed to a land
and a life about which we knew nothing.

We leaned over the railing and watched as our crates of
books and dishes, our trunks of clothing, were carried off the
Tigre and onto the small launch wobbling in the water below.
Everything was carried on the heads or the backs of coolies.
One very tall labourer, clad only in a loincloth, bent himself
and braced his broad bare feet while the others heaved onto
his back our largest trunk. His legs were so thin and reed-
like, his sweating and trembling body so emaciated, that he
looked as though he must buckle and break under the load.
No one seemed concerned. The only anxiety was that the
trunk might slip off and plunge into the harbour. Goods were
more expensive than men, here. There were millions like him,
in every city throughout the East, men with names and meanings, but working namelessly and with no more meaning than
any other beast of burden. It occurred to me that Markham's
lines were more applicable here now than in Europe.

> *How will it be with kingdoms and with kings –*
> *With those who shaped him to the thing he is –*

> *When this dumb terror shall rise to judge the world,*
> *After the silence of the centuries?*

The *Velho*, which had been chugging from Aden to Berbera and back again for more years than anyone knew, was a ship inhabited by ghosts. The presence of Englishmen long dead clung around the saloon, where the bolted-down tables were once glossily veneered but were now chipped, their surfaces ringed with the wet glasses of innumerable greetings and partings. Behind the bar, a gilt and curlicewed mirror reflected leadenly the bottles of gin, orange squash, Rose's lime juice. The air reeked heavily of tobacco smoke, curried soup, foul dishwater. The brass bar-rail was worn with decades of boots, men leaning there lazily, joyously, on their way to Aden and then home on leave, or heavily, tensely, on their way back to Somaliland again. In some cases, it would have been the other way around, men who went on leave only because it was compulsory, men who could hardly wait to leave London behind and get back to an exile that had become beloved. They were all there that evening, as we sipped our gin-and-lime and reflected on the place and those who had passed this way before us.

A firm of Bombay merchants owned the *Velho*, which had room for nine first-class passengers, eight second class and an indefinitely large number of third. She was the flagship of the fleet, our fellow passengers informed us. Her sister ship, the *Africa*, was not so grand. We found our first-class cabin something of a contrast to our suite on the *Tigre*. The room was approximately the size of a matchbox, and the Indian clerk who had accompanied us on board had advised us to cram as much of our baggage as possible into the cabin with us.

"Otherwise, sar, you might enquire after it next morning quite in vain, oh my goodness yes."

The mattresses on the narrow, rough-plank bunks were straw, and of an indescribable skimpiness. The grey hue of the sheets suggested that they had been used for the last dozen voyages or so. I had an unpleasant suspicion that we were not the only living creatures in this cabin. I would have preferred to encounter the bar-room ghosts in any visible form rather than the host of winged and many-legged things which my imagination assured me were ready to attack from every crack in the timbering, every straw in my palliasse. The rustlings and faint scratchings went on all night, and I remained stiff as bronze, open-eyed.

Jack, with his usual calm logic, decided that nothing constructive could be done about the cabin, so he crawled into his bunk and went to sleep immediately. As a result, the next morning he felt fine, ready for anything, while I felt queasy and jangled.

"In this part of the world," he said, recalling the years he had spent in India during the war, "you have to learn that if you can't change something, you might as well not worry about it."

He was right, but it was many months before the time came when I could curl up on the seat of the Land-Rover and quietly conserve myself in sleep, when the road had somehow got lost in the desert and we had no idea where we were. That night on the Gulf of Aden I could not have conceived of a time when the bunks of the *Velho* would have seemed like the silken beds of a sultan's palace.

The vessel's mate had a lean intense face and a flaming beard. His eyes must surely have been penetrating, but they were always concealed behind sunglasses. He stalked silently around the boat not exchanging a word with anyone. Maybe he communicated with the captain, but we never observed them speaking together. The captain was an elderly Scot who had worked in the East for many years. He was dressed meticulously, a contrast to his grubby craft. What had brought him here, to skipper this pint-sized wreck from Aden to Berbera and back to Aden, eternally, under the blazing sun? We would never know. When I talked with him, he spoke of only one thing – his last leave in Scotland. I imagined he must have returned from there only recently.

"Oh no," he replied, when I asked him. "That was seven years ago, lass."

The wireless operator was a young Egyptian, a Coptic Christian. He led a lonely life in Aden, for he belonged in neither the Christian nor the Muslim communities there. He was fond of jazz, and homesick for Cairo. When we were a short way off from Aden, he laughed ironically.

"I can hear them now," he said, "but they can't hear me."

His wireless set with its spark-gap transmitter was so antiquated that he could communicate only when the vessel was within a mile or so of shore. As soon as we decently could, without appearing too obvious about it, we went up to have a look at the lifeboats. There did not seem to be very many of them.

Among the Europeans on board were two Army sergeants, reluctantly returning from leave.

"This your first time out?" one of them said, gloomily gloating. "You'll hate it. Nothing there but a bloody great chunk of desert. It's got the highest European suicide rate of any colony – know that? Good few blokes living very solitary there in outstations, that's the reason. They go round the bend."

Another fellow passenger was a civilian, a member of the administration. He told us, confidentially, to watch out for the Public Works Department.

"It's really gone beyond a joke," he said sorrowfully, "the way those P.W.D. fellows look after their own people first. They corner all the best furniture and the most workable plumbing. Shocking."

When he learned that Jack would be associated with the P.W.D., his manner became slightly withdrawn for a time, but he later grew friendly once more and told us how much better the trip from Aden to Berbera was than the return voyage.

"Going back to Aden," he said, "the boat's full of camels. They ride with the Somalis, down on the third-class deck. They bawl and groan the whole time, and the stench is terrible."

The Somalis crowding the third-class section slept out on the decks that night. They were tall gaunt men, most of them, their features a cross between negroid and Arabian. They wore tunic-like robes called *lunghis*, knotted around their waists and reaching just below their knees. The cotton materials of their robes were of every shade and variety – splendid plaids, striped or plain, green and magenta and mauve. Around their heads were loosely constructed turbans, pink, white, blue. The few Somali women on board seemed a contrast to the brash, assertive men. They had soft features and enormous liquid brown eyes, and many of them had lighter skins than the men. The young unmarried women wore long robes of many colours, but the married ones were clad in black and red. All wore headscarves that billowed out behind them in the breeze. The women walked so shyly, so lightly, with downcast eyes, that I imagined they must be very meek and gentle creatures.

Beautiful a great many of them certainly were, and gentle they certainly could be when it pleased them. But meek – meek as Antigone, meek as Medea. I did not then know Safia, or Shugri and her mother, or proud Saqa, or the old woman of Balleh Gedid.

Berbera from the water looked beckoning. The sea was calm and turquoise, and the level shoreline was yellow sand. A few palms and pepper trees grew around the town, and the houses appeared pure white, their blemishes concealed by distance. The sharp thin minaret of a mosque rose above the squat dwellings. Beyond the town the blue-brown hills looked softer, less treacherous than they really were. Berbera had no harbour, so we anchored off shore and a government launch came out. Jack went ashore to discover what arrangements, if any, had been made for us, and I stayed on the *Velho* to guard our belongings. After a while Jack returned, accompanied by a Somali boy.

His name was Mohamed, and he looked about eighteen, a boy of unprepossessing appearance, clad in a purple robe and a clean white shirt, and sporting a small black moustache that looked incongruous on his youthful face. He was to be our houseboy. I felt, uneasily, that he had been hired too quickly. We didn't know the first thing about him. He might be the most cunning crook in Berbera, for all we knew.

"The P.W.D. foreman knows him," Jack reassured me, "and thinks he's probably okay. I've only taken him on trial. He'll do for the moment."

It still seemed absurd to me. I could not see why we needed anyone so soon. With dwindling patience, Jack tried to explain.

"This isn't Winnipeg or London. You don't tote your own luggage here. It just isn't done. Maybe we don't agree with the system, but there it is. Another thing – he'll be useful in the shops. If you buy anything by yourself, before you know what's what, you'll likely get cheated by the local merchants."

Mohamed's function in the situation, apparently, was to look after our interest, and that day he put on a wonderful display of enthusiasm, for he obviously was anxious to have the job. He carried suitcases, conveyed Jack's instructions to the Somali coolies, cautioned me as I climbed down into the waiting launch.

"Memsahib – must be you step carefully-carefully –"

The whole performance amused and distressed me. I could not face the prospect of being called "Memsahib," a word which seemed to have connotations of white man's burden, paternalism, everything I did not believe in. Furthermore, I was not sure I would be able to cope with servants. We had a series of "hired girls" when I was a child in a prairie town, but they could not have been called servants – they would have been mortally offended at the term. Mohamed's deference embarrassed me. I need not have worried, however, for he was not humble in that detestable way, nor was any Somali I ever met. But I had no way of knowing that at the time.

Mohamed, employed so hastily and on a temporary basis, was the first person I met and spoke with in Somaliland. It would have surprised me then to know that many months later he would also be the last person we saw when we left.

The launch set out for Berbera, and I held onto my broad-brimmed straw hat and felt the warm salt spray on my arms. Perched on the prow was a Somali coolie, and as the boat rode high, caught in a sudden swell of waves, I saw his face against the sky. It was a face I could not read at all, a well-shaped brown face that seemed expressionless, as though whatever lay behind his eyes would be kept carefully concealed.

I wondered if his was the face of Africa.

Footsteps

SIR RICHARD Burton, surely the strangest and most compulsive traveller of them all, had an extremely low opinion of Somalis. In his view they were stupid, dirty, and most damning of all, poor Muslims. As he had thought all along that they would be. Before he ever began the journey which he later described in *First Footsteps in East Africa*, his bias had been firmly set. As a scholar in Arabic literature and philosophy, and as a man who had found his true and inner home in the deserts and the bizarre cities of Arabia, Burton disliked the Somalis on sight, chiefly, I believe, because they happened not to be Arabs.

Every traveller sets foot on shore with some bias. Not being a scholar in Arabic literature or anything else, I had no specific pre-conceived ideas of what the Somalis would be like, or ought to be like. My bias lay in another direction. I believed that the overwhelming majority of Englishmen in colonies could properly be classified as imperialists, and my feeling about imperialism was very simple – I was against it. I had been born and had grown up in a country that once was a colony, a country which many people believed still to be suffering from a colonial outlook, and like most Canadians I took umbrage swiftly at a certain type of English who felt they had a divinely bestowed superiority over the lesser breeds without the law. My generation remembered the last of the "remittance men," languid younger sons of country families, men who could not have fixed a car nor driven a

tractor to save their souls and who looked with gentlemanly
amusement on those who could, men who had believed they
were coming to the northern wilds and who in our prairie and
mountain towns never once found occasion to change their
minds.

The first Englishman I met in Somaliland was Alf. In his
middle thirties, he was a lean sharp-faced man, slightly
stoop-shouldered, with a straggling moustache and a rather
anxious look, pessimistically anxious, as though he were certain that his was the foot destined to skid on the banana peel
over which thousands had passed in safety. He was a P.W.D.
foreman and a bachelor, and he offered to put us up for the
night.

"Of course, the telegram you sent from Aden only got here
an hour or so ago," he said morosely, in his strong midlands
accent. "That's why no one went out to the *Velho* to meet
you. It never fails. It's the only thing you can really depend
on, here – nothing ever happens in the way it's meant to."

He lived alone in a high barn-like structure of truly antique
appearance, a two-storey house with enormous windows and
heavy wooden shutters. Somali knives and spears were
tacked up on the walls, but apart from these meagre decora-
tions the dwelling had a bare and almost unlived-in look.
Geckos, tiny lizards transparent as gelatine, raced restlessly
across the ceiling, displaying their palpitating vitals and their
spines, staring with cold eyes on the humans below.

"What'll you have to drink?" Alf asked.

In England we had been able to afford only the occasional
bottle of cider, and we had smoked Weights or Woodbines,
half the price and half the size. Now, seeing Alf's amply
stocked liquor cabinet and the open tins of full-size cigarettes
sitting casually around on small tables, we had the feeling
that whatever the drawbacks of this country it would not be
entirely without its advantages.

Alf had been here for twenty-one months without leave,
and that was a long time in Berbera, too long, especially
during the *kharif*, the hot wind of the monsoon season. Tell-

ing us about himself and his work, he would suddenly begin to stammer a little and his words would peter out, as though he had forgotten what he was going to say. Sometimes he did not hear us when we spoke.

"Sorry," he would say, with a bewildered frown, "I'm afraid I missed that."

Wandering around the house after dinner, before we all settled down again to talk, he sang in a hoarse tenor, and talked to himself quite naturally and unaffectedly, telling himself he ought not to smoke so much or that he must remember to tell Jama to get cracking on the Police Land-Rover.

Alf was a plain and practical man. He liked to see things done properly. Mostly, here, they were not done properly, and it was always hard to see whose fault it was. He had become saddened and discouraged by what he called the Somalis' "obstructionism." He wanted to show them how to look after machinery, how to build and repair roads. Why wouldn't they let him? He did not know. He knew only that he had to keep on with his job and try not to let things get in too much of a mess. He was not bitter, only overworked and frequently mystified by the fact that the Somalis did not take the work as seriously as he did. But he was careful not to group Somalis together. When he spoke of his staff, he grew keen once more – Ali was a promising mechanic, and you wouldn't find a better driver than Farah.

But there were so many difficulties. Equipment was always breaking down, and the spares took months to arrive from England. There was never sufficient money in the department's allocation to get enough new equipment. And there was always trouble with the gangs of labourers. Often it was impossible to see what their current grievance was, for everybody talked at once. The Somalis were the damnedest talkers, he said – they'd argue all night if they could find any one to listen.

How to explain such a person? It is easy enough to label someone from a distance, but how could you possibly think of a man as an imperialist when he told you, sorrowfully and in perplexity, that he tried to start a football team but the Somalis didn't seem to take to the game?

Alf's frayed moustache, his worried eyes and pale untidy hair became a familiar sight to us in the next few months, when we drove from Sheikh to Berbera to get supplies. Gradually I came to believe that if he had ever fully realized how difficult his job was, he would have given up. He had no gift for analysis, however, and perhaps that was just as well, for in trying to turn camel herders into truck drivers, desert tribesmen into town-dwelling mechanics, he was trying to construct a bridge that would cross centuries and oceans in a single span. He went on speaking to them in terms of one culture, and they continued to hear and interpret his words in terms of quite another. Small wonder he was at cross purposes with them half the time.

His business was with solid tangible things, lorries and road-graders, and yet a host of intangibles plagued him like malarial mosquitoes. What did the road gang mean when they complained that the headman was like a hyena in the dry season? Was Jama telling the truth when he said the spanner got lost? Did Abdillahi really understand the gearshift on the new three-ton, or did he only claim to understand, thinking it best to be agreeable? Who was the weird old bearded geezer who had come along and talked non-stop for an hour yesterday, and why had he presented that petition on behalf of Omar, sacked three months ago? There were never any answers.

In later months, we overheard a few of the young English administrators speaking with Alf. *Good old Alf* – the tone was jovial when they were asking him to give priority to the repair of their vehicles. But they did not invite him to their dinner parties.

He became depressed sometimes, and would mutter irritably about both the Somalis and the administration. But he did not give up. The roads got repaired, ultimately. The lorries got serviced. The transport section often had an air of almost lunatic comedy about it – instructions wildly misunderstood, tools lost or broken, vehicles giving up the ghost – but it kept going somehow.

Alf was not unique. He was not even unusual. In other years and other places, we met many other foremen like him, men who were not socially accepted by their better-educated fellow expatriates and who were regarded by Africans as impossibly finicky.

I came at last to see a kind of heroic quality about the man, something which he would have denied utterly and with embarrassment. He was an ordinary bloke – he never pretended to be otherwise. The job was all right, in his opinion, better-paid than jobs at home, but he could never feel he was making much headway.

There are roads that criss-cross Africa, not good roads but at least passable ones. There are trucks on the roads and a generation or two of Africans who know how to operate and maintain those trucks. A great many Europeans do not know and a great many Africans do not consider one aspect of this network, and it really matters very little that they do not. But sometimes I wonder if even Alf himself realizes who put the roads there and showed the village boys and the young camel-herders how to drive.

In a borrowed and bone-rattling truck, we made our way across the scorched plains of the Guban to Hargeisa on our second day in the country. Only a few wizened and prickly bushes grew in that expanse of desert, and sometimes one could see a murky waterhole or a dried-up river bed. The land was incredibly empty, the sky open from one side of the horizon to the other. The light brown sand glistened with mica and slid down into long ribbed dunes. It seemed to be no place for any living thing. Even the thorny bushes, digging their roots in and finding nourishment in that inhospitable soil, appeared to have a precarious hold on life, as though at any moment they might relax their grip, dry up entirely and be blown clean away.

But the land was not empty. A figure appeared, standing

against the sky, a Somali herdsman, very straight and calm, looking at us with a haughty detachment. He wore a brownish orange robe, cotton that once might have been white but had taken on the colour of the muddy water from the wells where the camels drank. He carried his spear across one shoulder. Around him his sheep clustered, spindly legged creatures, white with ebony heads and no wool at all, only short hair like a deer's hide. He did not move or turn his head as we jolted dustily past him. To him, we might have been as ephemeral as dust-devils, the columns of wind and sand that swirled across the desert and then disappeared without a trace.

The landmark of Hargeisa is the pair of hills called by the Somalis *Nasa Hablod*, the girl's breasts. As we drew into the town I realized the meaning of oasis – after the interminable rock and sand, after the barren places where no water could be found and no trees grew, the sudden sight of greenery and the walls of human dwellings.

The Hargeisa Club actually meant the English Club, for no Somalis and very few Italians were ever invited in. It stood, like the European bungalows, at a considerable distance from the *magala* or Somali town, and was a low rambling building surrounded by feathery pepper trees and flat-topped acacias. In the front garden, the staunch zinnias grew, the only familiar flower one can be certain will take root in alien soil, although even these plants had been altered here, their colours faded or diluted into an assortment of muted pinks and muddy yellows.

When we wakened in the early morning we heard a harsh squabble of bird voices, and looking out we saw birds whose wings of peacock blue and breastfeathers of gold seemed out of place in the dull-toned land.

"Morning tea, sahib." Mohamed knocked at the door and entered with the imposing tray, and once again we had to explain that we did not like tea in the morning.

"I think you no be same as other sahibs," he said in a puzzled voice.

It was a remark he was to make often. Sometimes he

meant it as a compliment. More often, it denoted a kind of confusion. In the relationships of servants and employers here, the patterns of behaviour were formal, clearly laid down. If one broke with the traditional patterns, how could anyone know what to do or how to respond? It was not easy for us to become accustomed to colonial life, and it was not easy for Mohamed to get used to our departures from it. Ultimately he discovered a satisfactory explanation. We were neither *Ingrese* (English) nor Italiano. We came from another and unknown tribe.

"Canadian peoples different," he would say, and this covered a multitude of lapses.

Jack spent several days making plans for the commencement of his work. I, in the meantime, was introduced to the European community through that time-honoured institution, the morning tea party. At these gatherings, some of the English women of the station were kind enough to impart to me various pieces of advice. My only trouble was in knowing which to follow, for there was a marked lack of unanimity. The adages ran something like this:

Always lock the storeroom door, or you will be robbed blind by your servants.

Never lock the storeroom door, or your resentful servants will find other ways to pilfer food.

On no account be so foolish as to advance pay to your cook or houseboy, for it encourages them in financial carelessness.

It is quite acceptable to advance pay, provided they understand clearly how much is to be paid back each month.

Never eat curry puffs made in the town, or you will get enteric dysentery.

Curry puffs are perfectly safe, for the curry acts as a preservative.

Never buy Kenya bacon; it is too expensive and will probably give you trichinosis.

By all means purchase Kenya bacon; it is excellent and reasonably priced.

Never hire a Somali *ayah* to care for children; such girls all have loose morals – otherwise, as Muslim women, they would not take employment.

Always employ an *ayah*; children are in deadly peril from snakes and scorpions and must be watched over constantly.

I told them I had no children yet, but that if I had I would certainly not entrust them to the care of anyone else, not even a trained English nanny.

"Oh well," they said, eyebrows lifting only slightly, "in that case –"

Their explanation of me was in essence the same as Mohamed's. I was from another country. They shrugged and smiled, a trifle stiffly, perhaps, but politely. Later, it seemed to me that in those early days of our tour quite a few memsahibs must have looked upon me with a greater generosity than I afforded them. At the time, I saw only the distance which they put between themselves and the Somalis, whom they tended to regard either patronizingly or with outright scorn. I did not appreciate then the really desperate boredom of some of these women, the sense of life being lived pointlessly and in a vacuum. Nor did I perceive the need many of them felt to create a small replica of England here in the desert and the enormous effort they put into a task that must inevitably fail.

In only two pieces of their advice was a general and immediate agreement evident. I decided it would be prudent to follow these two.

Boil all drinking water.

Take an anti-malarial pill every day.

The Hargeisa *magala* looked best at night, when the milky moonlight was spilled over the town, blanching its stained daytime countenance. The festering gutters, the leprous white-wash of the mosque, the jaundiced mud walls of the tea shops that squatted around the market-place – by moonlight the sores of all these places were made to appear sound. The Somali dwellings, hive-shaped huts of coarse woven grass steeped in smoke and brown-splattered by past rains, were

mellowed then, and even the cloth-merchants' shops, stony
hags whose angularity showed through their *purdah* of grey
shutters, seemed softer and more benign.

In the hard glare of the sun it was another matter. Soon
after our arrival, I decided I would go to the town and look
through the shops. I had no transport, so I walked, for it was
only about a mile. Mohamed accompanied me. At first he
had been reluctant.

"You no go there, memsahib."

But when I asked why not, he would not say. He hinted at
unspecified danger.

"May be some small trouble –"

I could not take his warnings seriously. With a shrug he
resigned himself and shuffled with some embarrassment
beside me along the dusty road.

By day the town was a vivid and shabby conglomeration of
people, a tumult of voices. In the marketplace, shrivelled old
men and women sat, gossiping under the thorn trees. Hordes
of children, quick and nimble as geckos, darted among the
crowds. Camels plodded and sneered. Men from the interior
plains of the Haud stacked up the piles of dried sheepskins
they had brought in to sell. Somali labourers chanted a high-
pitched song as they worked to repair the road. An Indian
merchant, dark and plump as a damson plum, sipped spiced
tea in the shade. Somali girls walked enticingly in their scarlet
or green robes, flicking their eyelashes at the young men.
Some of them affected *purdah*, never worn by the desert
women but only by women in the town, and these would
coyly hold their gauzy veils just above the bridge of their
noses, leaving only their eyes to be seen by passers-by. But so
expressive were the eyes that the girls seemed to have no
trouble in making their meaning plain to the grinning boys
who lolled in the doorways.

"*Baksheesh! Baksheesh!*"

The eternal appeal for alm. All at once I was aware of
them, the ranks of beggars whining their monotonous plea
outside the shops. The old and withered among them smiled
with senile serenity, forever hoping for the miracle forever

denied, the grace of Allah forever withheld. Their tattered remnants of robes fluttered like ancient prayer flags from a mosque, and the claws that held the wooden bowls were separated from skeleton only by skin as crinkled and brittle as charred paper. One dragged himself along with two blocks of wood strapped to his hands, because he had no legs.

Many of the begging throng were children, the marks of their profession plain upon them – running sores on twig-like bodies, a twisted shoulder, a stunted stump of a leg dragged heavily, patiently, through the dust. They were the misshapen ones, the weak in a land where life came hard even to the strong. Muslims, traditionally alms-givers, look after their poor and afflicted where they can. Here they could not.

"*Baksheesh,*" the children chirped, "*baksheesh.*"

What does a person do? I gave them money. The blessings of Allah were placed upon my head, and I was mercifully released, enabled to get away. I could not deceive myself that the giving of alms did anything except momentarily soothe the conscience of the giver, permit him to leave and turn his eyes away. What happened to those who did not receive even these occasional coppers? What happened when there was no money? If they could not live, they died.

When I returned to the Hargeisa Club, I discovered that I had unwittingly caused a scandal. European women did not go to the Somali town alone, and no European ever went on foot. It simply wasn't done. Many European women, I was told, were afraid to visit the Somali town at all, and never did so. I asked why. Well, stones might be thrown, names called. The Somalis could be very awkward. It transpired that someone had reported me to the police, and all afternoon I had been unobtrusively trailed by two Somali policemen. I was amused and angry. "Perhaps it is the sight of poverty that the memsahibs shrink from," I wrote in my diary. And of the police, "much ado about nothing."

I did not then know how much the Somalis resented the Christian conquerors, or if I suspected it, I felt somehow that I would be immune from their bitterness, for did I not feel friendly towards them? Surely they would see it.

But they looked at me from their own eyes, Later, when I had seen the thronging beggars again again, and the half-starved men of the desert who brough their lean camels to drink at the town's shrunken wells, I wondered if all the well-fed ones of this earth, of whom I was one, did not have reason to fear the dusty streets of the crowded town. The hands would not always be stretched out in blessing over the giving of the easily spared coin that made life possible today but tomorrow.

...se in the Clouds

A T THE TOPMOST part of that world, in the hills that
jutted blue-brown and jagged out of the flat hot plain,
Sheikh stood, a few dwellings scattered along the slopes and
across the valley where the grey twisted fig trees were nested
in by green pigeons. The settlement took its name from a
revered sheikh who lived here long ago. On holy days the
devout walked out and said prayers at the white tomb.

Once Sheikh was the administrative capital during the hot
season, in the days when Berbera was the government head-
quarters, but now the old Government House was rarely
used. Its garden was a tangle of purple bougainvillaea, and in
the dried pond where once the goldfish glinted, now only the
sleek striped lizards slid and hid themselves under the fallen
flowers.

We were based in Sheikh, and lived in a small dark-green
house on a ridge away from the main settlement – the bungalows of the few English schoolmasters and their wives, and
the Somali boys' school, the country's largest. Our house had
sandbags on top of it so the roof would not be blown away
during the *kharif* wind. These imparted a look of patchiness
to it, like a child's house fashioned of coloured blocks and
daubed with plasticine. The floors were gritty concrete,
inadequately covered by our one thin cotton carpet, purchased in Aden, patterned with oriental flowers in blue and
magenta, and labelled *Made in Amsterdam*. The stone fireplace, wonderful in appearance, did not draw. Our house was

lighted with paraffin pressure lamps that puffed and splut-
tered, and our scanty water ration was kept in galvanized
buckets. To my eyes, however, this house was perfect, for it
was the first we had ever had. Always before we had lived in
apartments or bed-sittingrooms.

I rushed around, re-arranging the plain furniture, hanging
our few pictures, swiftly sewing curtains from cheap flimsy
cotton, making cushions for the chairs and embroidering
them with giant snails in olive and yellow wool because this
was the only design I could draw and the thick mending
strands made the shape appear quickly. I had flair, but no
patience. Everything had to be done right away, this minute.
Mohamed watched and shook his head, impressed and distressed by my fever to be settled.

I stopped my buzzing after a while and looked around, and
then I noticed that everything was calm. The land was not
aware of me. I might enter its quietness or not, just as I chose.
Hesitantly at first, because it had been my pride to be as
perpetually busy as an escalator, I entered. Then I realized
how much I had needed Sheikh, how I had been moving
towards it through the years of pavements, of doom-shriek-
ing newspapers and the jittery voices of radios.

At night we went to sleep to the shushing sound of the
wind, and in the morning it was the only sound we heard
when we wakened. I rose and looked out the window – the
whole valley was filled with clouds. The dawn light was still
wavering and uncertain, and the sun had not yet climbed
Sheikh Pass. We walked out to explore our territory, and
found that the early clouds swept so low that we were actually
walking through them. They billowed around us like cloaks
or gusts of smoke, and I was amazed that such a thing was
possible, to walk in the clouds.

Later in the day, when the clouds disappeared, the air was
dazzlingly clear, like spring water. The *Jilal*, the dry season,
was at its height, but at Sheikh the hills were still speckled
with green acacias and pepper trees that grew along the gul-
lies and gorges. Looking out our front door, we saw the line
of hills dark against the sky, and flocks of sheep like white

dots on the slopes. Across the valley, the sheikh's tomb, in reality mudbrick and whitewash, shone like pale marble in the sun. Near our house the sheep and goats grazed. The sheep would eat only the coarse stringy grass, but the goats would eat anything. They craned their necks to nibble the leaves from bushes, and we could see why they were called "the scourge of Africa," for they were like locusts and no plant was immune from their insatiable mouths. The animals were tended by a placid brown-robed woman with a scarlet headscarf. Sometimes she was assisted by a little boy who carried a switch of dried grass which he used to round up the stragglers.

By day, the only sounds other than the wind were the fragments of bird song, the minor-key chanting of Mohamed and Ismail as they worked, a shrill cry from the herdboy as he leapt over rocks and bushes to trace the sadly bleating lamb or young goat that had become separated from the flock. No telephone or radio, no traffic or crowds.

We had a plentiful supply of crises, but they were of a mild variety, and even the terrors were not really threatening.

"It's an unlucky house that doesn't have a gecko." If this common saying was true, our house must have been exceedingly lucky, for whole tribes of geckos dwelt with us. At night they chased each other around the walls, playing hide-and-seek behind our pictures, chittering continually.

"Chik-chik-chik –"

My eyes followed them in their peregrinations. I was afraid to look away, certain that if I did, they would immediately be on the back of my chair or struggling in a reptilian panic in my hair. They were quite harmless, but my flesh crawled all the same. In corners, stuck to the walls in clusters, we found their eggs, pink and china-like. When the infant lizards hatched out, it took them a day or so to learn how to cling competently to walls and ceiling. In the meantime, they twitched and wriggled across the floors, creatures no larger than a needle but lively as tadpoles. Mohamed noticed my fear and capitalized upon it. He carried in buckets of hot water for the bath and suddenly shrieked as though he had just discovered a cobra.

"Memsahib – come quick!"

Cautiously I approached, and found that several fullgrown geckos were stretched out languorously, for coolness, at the bottom of our concrete bathtub. I recoiled, and Mohamed bent double in a paroxysm of silent laughter. Imagine anyone being frightened of a gecko! Helpless with mirth, he staggered out to the cookhouse, and I heard him regaling the *yerki*, his young helper, with the tale.

"*Wallahi!* Memsahib –"

A spate of Somali, gulped and hilarious. I could not understand the words, but I could imagine them well enough.

"By God, you never saw anything like it in your life –"

On the hills we saw *dik-dik*, deer scarcely larger than rabbits, with short grey-green hair on their backs and pale rusty hair on their bellies. They merged perfectly with their surroundings of scrub bush and rock, and we were never able to see them until they suddenly darted up like fearful birds at our approach. They were almost too shy and timorous for this world. John, one of the English schoolmasters, told us how his dog once chased a *dik-dik*.

"The little thing dropped before the dog touched it. You may not believe it, but I swear it died of fear."

To die of fear – there was something pathetic and repulsive in that death.

Mohamed called us out one morning to see a herd of hairy wild pigs led by a bristling and evil-tusked old boar.

"Somali bacon," he said, grinning at his own wit, for no Somali would touch pork in any form, and even the *Ingrese*, such as ourselves, who ate unclean food, would not eat the diseased and worm-infested wild pigs.

We sighted a family of baboons, and chased them far across the slopes in an attempt to see them at closer range. They were big grey-furred animals, agile and dog-faced, with hairless crimson buttocks. The young perched comfortably on their mothers' backs. The males glanced back at us over their shoulders, leered and barked a little, then loped on. When we told John of the encounter, he laughed and frowned.

"That wasn't a very bright thing to do, actually. Those fellows will turn on a dog sometimes, if it chases them, and tear it to pieces."

If the baboons had turned on us, I could not have said *I will now wake up*, as one does sometimes in nightmares. How absurd it was to be frightened of geckos, harmless as butterflies, and yet to be totally unafraid of a baboon pack. I began to see that these hills in offering their quiet also required a person to tread carefully.

To tread carefully with wild creatures is relatively easy. With people, it is not so easy. Jack drove to Burao, and in his absence three Somali elders came to see him. I undertook to explain Jack's work to them, feeling that although I knew little of the technical aspects, they knew even less. Summoning all possible graciousness, I invited them in and asked Mohamed to bring tea. The three old men sat on the edges of their chairs, their hands clasped around the knobbled canes they carried. Mohamed clattered in with the tea tray and stayed to act as interpreter. He seemed ill at ease, and fidgeted from one foot to another, avoiding both the elders' eyes and mine, focusing his gaze on a ceiling beam.

The old men were exceedingly polite. They nodded their heads at everything I said, but made no attempt to ask questions or discuss the matter. One of them observed that never in his entire long life had he known such a fine memsahib.

For the sake of decency, one always pretends not to be pleased by flattery, but underneath the hopeful question lingers – perhaps he is telling the truth? I ushered them out, finally, poured myself a cup of lukewarm tea and sat down among my snail-embroidered cushions to review the visit. *I handled that pretty well, I think; yes, I'm sure I did.*

Mohamed blew in like a wind, agitated.

"Memsahib – never do so like that, never no more."

"What?" I was startled, uncomprehending.

He sighed deeply, wiped his sweating forehead, and told me in consternation that a woman alone in the house must never invite men in, not even if they happen to be about eighty years old. To do so was a terrible breach of etiquette. Further, the elders could certainly not discuss any serious matter with a woman.

The elders' flattery, I saw now with painful clarity, was pure tact, directed at what they felt must be my feeling of awful shame at having thoughtlessly committed such a series of errors.

The next time the elders came to visit, Jack was at home, so all I had to do was to stay well in the background, which was not so easy for me, at that. The elders walked in and settled themselves in the armchairs, with none of their former reluctance.

Haji Abu Jibril was a heavily built man, big-jowled, with the hennaed beard permitted to those who have made the *huj*, the pilgrimage to Mecca. His embroidered turban was slightly askew. Over his long white robe he wore an incongruous khaki jacket with bulging pockets. His boots were tremendous and unlaced. In one hand he brandished a silver-headed cane. I tried to size him up rapidly, imagining this ready-reckoning process to be feasible. A man of power, I thought, but not to be trusted. Was there not something evasive, almost shifty, about his eyes? So much for my cleverness. In later months I discovered that he was in fact widely regarded as one of the wisest and worthiest elders in the country.

Haji Yusuf followed close behind, as though in attendance. He was a scrawny and shrewd-looking man, wearing a mauve and beige striped sweater over his skimpy pink robe, a man with a sly face and a habit of winking one eye sagaciously. I tabbed him at once as the lion's jackal, and this assessment turned out to be not totally wrong.

The third looked just as an elder should. From the corner where I sat silently, feeling almost as though I were in *purdah*, I glanced with complete approval at Haji Adan. He strolled in, neither boastfully nor apologetically, a tall old man with a well-trimmed grey beard and strong handsome features. He had a neat red and yellow turban, a green and spotless robe, a courteous and dignified manner. I trusted him at once, charmed by the suitability of his appearance. He turned out, however, in the following days, to be something of a business shark, and used to send his emissaries to sell me beaded mats and carved wooden spoons at exorbitant prices. I never lost my initial liking for him, though, for he had a quiet sarcasm that appealed to me. He harked back often to the old days and mocked the young men, who did not have, he claimed, the courage of their sires. When we heard rumours of lions in the Sheikh hills, Haji Adan told me scornfully that every time a young man saw a rabbit he thought it was a lion. It was different in his day. *We had men then*.

When we finished tea, the elders questioned Jack closely and suspiciously. Mohamed, acting as interpreter, became nervous at the amount of tact necessary to convey one side's words to the other without offending anyone.

"We have heard that the *Ingrese* are going to make *ballehs* in the Haud," Haji Abu Jibril said, a *balleh* being the Somali term of any dug-out pit that would hold rainwater. "What we want to know is – why are they doing this thing"

Jack was anxious that they should understand. He explained that the government had undertaken the project because the Somalis needed watering places in the Haud. The elders' eyes narrowed and their faces crinkled into small cynical smiles. They did not believe a word of it.

"We have heard," Haji Adan said, "that the *Ingrese* plan to build large towns for themselves beside these *ballehs*, so there will be no room for our people there."

How to deal with these three maddening old men? Jack, who was logical himself and sometimes impatient with people who were not, asked them if they could really imagine large numbers of English living permanently in the desert areas of the Haud for no reason at all. They looked at him blankly. They could imagine it quite well. It would be no more insane than anything else the English did. Jack was annoyed, and annoyed at himself for being annoyed. He would not let them see it, not if it killed him. He became exaggeratedly calm. This session of gabbing seemed a waste of time to him. He wanted to get on with the job, not talk pointlessly and in circles. But here, this kind of talk was necessary, and the elders were not in a hurry.

"The rumours are false," Jack said. "There will be no European towns beside the *ballehs*."

Haji Yusuf, the sly winking one, insinuated himself to the fore, with a sidelong glance at his master. Haji Abu Jibril's face remained impassive, but almost imperceptibly he nodded his head. Had they planned their entire approach beforehand? Very likely. We were no match for these accomplished plotters.

"Some people are saying," Haji Yusuf suggested, "that the *Ingrese* plan to make *ballehs* and then poison the water so all our camels will die."

Mohamed, translating that one, was in an agony of apprehension. Who would be angry, and at whom? He looked as though he wished he were a hundred miles away.

"What interest could the English possibly have in poisoning your camels?" Jack parried.

Back and forth, back and forth – the talk was like a tennis ball. It seemed never to get anywhere. Indeed, this was probably the elders' intention. They might or might not have believed the rumours. All they were after, really, in this game of wits, was Jack's reaction – how did he argue, and what manner of man was he?

Finally, and surprisingly, as though upon an agreed signal, the elders nodded their heads. All right. The rumours were false, they conceded. But if this was so, why did the government not simply pay Somalis to dig their own *ballehs*?

"The *ballehs* will be made with machines," Jack said. "No man could make a *balleh* of that size by hand."

They appeared to be satisfied for the moment. They rose and ceremoniously bade us farewell.

"*Nabad gelyo* – may you enter peace."

"*Nabad diino*," we replied. "The peace of faith."

But as they went out, we wondered for the first time if it really would be peace. The gist of Jack's words would be conveyed to nomads all across the Haud. How would they interpret what he had said? Would the meanings become distorted and lost? We had assumed that the Somalis would naturally be pleased at a scheme to provide watering places in the desert. Now we saw that they were by no means convinced that the project was designed to help them.

We both sensed that this same scene would be re-enacted, in different places, time and again. It was not a cheerful prospect.

A stroke of luck. We met two people with whom we could discuss anything, freely, not worrying what we said. Jack was better than I, at simulating the English reserve, an extreme caution in speech, but it did not come naturally to either of us. Now we could occasionally shed it.

Guś (whose real name was Bogomil and whose nickname was pronounced "Goosh") was Polish, a tall man with an expensive and almost oriental face, high cheekbones, faintly slanting eyes. He was a poet in his own language.

"Of course, it is useless," he said with deep Slavonic melancholy. "My poetry can't be published in Poland, and in England who is interested in publishing poems written in Polish?"

His moods would swing like a pendulum. Suddenly he would be laughing, regaling us with Somali jokes or his own brand of slightly macabre humour. He spoke Somali more fluently than any other European in the colony, for he was here to do research into the Somali language and its phonetics.

"Listen to this Somali joke about a Midgan. His wife had a miscarriage, and the man was very angry. When his friends asked him why he was so furious, he replied – *There! That will teach me not to pour anything into a vessel that's upside down!*"

Guś's wife, Sheila, was an attractive and capable English girl. She did everything with so little fuss that only gradually did it dawn on us that she was probably the only English woman in the colony who did her own cooking.

"I like cooking," she said, "so why not?"

Guś ate compulsively but never gained any weight. During the war, when he was escaping from Poland, he was close to starvation many times. When he finally got to England, he joined the Free Polish Forces, and after the war he went to Oxford. Now Sheila cooked for him with a kind of tenderness, as though she hoped to make up for whatever hardships he had suffered once. She cooked everything on a tiny primus stove, and even ingeniously managed to make cookies, known to her as biscuits, by fixing up an oven of sorts with a saucepan.

"I don't really feel I was cut out to be a memsahib," she admitted.

This was my exact feeling, too. We were heartened to have discovered one another.

Guś's Somali assistant was Musa, a thin and strikingly handsome man with a pirate-like moustache. He was something of an orator, and was a well-known poet in the Somali language. He had a fine and subtle sense of dramatic irony that could overturn an adversary in an argument. In the evenings, we all used to gather and discuss Somali customs, language, poetry.

"Somali is a difficult and complicated language," Guś told us, "but very expressive."

A language well suited to poetry, I discovered, for so many of its words were of the portmanteau variety, containing a wealth of connotations. One word described a wind that blew across the desert, parching the skin and drying the membranes of the throat. Some words were particularly lyrical, some were acutely specific. A low bush with soft broad leaves and delicate purple flowers was called *wahharawallis*, which meant "that which makes the little goats jump." There was a word for anything tasting sweet, even the fresh air. The word expressing a state of well-being meant literally "to have enough water in one's belly." A risk or any dangerous situation was *saymo*, the net of God.

"*Marooro* is a plant," Musa said, "that has an acid taste in the morning but tastes sweet in the evening."

Sheila and I, sitting like acolytes, listening to his words, possibly in the hope of total enlightenment, had to question that one. So what? What was so expressive about that? Musa grinned wickedly.

"Well, you see, the Somalis often use the word as a nickname for a woman."

One evening an idea came to me. Could some of the Somali poems be put into English?

"Absolutely not. Impossible." Musa's deep decisive voice. He felt protective towards his own literature. No one could do justice to it. He did not want to see the poems mangled in translation. He felt no English person could comprehend them, anyway. They would be wasted on the cold and unemotional English. As he was unacquainted with English poetry, he found it hard to believe that English people ever felt despair or exultance.

"But listen, Musa –"

Think of all the English here who had no idea that the Somalis had ever composed poems – think of showing them some of the epic *gabei*, the lyrical *belwo*. This was my line of persuasion. Guś saw the possibilities immediately. But Musa had to have time to consider.

"Well, I don't know –"

We dropped it then, not wanting to press the issue. But we would return to it. I knew that I had found what I would like to work at, here. But I could not do it alone. Would I be able to find people who would help me? I was certain that I would. As we walked home across the valley that night, I was filled with enthusiasm.

"Take it easy," Jack said, wanting to protect me from disappointment. "It may not work out."

"Oh, I know that."

But I did not know. What I really knew was that it would

work out. Incredibly, and much later than I would have
thought, it actually did. What I did not at all suspect, however, was that it would be an "imperialist" who would make
the publication of these translations possible.

Hakim came for tea. How handsome he was, hawk-nosed and
deep-eyed, wearing his Somali robe and an embroidered cap
like a white *tarboosh*. With him came Nuur, dressed with
scrupulous neatness in khaki trousers and white shirt, and
carrying a folder which contained some of his paintings, birds
and twisting trees and flowers that looked as though they had
been delicately transplanted from some Persian tapestry.

I felt I must discover everything about Somali beliefs, customs, traditions. I assumed that these young men, who were
teachers, would be delighted to tell me. What did the Somali
bride-price actually involve? Did men love their wives or
merely regard them as possessions? Could a woman divorce her
husband for infidelity? Did Somalis believe in magic? Did the
clitoridectomy make it impossible for Somali women to enjoy
sex? When a man was enjoined by the Qoran to marry his
deceased brother's wife, how did he feel about that? Hakim
and Nuur smiled and said they did not know. All at once the
brash tone of my voice was conveyed to my own ears, and I was
appalled.

Hakim told me about *faal*, the way in which the future could
be foretold by the counting of beads of the *tusbahh*, the Muslim rosary. It never occurred to me to attempt to glimpse the
future myself, in another way, by asking Hakim what he hoped
would happen here in his lifetime. Independence seemed a long
way off then, but longer away to me, probably, than to Hakim.
He implied as much when he offered to teach me a few verses
of *Somaliyey Tosey*, the song of the Somali Youth League,
which was becoming a popular national song.

> *Somalia, awake!*
> *Unite the warring tribes.*
> *Give help unto the poor*

And strength unto the weak.

If one of your camels is stolen,
To save it you risk your lives.
But for our whole lost land
No man even raises a stick.

The tribes were at constant loggerheads with one another, but they were unanimous in their resentment at being governed by infidels. When independence came, it would be men like Hakim who would be the leaders. There were not many educated Somalis in the Protectorate, men who had some knowledge of the world outside their own land. When Hakim set foot on that path, it would not be a straight nor an easy one, for he was divided between two ways of thought. One day we chanced to talk with him about insanity. A common Somali belief, he told us, was that insanity is caused by the possession of a person by evil djinn.

"Sometimes," he said with a smile, "a mad person is told by an elder to slaughter a white sheep and wash in its blood, to drive forth the bad djinn."

I, too, smiled, and was astounded when the young Somali turnéd to Jack with a slightly puzzled frown.

"Can you tell me," Hakim asked, "what does science think of these djinn?"

But the events of the future, like the drought in the Guban and the Haud, were still only far-off murmurs to me. The reality was the peace I felt at Sheikh, and the interest in all things new and strange, customs and costumes and the country itself with its weird candelabra trees or the lizard I saw sunning itself on a rock, its head a piercing yellow, its body an iridescent teal-blue, its legs a greenish gold.

Minor adventures provided just enough excitement. We drove to Berbera to get petrol. When we returned, the hills were black and tigerish, crouched above the plain. We wound our way through Sheikh Pass, and as we looked at the narrow road and the sheer drop, we felt apprehensive, for behind the Land-Rover was hooked a trailer loaded with drums of petrol. The fifty miles seemed five hundred. As we climbed and twisted, our old driver Abdi smiled sardonically and told us gruesome tales of the lorries that had gone over the edge.

"Were many people killed?" we asked, as he related the most recent calamity, for the trade-trucks were always covered with people who swarmed all over the top like ants on a sugarbowl.

"Oh no," Abdi replied, surprised. "Nobody get kill. They jump."

They became accomplished jumpers, it seemed. The trade-truck drivers had a gay recklessness about them, more verve than mechanical know-how. If their lorries broke down, they always managed to fix them up with a bit of string or a piece of wire. At the top of Sheikh Pass we crawled past a truck which was plastered at the front with handfuls of ripe dates to plug a leaky radiator, and Jack, who had a feeling for machinery, at first stared in cold disapproval and then burst into incredulous laughter.

The sweeping out of houses was not done by Somalis. This menial work was carried out by Midgans, an outcast tribe. They had a separate language, and long ago they were the hunters of the country, using their poisoned arrows on the elephants that used to roam here, much in the same way as the pygmies further south still did. The Midgans did most of the leatherwork, sandal making and suchlike, and were often attached to Somali *rers*, or tribal groups, as servants. Once they were slaves of the Somalis. They were still looked upon disdainfully and regarded as inferior, despite the fact that the Midgans had always been more skilled in crafts than the Somalis. The supposedly dim-witted Midgan was a favourite figure in Somali jokes.

One of these Midgan jokes concerned a family who journeyed out at night to fill their water vessels at a well. With them they carried a baby. When the vessels were filled, they discovered they could not possibly carry the baby and the heavy water jars at the same time. They decided to leave the child and return for him later. But where, in all that unvarying desert country, could they leave him in a place sufficiently well marked for them to be sure of finding it again? Finally they thought of a wonderful idea, and went off happily, having left the baby right underneath the moon.

Another outcast tribe was the Yibir, who were magicians and sorcerers. These were an ancient people, tracing their ancestry far back into pre-Islamic times. When a Somali child was born, the parents gave a gift to the local Yibir, for if they did not, the child would be followed by bad luck all his days. After receiving the gift, the Yibir in return would give an amulet to the child, which was worn always, a protection against the evils that are seen and the evils that are unseen.

The Qoran, usually referred to by Somalis simply as the *Kitab* – The Book, warned against sorcery and against "the mischief of women who blow on knots" to make magic spells. Somalis, I discovered, were reluctant to speak of such matters. Mohamed and Hersi, our quick-thinking and stutter-tongued interpreter, denied all knowledge of anything pertaining to the black arts.

Would a man go to a Yibir to have him make *faal* to predict the future? Mohamed's face assumed a total blankness at my question.

"I never no hear such thing, memsahib, never at all." Apparently shocked to the marrow, he raised both hands to heaven as though seeking divine confirmation for his words. "Only Allah know what will happen. Man, he don't know."

Hersi's answers, on the other hand, were always lengthy and ornate. He spoke slowly and with great emphasis, making every speech sound like a sermon.

"Memsahib, I wish to telling you – this Yibir matter is not for our highly considerations. We have no use for bloody these people. We are Muslims, memsahib, Muslims. These Yibir matters, they are going against our religion – absolutely."

The same answers applied to prostitution or any other

subject which might be thought questionable. No such prac-
tices went on in Somaliland. Their virtue, as self-declared,
was remarkable. They belonged to a nation of paragons. I
was somewhat irritated at their pretence, and then amused.
But finally I perceived that it was no more than I deserved.
People are not oyster shells, to be pried at.

Hakim, the sphinx-eyed, when I no longer bludgeoned him
with questions, offered to tell me more about the outcast
tribes. The Yibers were still widely consulted, despite the
necessarily concealed nature of magic among people so
strongly Muslim. Some of the old warlocks still made clay
figures and stuck thorns in them, in order to injure those
whose effigy had been pierced. But the Yibers also knew of
herbs with genuine powers of healing. A common belief was
that no one had ever seen the grave of a Yibir.

"When they die," Hakim said, "they vanish."

The third outcast tribe was the Tomal, the workers in
metal, who made spears and knives. One of the Tomal came
around with his assortment of hardware for sale, and
Mohamed and I looked over the weapons carefully. I decided
to buy a *torri*, a sharply pointed knife in a leather case.
Mohamed badly wanted a knife also, but he had a problem.

"All this knife—" he said, fingering them, "too long. Must
be police will see I am wearing this one. Then – *wallahi!* – big
trouble."

He ordered a shorter knife from the Tomal, one that the
police would not be able to see.

I persisted in my attempts to learn Somali, but found it slow
going. A constant difficulty was that most Somalis, when I
spoke to them in what I thought was Somali, appeared to
have the impression that I was speaking English or another
totally unknown tongue. The old watchman, Hussein, was
convinced that I need learn only one Somali word.

"*Rob* – rain," he said to me. "Somali call rain *rob*."

I prepared a few Somali sentences carefully in advance and

delivered them like a campaigning politician, ringingly. But Hussein was unimpressed.

"*Rob* – rain," he repeated.

I recalled hearing some of the sahibs and memsahibs speaking very loudly to Somalis, as though a greater volume of sound would be bound to pierce the language barrier. Now, some of the Somalis, humouring me in my determination to learn their language, raised their voices and bellowed manfully, shaking their heads in bewilderment when still I did not comprehend their words.

While in Hargeisa and Berbera, at the morning tea parties and the evening gatherings at the Club, numerous expatriates still persisted in the belief that the Somalis were of an inferior mentality because they did not speak English as well as the English did.

Jack prepared to go off on trek into the Haud.

"I'd rather you stayed here," he said. "I want to travel with as few people as possible, and as little equipment. I have to make a rapid preliminary survey along the Ethiopian border. Mohamed can stay here, and I'll take Ismail with me."

We had decided to let Mohamed be cook, and had hired Ismail as houseboy. Ismail was young, but he had worked in domestic service for a long time and had a fantastically strong sense of what was fitting. This insistence upon formality seemed to protect his own status. No Somali wanted to work for an Englishman who did not know the proper thing to do – this was Ismail's attitude. For trek, everything had to be correct – sheets, pillowcases, two pairs of pyjamas, six handkerchiefs. All these had been ordained ages ago, apparently, by some higher power.

We were sitting in the livingroom after dinner. In the kitchen, Mohamed and Ismail were packing the cooking utensils for the journey next morning. Suddenly – chaos. Loud and furious shouting. Wild accusations. Pained denials. We rushed out to the kitchen and found a domestic war in progress. Ismail was sitting on the floor, surrounded by every pot and pan we possessed. Mohamed was screeching like a madman.

"Ismail, he take all my pans. How I can do my work? He is *shaitan*, a devil!"

Ismail sat there unmoving as a statue, clutching the aluminium ware as though it were his hope of heaven. He shrieked back at Mohamed.

"How we go on safari if we never got nothing?"

Jack tried to calm the pair. No use. Finally he lost all patience and shouted louder than either of them.

"Stop this nonsense! Cut it out right this minute! My God, I wish I could just go off quietly to the Haud by myself, without all this damn silly fuss."

They gazed at him in astonishment. What on earth could he be annoyed about? This argument was perfectly normal procedure. Jack succeeded at last in wrenching some of the utensils from Ismail, and pacified him by telling him he would be able to get any really essential pieces of extra equipment when they stopped at Hargeisa. Ismail instantly reeled off a lengthy list of things essential for safari – pans, spoons, another charcoal burner, egg-beater, china cups, glasses, soup-strainer.

"All sahibs have soup on trek," Ismail said, over and over again.

Several week later, when Jack had returned from the trip, he told me of the sequel to this evening. At Awareh, he found he had forgotten his shaving mirror. Ismail remedied the oversight by borrowing one from an English major stationed there.

"I never told him you forget," Ismail said triumphantly. "I tell him yours get broken on the way."

Alone at Sheikh, I never felt afraid in our isolated house, for I had a kind of faith that nothing could harm me here. The other bungalows, however, were about a mile away across the valley. Mohamed's quarters were down the road at a distance from our house, and although old Hussein occasionally plodded past the windows in the evening, as he made his watchman's rounds, there was usually no one within hailing distance.

"Some very bad thief staying in Sheikh now," Mohamed informed me one morning.

They were well-known thieves, it appeared, and the knowledge of their presence quickly spread.

"You'd really be better to have a watchdog there with you," John, the schoolmaster, said to me. "Would you like to borrow Slippers?"

Slippers was a good-natured black dog of undeterminable breed, and I was glad to have him with me. The only trouble was that he refused to stay. Each day he went back to his old home across the valley, and each evening John patiently fetched him back again. Then John became ill with malaria and was unable to bring Slippers back. At dusk I set out to fetch him, although it seemed to me rather odd to be wandering around at night by myself in order to find the watchdog that was supposed to be protecting me.

The sky was a dark shadowy blue when I started out, and the clouds scudded across the moon, making it look as though it were hurtling through the sky. This was my first solitary nocturnal trip, and when I started back with the dog, the darkness was complete and the moon was hidden. The valley was full of thorn trees and bushes, and there had recently been rumours of lions in the vicinity.

Then the moon came out from behind the clouds and lighted the whole valley. The stars were clearer than I had ever seen them. The only sounds were the faint dry rustling of the trees and the scraping of my sandals on the stones. The mountains could be seen in the starlight, looking blacker than the sky. I felt the splendour of the night, and fear seemed trivial.

But when the alien noise came, fear returned with a rush. A scratching in the bushes, the sound of breathing, a low cough. I stood absolutely still, certain that the next instant I would be face to face with a lion. Then I heard a tiny voice which seemed to be coming out of a bush.

"Good morning!"

It was a small Somali boy, and this was the extent of his English. He emerged and gravely put out his hand for me to shake. I did so, and replied "Good morning" to him. Perhaps he had imagined I was a lion, too. We smiled and went our separate ways, having reassured one another in the darkness of the valley.

Each morning Ali Ma'alish's wife climbed our hillside to bring the allotted two donkey-loads of water, our day's ration. Soon after dawn I would hear the clonking and rattling of the old paraffin tins which were used for water containers, and the sloshing sound of the precious liquid being emptied into our buckets. Ali was the school gardener, and Ma'alish was a nickname, an Arabic word which meant "never mind" or "it doesn't matter a damn," applied to him because he habitually shrugged off all events in this manner. If the ants devoured the two puny cucumbers he had been cherishing, he said "ma'alish," and if the news arrived that the Ogaden had raided the camps of the Dolbahanta, his comment would be exactly the same.

Ali's wife always carried her baby on her hip in a sling tied around his bottom, so that his back was bent like a half moon. His legs stuck out of his queer cradle and occasionally landed an outraged kick at his mother's spine. He was about nine months old and was named Ibrahim. He had a fat firm little body, and skin a soft cocoa colour. Usually he wore only a string of white and silver beads around his neck, and looked like a water-baby clad in a necklace of shells. I decided to take his picture one day, as he sat on the ground, so placidly, sifting the dust through his fingers. I brought out my camera, but Ibrahim's mother hastily picked him up and covered his nakedness with her headscarf. No Muslim man, however small, her reproachful glance seemed to say, could possibly be peered at through the camera's eye when insufficiently clothed. Was not modesty next to piety?

Modesty of women, of course, was even more essential. European women, as far as I could gather, were not really regarded as women at all but rather as some kind of hybrid creatures who could, on markedly rare occasions, conceive and give birth to their young by some unusual means, possibly parthenogenesis. This view was confirmed by the odd way in which European women dressed. Bad enough that they shamelessly displayed their legs, but when they sauntered around in trousers – the Somalis could only snicker at it; their imaginations boggled at the thought of what sort of hermaphroditic features the shocking garments must conceal. I was wandering around in the garden one morning, wearing slacks, when some Somali women paused on the road to gawk at me. I could understand enough Somali by that time to catch their remarks.

"Look, Dahab! Is it a man or a woman?"

"Allah knows. Some strange beast –"

I went back into the bungalow and put on a skirt. Never again did I wear slacks in Somaliland, not even in the desert evenings when the mosquitoes were thick as porridge, not even in the mornings when the hordes of glue-footed flies descended.

"Two she come to see you," Mohamed said.

The visitors were the wives of two of the local elders. Both were extremely young. Zahara was small and slender, with lovely features which showed to advantage only when her mouth was closed, for she had very bad teeth. Her robes were blue and maroon, and in the long folds of her skirts her little daughter, a shy three-year-old, tried to hide.

Hawa, the other, seemed more a girl than a woman, a tall and awkward girl, dressed in robes of blue and white, with a pale blue headscarf. She wore lightly musical gold bangles on wrists that seemed gauche, as though her long slim hands were an inconvenience, appendages that would not yet move gracefully to her bidding. She had no children, which might partly account for her lack of ease. When I told her I had none yet, either, she seemed to loosen a little. We said to one another the traditional prayer.

"*In sha' Allah* – if God wills it, you will have a son."

She had been married only a year. Her husband was a man old enough to be her grandfather. What her chances were of bearing the children she wanted so much, I did not know. I wondered how a girl her age, which could not have been more than fifteen or sixteen, felt about being married to an old man. I had no way of knowing that, either, but the look of resignation in her eyes said that her life was a bitter one. When she walked through the town, if her glance caught a group of the young men, she must forever look away from the one she would have chosen if the choice had been hers.

I had brought with me from England a number of tubes of textile paint, and had done potato-block prints on unbleached cotton for our curtains. Zahara and Hawa fingered my curtains with interest, for the bold and simple designs caught their eyes. I explained to them how the work was done, and they were enchanted. It seemed enticingly easy to them. Their own embroidery, the stylized birds and flowers which they put on pillows or coverlets, took a long time to finish. Touched by their eagerness, I offered to teach them how to do block-printing. I would buy some more cotton, I told them, and let them know when to come for lessons.

Shortly afterwards, I talked with the wife of the Director of Education. She had spent several years in convincing the local elders that some kind of education was desirable for Somali women, but not the highly theoretical education which at this stage of the country's development would inevitably separate a woman from her people and turn her into a prostitute. She had a class of Somali girls now, the first in the country to be educated.

"When they were nomads, the sanitation problem didn't exist. They packed up their huts and left all the debris behind. but in a settled community such as Sheikh, new ways have to be learned."

She was teaching them how to care for their houses and children in this different kind of community. In her class, the girls worked with materials they would find available to them when they left school and got married.

I went home and put away my imported paints, and no more was said on the subject.

Jack returned from the Haud. He was sunburned and smelled attractively of sun and wind. But when he walked into the house, his khaki bush-jacket and his old grey fedora thick with red dust, I saw how tired he looked.

"Didn't it go well?"

"Oh yes," he said. "I got the data I needed. But it was pretty grim."

And then he told me. I could hardly believe it. In the Haud he had met Somalis who were dying of thirst. He had a spare tank of water in the Land-Rover, but no containers with him in the car, so he put the hosepipe directly into people's mouths and let them drink that way. It was, as he pointed out, merely a spit in the ocean. All along the road were the bodies of camels that had died before they could reach the wells. Most of the nomads were on their way back to Hargeisa, the nearest watering spot. Jack had been troubled at the apparent improvidence of the Somalis.

"I know they couldn't do very much in the situation, but even the slight precautions they could have taken simply weren't done. I met one family beginning a hundred-and-fifty-mile trek across the desert, and only twenty miles away from the Awareh wells they were already out of water, or hadn't taken any with them."

Hersi had tried to explain.

"You see, sahib," he had said, "it is no greatly use for them to taking water. If Allah wanting them to reach the Hargeisa wells, they get there. If not, they die."

To us, this point of view was at first incomprehensible. Our lives had placed us in very few situations in which we had been virtually powerless. The Muslim fatalism was essentially foreign to us for other reasons as well. Our roots were closer to Luther's "Here stand I; I can do no other" or Brigham Young's "Trust in the Lord but keep your powder dry." Individualism and self-reliance had been woven into us all our lives. The total subservience of the individual judgement went against our deepest grain.

But *Islam* means "submission to God." Gradually we began to see why Islam is a religion of the desert. Even had the tribesmen taken full water vessels with them on their trek, it would have made little difference in the long run. Some would still have died on the way and some would have reached the wells. The Somali tribes had always been dependent upon moving from place to place, seeking grazing for their herds and flocks, dependent upon brackish pools of water hundreds of miles apart. When they had watered their animals and filled themselves with water, they moved on to grazing grounds where there were no wells. This was the inevitable pattern of their lives.

A cruel saying of the Arabs used to be that Allah had created the Arabs, and then He had created all other peoples, and then He had created the Somalis, and then He had laughed. This country's irony began to be apparent to us – a forceful and imaginative people in a land that had no resources. We recalled the comments of some Europeans in Hargeisa and Berbera – the Somalis were stiff-necked, recalcitrant, difficult, hard. Yes, they were hard. They had need to be. And yet they maintained their faith – or were maintained by it.

A few days after Jack returned from Awareh, Hakim came to see us.

"Oil will be found some day in Somaliland," he said with confidence. "You wait and see."

Why was he so certain, we wondered.

"Because," he said, "Allah, who is merciful, could not have been so merciless as to create a country with nothing of wealth in it."

Jack's reports from the Haud were such a contrast to our life at Sheikh that I found them difficult to grasp. Even the nomads dying in the desert were distant and insubstantial. I spoke the words – how terrible that people should die of thirst. But the imagination is depressingly limited. I had not seen them die, and so I did not really know at all.

My gentle introduction to this land was drawing to a close.
At the peak of the dry *Jilal* season, we left Sheikh and went
out south into the Haud. At the time we planned to return
from camp fairly often, but as it happened we returned only
once.

We came back to Sheikh after the rains, when all things
had been renewed. New grass sprouted from every rock crev-
ice, and the mountains were covered with a haze of green.
The fern-like boughs of the pepper trees were pale green with
unfolding leaves.

The cactus plants had put forth yellow waxen blossoms,
and on the hills all kinds of wild flowers grew. The wilted
aloes had filled with moisture and become succulently firm
again, rosettes of broad pointed leaves mottled green and
brown, edged with rust-coloured barbs like a shark's teeth,
and in the centre a thin stalk culminating in a scarlet flower,
really a cluster of innumerable tiny flowers. Weird insects
emerged – a crimson beetle patterned in gold and black,
looking like a small heraldic shield, and another that looked
like a piece of Italian mosaic, a delicate turquoise with pastel
markings in coral. Near the stony river-bed the green pigeons
had returned to the gnarled fig tree.

Early one morning we began to climb Malol, the highest
mountain around Sheikh. The path was covered with fissured
rocks and piles of rock rubble, and the climbing was hard.
We did not reach the top of Malol, but when the afternoon
heat was at its height we came to a hidden valley. Clambering
through a narrow rock pass, we came upon it suddenly, a
green place where the grass was thick and soft, hair-like, and
where mauve flowers grew.

This valley was full of clumps of euphorbia, the candelabra
trees, the milk of which was poisonous. Their trunks were
creased and dark, almost like oak, but instead of branches
they bore a collection of thick stalks, green and smooth,
uplifted like long tapers. The trees were curiously filled with
shadows. Vines had threaded themselves through the stalks
and hung down like lace around the heavy candelabra. The
loose heaps of rock and shale that littered the ground could

almost have been the decayed remains of some temple or
court that died ages ago, before any Somali voices came to
break the silence once more. That Somalis had been here was
proven by the little brushwood *zareba*, which seemed out of
place, as though a nomad's hut had found itself by mistake in
the garden of a sultan. The clouds were swept along by the
wind, and their moving shadows gave flecks of shade to the
hills. Further into the heart of the mountains we could see
Sheikh Pass. Far away and lower down was the settlement,
the bungalows and the sheikh's white tomb, all miniature at a
distance. Around us, the swallows darted and the cream-
winged butterflies trembled lightly on the flowers. The only
sounds were the whirring of the insects and the stirring of the
wind.

We rested for an hour or so in the valley of the candelabra,
among the forgotten enchantments. Then we went back,
down the steep slopes, back to our house. When we got there,
the dusk had come and the lamps were already lighted. We
went to sleep that night to the sound of the wind that was
never still. We would know other winds, some of them blowing like flame, whirling the dust-devils across the desert,
moaning like the voices of the uneasy dead. But the wind at
Sheikh, however deep its voice, never seemed to carry any
threat.

We did not go back again to our house in the clouds. But
we carried the memory of its peace with us as a talisman.

CHAPTER FOUR

Jilal

Praise be to Allah, Lord of the worlds.
The compassionate, the merciful.

IN THE PLAINS of the Haud, no rain had fallen for a year.
No green anywhere, none, not a leaf, not a blade of grass.
In stretches where the wind-flattened grass remained, it had
been bleached to bone-white. The earth was red, a dark
burning red that stung the eyes. The sun was everywhere;
there was no escaping its piercing light. The termite mounds,
some of them three times the height of a man, rose like
grotesque towers, making part of the plain seem like a vast
city of insects where the minute knife-mouthed *abor* reigned
supreme. In other places the thorn trees stood, grey and
brittle, and on the ground lay littered the broken skeletal
branches that had been snapped off by the wind. The clumps
of aloes were shrivelled, all their moisture sucked out by the
sun. The antelope and gazelle – the swan-necked *gerenuk*, the
small white-tailed *dero*, the light brown *aul* – most of these
had gone further south in search of water. Only the people
and their herds did not attempt to escape the *Jilal* season.

They shuttled between the northern wells of Hargeisa,
Odweina, Burao, and the wells of the south, Bohotleh, Las
Anod, Awareh. The two lines of wells were several hundred
miles apart. Only dry grazing could be found now, and even
this was not plentiful, so the tribes had to seek it continually

for their herds. The camels moved along the road in a falter-
ing line, the lean exhausted ones returning to the northern
wells, the scarcely less lean ones coming back out into the
Haud. The beasts' humps were shrunken, and hung flabbily
on their bony backs. They moved silently, ploddingly, and
the men beside them walked silently, not speaking. What was
there to say? They knew that if they stopped, they would not
be able to rise again.

When we passed them in the Land-Rover, travelling as far
in a day as they could go in a week, sometimes they held out
their water vessels of clay or dinted tin. If we had any water
left in our spare tank we stopped. If not, we drove on. There
was not much difference between the occasions when we
stopped and those when we did not stop. A cupful of water
might take them another half-day's journey, but that was all.

The *Jilal* was a good season for the vultures. They
swarmed and shrieked around the dead camels that had suc-
cumbed to the drought. They stuffed themselves with carrion
until they were too full to fly. Their bloated black bodies
would run a little, try to take off, fall back again to earth.
Their beaks and the dirty white ruff of feathers around their
necks were crusted with red. Their snake-like necks craned
interminably and their eyes searched for more dead flesh.
Sometimes they could not wait for a camel to die before they
descended, picking first at the greatest delicacy, the still-see-
ing eyes.

By the roadside were the graves of people who had not
reached the wells. So little stone existed here that grey acacia
branches and piles of brushwood were used for the marking
of graves. People were buried in a shelf jutting from the pit,
in the hope that this might protect the bodies from the hyenas. The body was faced towards Mecca; the prayers were
spoken and the tribe moved on for no one dared linger to
mourn the dead.

At the wheel of the Land-Rover, Abdi's hands tightened
whenever we stopped or did not stop beside the stumbling
herdsmen. His face was set and rigid. His wife and younger
children were out here in the Haud, with his tribe. Hersi's

family was out here, too, his wife Saqa and his two young daughters. His myopic and enquiring eyes expressed now only resignation.

"Allah has placed a hard situation on His people. But if He is willing us to live, we will live."

At dusk, when the evening prayers were said, Hersi led the others in the low-voiced chanting. The Arabic words seemed to be suspended momentarily in the still air.

Bismillahi'rahhmani'rrahheem –
In the Name of Allah, the Compassionate, the Merciful –

How could they? Like Job, they could find it within themselves to say – *Though He slay me, yet will I trust in Him*. We had to accept faith's intense reality for them. They lived in the palm of God's hand. If His hand crushed them, so be it. Only in this way, in this land, was the heart saved from breaking. They were not a passive people. They struggled against terrifying odds to get through to the wells. But always in their minds must have been the feeling that if Allah intended them to make it, nothing would prevail against them, and if He did not intend them to go on living, no effort of theirs would be any use. This fatalism did not weaken them. On the contrary, it prevented them from wasting themselves in fury and desperation.

But for myself, it did not apply, this faith, perhaps because I had never needed it the way they did. I viewed it from the outside. As far as I was concerned, God was deaf. If we did not hear the sound of each other's voices, no one else would.

The situation at the Awareh wells was said to be "very tense." The tribes in the Protectorate were not allowed to own rifles, but a certain number were smuggled in. The Ogaden who dwelt in the protected area of Ethiopia were said to obtain arms from the Ethiopians. Most of the tribes in British Somaliland belonged to the large tribal group of Ishaak, whereas the Ogaden belonged to the tribes of Darod. Feeling had always run high between the two, but now the ancient animosity was greatly enlarged by the fact that the Ogaden were selling water at the Awareh wells for ten rupees a drum. If the incoming Ishaak tribes did not have the money, they and their herds died. The government feared a full-scale tribal war. In the manner of this country, there were any number of additional factors – tribal and personal jealousies too complicated for us to penetrate. But the main factor in the warring of the tribes could be expressed in one word. *Biyu.* Water. Each day the clouds drifted in shreds across the sky. But no rain fell.

"*In sha'Allah,*" the Somalis repeated, eyeing the clouds. "If God wills it."

One day Hersi showed me an *abor*, the insect which made the towering earth mounds on the plains. They used only the red soil and their saliva, he told me, and they worked only at night. The creature was half the size of my smallest fingernail, and its mouth was equipped with a blade, for I put it on my hand and although I could feel nothing, in an instant there was a little slash and the blood was oozing out. Hersi removed the bug and turned to more serious matters.

"Memsahib – will you asking the sahib if he allowing us to go hunting evening times? We have no meat in bloody this place, and the men saying they cannot working without some little strength in their stomachs. Abdi is very good shot. I think maybe he is succeeding for some *gerenuk* or *dero*."

Just before dusk we set out in the Land-Rover, Abdi and Jack and myself in front, Hersi and one of the labourers in the back. The canvas top of the car was down, and as we bumped across the desert, over hillocks and clumps of grass, Jack on wild impulse stood and took a pot shot at a fox. Astonishingly, from the moving vehicle, he hit it. Hurrah – fantastic jubilation! The Somalis shouted themselves hoarse. A good omen – now, obviously, we would get a *gerenuk*.

Although so few gazelle remained in the Haud, we sighted one almost immediately. We were all terribly excited. Abdi seemed to be trying to drive softly, crouched over the wheel in deep concentration, as though he could coax the vehicle to make less noise.

The *gerenuk*, like a shadow, slipped from the tangle of thorn bushes. We saw its beautifully arched neck, and as it leapt it seemed to be held there for an instant against the pale sky, an image of perfect proportion. I was struck, hypnotized almost, by the unbelievable grace of it. Not so the Somalis. They were too meat-hungry to consider anything else.

"Shoot, sahib!" Abdi hissed urgently, halting the Land-Rover.

With this weight of responsibility heavy on him, Jack fired. He missed. The *gerenuk* darted away.

"Hell and damnation! Well, let's go after it, Abdi."

Off we went again. Even I was infected now with the spirit of the hunt, and would have seen the creature destroyed for the sheer triumph of scoring, even apart from the need for meat. Miraculously, we sighted it again. This time Jack handed the rifle to Abdi.

"Here. You try."

Abdi, who was by no means a young man, jumped lightly out of the Land-Rover and began to stalk the *gerenuk*. We waited, hardly breathing. At last he fired. The *gerenuk*, untouched, bounded away and was lost in the gathering twilight.

Abdi swore under his breath as he started driving once more, but Hersi was philosophical.

"Allah is not intending we should have meat this day."

On the way back to camp, Abdi all at once swerved and headed off in another direction. When we asked him where he was going, he refused to reply. Finally we found ourselves in a Somali encampment, a few brown grass huts, a camel or two, a boy herding the sheep into the brushwood enclosure for the night. Abdi jerked the car to a halt, climbed out grimly and launched into a long harangue with an old man who appeared from one of the huts.

"He is buying one sheep," Hersi explained. "He will paying with his own money, sahib."

"He mustn't do that," Jack protested.

"He is wanting to do it. This *gerenuk* business is a heavy matter for Abdi."

Abdi came back with the live sheep, its forelegs tied together. He shoved it into the Land-Rover, practically on top of Hersi, and it bleated all the way back to camp. Mohamed came rushing out to greet us.

"Meat!" he shouted ecstatically.

He grabbed the sheep and tugged it away. We heard its cries, fainter with distance, and then silence. Precisely fifteen minutes later Mohamed appeared with our dinner, two steaming plates of rice with large slabs of meat at the side.

"Liver," he said, smacking his lips, "and some small steak."

When he had gone, I looked at my plate and I seemed still to be hearing the revolting sound of that shrill bleating. The interval between life and death, creature and meat, had been indecently slight, from my point of view.

Evenings in camp were quiet. We sprawled in our canvas and leather-strapped chairs outside the tent, watching the dance of the moths around the lamp. The Somalis talked around the fire, or chanted songs. Sometimes we heard the high-pitched voice of Mohamedyero, ten years old and excited to be here among the men. The night was softly black, the stars white and startling. I felt I had never seen the stars before I saw them here. In cities and towns the electric glare detracted from the sky. Here there was nothing except our few faint lamps and the orange embers of the fire. If we walked past the edge of the camp, the human lights were lost and there was only the blaze of planets beyond ours.

With the arrival of dusk, the hyenas began to emerge, long shadows sneaking from bush to bush, prowling around the camp in wide circles that would narrow as the night wore on. They were scavengers, not fighters, these giant bastard dogs with massive shoulders and jaws that could have broken a man's neck in a single snap. They had strength but no heart, as a lion has, or a leopard. They would not venture inside our bushwood fence unless our campfires died untended and all humans slept. The great pale-furred throats gave forth their eerie groan as the wide nostrils caught the scent of the sheep guts with which our steel traps had been baited, just outside the camp. And the Somalis squatting around the fire heard the cry and grinned with anticipation, for they loathed the hyena who killed their sheep and young camels and sometimes even children but who would never stand to face a man with a spear unless thirst had given the beast the courage of madness. When the sudden yelp of pain came, every one rushed out to see the trapped animal and deal it the last blow. Another hyena would trouble the flocks no more. Praise be to Allah, who delivered this evil one into our hands.

Jack went away from camp every day, looking for the best sites for *ballehs*, drilling test-holes to determine the nature of the soil. I remained, writing to whoever was left in camp, trying to learn Somali. One day when he returned he had a story to relate. On the Wadda Beris, the Rice Road, he had come upon a mud-and-wattle hut, of the type called by Somalis "coffee shop," although in fact the only drink sold in such places was tea, usually thickly laced with spices. An old Somali with a ragged white beard had come out to greet him, and would not let him go.

"Wait, wait – I have something to show you."

Jack waited impatiently while the old man rummaged in his hut and finally emerged with a piece of paper, a letter worn with being folded and unfolded, and now almost falling to bits. Jack read it, and was so struck with it that he copied it down. It was dated the 15th of April, 1931.

"*Salaam aleikum*, Haji Elmi. I am very glad to hear again from you after so many years. After I left you in Djibouti many years ago, I was for a long time very ill with fever, and after, I went on a long voyage around the world. On my way back I stayed in western Canada and did not return to England again, which is perhaps why I never had your letters. I do not remember quite all about Mohamed Hassan. I remember he stole the double-barrelled 303 rifle which Lord de Clifford told him to bring me in Abyssinia. I think I made a complaint to Captain Cordeaux. I do not see why you

should have to pay any money to him. All that we shall talk
of when I come (*Insh'Allah*). Canada is a very fine country
and I had good *shikar* there, principally bears and big antelope. I came back for the war to England and was nearly
killed in France, and then I went onto the staff in Palestine. I
tried to get back to Somaliland, but could not get leave. I am
very glad to hear you have seven sons. I have one – he is now
thirteen years old. I wonder if there is still any kudu or oryx
left, and any bears at Bijeh. *Aleikum salaam –*"

Some feeling of restraint had prevented Jack from copying
down the name, so it is lost. So many echoes appeared in this
letter. Where in western Canada had he found such good
hunting? The Rockies, it must have been. As for Somaliland,
there were practically no kudu or oryx left, and if there were
any bears at Bijeh, we never heard of them. We wondered
what had finally happened to him, and if his son was still in
England or had been killed in the last war. We would never
know. Here was a man who had belonged to that race of
wandering Englishmen who had once roved the world as
though it were their own backyards, and who were now
tokens of an age that was gone. They were odd men, perhaps,
difficult, doomed never to fit in anywhere, but of a uniquely
individual calibre. We wondered where such men could go
now, with the world so mapped and known.

The Somalis from nearby encampments often visited our
camp. When Jack was away, I tried to speak with them. I
made an effort to communicate in Somali, but usually they
did not understand what I was attempting to say. Mohamed,
beside me, squirmed in embarrassment.

"I think you let me speak, memsahib."

Invariably I gave in, unable to bear their blank looks,
Mohamed's tortured expression, my own sense of verbal
inadequacy. A delegation of Habr Awal, one morning, was
particularly suspicious. Through Mohamed, we struggled to
convey thoughts back and forth.

"If the officer is here to dig *ballehs*," they began, their voices gruff and their faces surly, "why does he not dig them? What is he doing? We see no *ballehs*."

I tried to explain that the sites had to be chosen, and that the machinery for the work had not yet arrived in the country.

"Why are the *Ingrese* making *ballehs* at all," they asked, "if they do not intend to use the water themselves?"

I tried to meet fire with fire. They were always saying the government should help them, I remarked, and now that the government was actually embarking on a scheme to provide *ballehs*, they still complained. Their talk surprised me, I told them blandly. They answered, however, by evading the issue entirely.

"Why does not the government leave us alone?" they enquired plaintively, and then they added, somewhat paradoxically, that they really wondered why the government did not send out twenty truckloads of water to each Somali camp during the *Jilal* season.

With a growing sense of futility, I replied that only the rains could provide enough water for all, and that was in Allah's hand. The *ballehs*, however, would hold water at least during part of the dry season, once they were built, but such things took time to build. The Habr Awal men threw up their hands and looked at the sky, and Mohamed refused to translate their comments. But I knew enough Somali now to catch the gist.

"What does she know of it, the fool? She is insane, like all English. They are *shaitans*, devils –"

They went away. But they did not wish me peace. They went in silence, with malevolent eyes. It was not to be wondered at, that I had failed to get across anything to them. My grasp of Somali was too limited, and so was my understanding of the country. And for their part, they were men who deeply resented the British and their families and herds were now dwindling in the drought.

The rumours about the *balleh* scheme grew with each passing week. The tensions in the Haud were severe, and it would

not have taken much to set the desperate tribesmen at each
other's throats, or ours. Hersi came to Jack one day with a
disquieting report.

"Sahib – one man coming last night to see me. He is my
cousin. We are both Musa Arreh, and his camp is not greatly
distances this place. He telling me what he is hearing recently
times –"

A group of tribesmen, it seemed, had spent the better part
of a night outside the thorn-bough fence of our camp, fond-
ling their smuggled rifles and debating whether they should
raid our camp or not. We were saved by only one thing – the
Somalis' inclination towards oratory and argument. In
whispers they had discussed the question so heatedly that the
day dawned before they had reached a decision.

"The sun rising," Hersi said with a sour grin, "so it was
too lately times for all their considerations."

The next time, they might make up their minds sooner.
What attitude could one possibly take towards people who,
understandably enough, were liable to turn in their despair
against the first person who happened to catch their attention, when that person might be oneself? I was filled with
doubts and indecisions. Jack asked himself the same questions, but he had to consider another thing as well. I was here
in camp all day, with only Mohamed and several labourers,
while he and the others were away surveying.

"You'd better learn how to use the rifle," he decided, add-
ing as casually as possible, "not that I think for a minute
you'll need it."

Sombrely, followed by Mohamed, Abdi, Hersi and all the
rest, we walked out to the edge of camp. Jack loaded the .303
and showed me how to hold it. I had never fired a gun of any
description.

"Hold it close to your shoulder," Jack said. "Okay. Now
fire."

Whoom! Stunningly, I found myself sprawled on the
ground, the rifle beside me. In the background, the Somalis
were quietly guffawing.

"For pete's sake," Jack said, trying to hold back his laughter, "I told you to hold it tightly – why didn't you."

My pride was more damaged than my shoulder. I went back to the tent by myself.

At last Jack poked his head in through the tent doorway.

"Maybe it would be safer, at that, for you to rely on your gift of the gab. You've got that in common with the Somalis. If there's any trouble, you can send Arabetto out in the truck to me, and try to keep them talking until I get back."

So, in a manner of speaking, the problem was solved. The matter of the rifle was never mentioned again. Either luck was with us or else our fears had been exaggerated, for although we had many more delegations of tribesmen, some of them riled or suspicious, we never saw a suggestion of a rifle nor heard any more rumours about a raid on the camp.

As for the question posed by the possibility of an attack, that was not answered. I doubt very much if there is an answer.

Some report of our vulnerable camp filtered through to the District Commissioner, and we were assigned four Illaloes to accompany us. They were the "bush police," tribesmen to whom the government gave uniforms and rifles and a certain amount of training. They remained close to their tribes, for their duties were mainly concerned with patrolling the country to keep down fights at the wells, the looting of camels and other forms of inter-tribal bickering.

Our Illaloes were very enthusiastic. They watched over us like gauche guardian angels in khaki shorts and pugrees. Indeed, at first it was difficult to persuade the Illalo corporal that when I set out across the desert at night in search of a nearby thornbush, I did not welcome an escort.

Jack left three of the Illaloes in camp each day when he went off surveying. The corporal came to me one afternoon and complained that he had an excruciating ear-ache. The tin box that contained our first-aid kit was my special province. I had selected the medicines and bandages with care and I had the satisfying feeling that we were well-equipped. But I had nothing for ears. The Illalo stood there with a quiet and expectant face. It was obvious that I must do something. But what? I asked Mohamed to bring me a bowl of warm water. The Illalo watched with interest while I added a drop of Dettol. Ceremoniously, I stirred and the water turned milky. I swabbed out his ear and he thanked me profusely. It would not do his ear-ache any good, but at least he might feel that I had tried. If his ear continued to bother him, we could send him to Hargeisa the next time the truck went in for water.

That evening Hersi came to see me.

"The Illalo corporal wishing me to telling you, memsahib, that the ear medicine is highest qualities. His pain, it is gone, absolutely. He says a thousand thanks."

I gaped at him. How could it be? Faith, which could move mountains, could also cure ears, apparently. Surprised and delighted, I pretended to shrug it off.

I had a regular sick-parade some days. Gashed fingers, thorns to remove from hands and feet. Abdi's eyes became sore with the constant blown grit and dust, and I bathed them for him with boracic. Courteously, he thanked me.

"I pray Allah grant you a son, memsahib."

I was moved by his gratitude and his prayer, and I felt a growing sense of confidence in my medical skills. I doled out aspirins and "number nines," the standard Army laxative, usable only by those with bowels of steel, and I bandaged away with a will. What I had not noticed, however, was that nothing serious had yet come my way.

Then the Somalis from nearby encampments began to come to our camp in the hope of obtaining medicines. The gashes were deeper now, the thorn-slivers infected. Once it was a woman who had been bitten on the arm by a camel. The teeth had gone in on either side, and the festering arm looked as though it had been punctured right through. Camel bites frequently caused blood poisoning – this much I knew. I told the tribemen with her that they should take her to the doctor in Hargeisa.

They could not possibly do that, they replied. They had a small camp, and if two of them went in to Hargeisa with her, there would not be enough men left to care for the sheep and camels. So I bandaged her arm, uselessly. She thanked me, and I felt sick.

A Somali herdsman came to our camp one evening. His emaciated body, every bone showing through the dried and flaking skin, trembled as though with chill. He crawled like a shot deer under a thorn tree and lay there, breath fluttering only faintly in him. I stood aside, for I did not have any idea what to do. Hersi and Mohamed and the labourers knew, however. They did not give him anything to drink right away. First they bathed him with water, and then they gave him a very little water in a cup, refusing to let him drink more until later. If they had allowed him all he wanted, he would have been twisted with cramps and would probably have died. When he had recovered sufficiently, we heard his story. He had been down at Awareh and had been travelling back alone with his camels. Thirst had almost killed him, and he had managed to survive only by the appalling process of killing one of his camels every eight days and sucking the moisture of the beast's guts.

What had I known of life here at all? I recalled the faith-healing of the Illalo's ear, and the simple boracic treatment of Abdi's eyes. It seemed to me that I had been like a child, playing doctor with candy pills, not knowing – not really knowing – that the people I was treating were not dolls. Had I wanted to help them for their sake or my own? Had I needed their gratitude so much?

For a while, after that day, I could not stand to look at my toy potions and powders. I shoved the tin box under a camp cot. I would have no more to do with it. Then I saw that this way, too, was an exaggeration. Would I do nothing simply because I could not do everything? The searching sun of the *Jilal* exposed not only the land but the heart as well.

Practical considerations forced me to dig out the inadequate tin box once more. Mohamedyero had sliced his finger with a butcher knife and was yowling as though he had just had a limb lopped off. I bandaged the small wound, thinking that all a person could do was what they could, but at least in the knowledge that it was only slightly more than nothing.

"Some she come to see you," Mohamed announced.

They stood hesitantly at the edge of the camp, several women from the bush and desert, clad in their drab brown and black rags, their faces unveiled, for *purdah* was never worn by those who spent their lives leading the burden camels.

Among Somalis, only the women knew how to set up the portable huts, how to place the frames of bent roots in the earth and cover them with the woven grassmats. When the tribe set up camp, the women had to assemble the huts before they could rest. This division of labour was not as unfair as it sounded. The men protected the tribe with their spears, and led the herds to new grazing grounds, often going ahead to find the way. Men had to reserve their strength for their own demanding work, but the women's lives were harsh, and after marriage they changed from girls to lean and leather-skinned matrons in the space of a few years.

The women approached, eyed me penetratingly, whispered between themselves, and finally asked. Could I give them anything to relieve their menstrual pain?

Somali girls underwent some operation at puberty, the exact nature of which I had been unable to determine, partly because in our early days here every Somali to whom I put this question gave me a different answer, and partly because I no longer questioned people in this glib fashion. The operation was either a removal of the clitoris, or a partial sewing together of the labia, or perhaps both. But whatever was done, apparently a great many women had considerable pain with menstruation and intercourse, and the birth of their children was frequently complicated by infection. In the opinion of an educated Somali friend of ours, this operation was one custom which would take a very long time to die, for the old women would never agree to its being abandoned, he believed, even if the men would.

I did not know what to say to these women. They were

explaining, almost apologetically, their reasons for asking. Walking with the burden camels, at such times, especially during the *Jilal* season – it was not easy to keep going.

What should I do? Give them a couple of five-grain aspirin? Even if they had money to buy future pills, which they had not, the lunatic audacity of shoving a mild pill at their total situation was more than I could stomach.

"I have nothing to give you. Nothing."

This was the only undeceptive reply I could make. They nodded their heads, unprotestingly. They had not really believed I would give them anything. Women had always lived with pain. Why should it ever be any different? They felt they ought not to have asked. They hid their faces in their cloths for a moment, then spoke determinedly of other things.

The days went by, and the clouds gathered, but still it did not rain. Ahmed Abdillahi, a young chieftain, visited the camp and offered his assistance.

"I have heard much about the *ballehs*," he said to Jack. "If you want me to go with you across the Haud, and guide you, and speak with the people, I will do it."

The first sign that the *balleh* scheme might be gaining some acceptance. Jack was encouraged and accepted the offer. Ahmed Abdillahi stayed with us for some time, travelling along the border with Jack, everywhere talking with people, arguing, explaining. He looked rather like Robeson must have looked as a young man, very tall and broad, with strong features and muscular arms. He had a poise that seemed never to be shaken. Whatever questions or suspicions were raised by his fellow tribesmen, Ahmed Abdillahi replied in the same deep firm voice, never losing his temper.

I drove with Jack and the others to Lebesegale. While Jack examined the possibilities of the place as a *balleh* site, I looked around. It was a tiny settlement, dark brown huts, a few camels, a mud-and-wattle tea shop with roof of flattened paraffin tins. The inhabitants were thin and in rags, haggard with the long *Jilal*. The water hole, once a large one, had dried to a small pool of muddy liquid which somehow sustained the few people here, but could not have done so if even one more family had arrived.

Beside me, Hersi trudged. "Nothing here, memsahib. The people are very poor presently times."

I nodded. There was certainly nothing much here. Only the bare red Haud soil, hard as stone, and incredibly, these few people, the old man who had come out of the tea shop to greet us, his two young grandsons, the three women with the flock of black-headed sheep. The rest of the villagers had left with most of the camels, to seek water and grazing elsewhere. Then I saw a small round brushwood enclosure within the almost-empty village. I asked Hersi about it.

"That is the mosque," he replied.

I looked again at the thorn boughs that formed the place of worship. It seemed to me that more genuine faith might reside in this brushwood circle than in the jewelled and carved magnificence of the Blue Mosque at Istanbul.

Driving along the Awareh-Hargeisa road, we saw two burden camels laden with the crescent-shaped hut-frames and the bundled mats. They were halted by the roadside, and as we drew near, we saw one of the beasts slide to its knees, sunken in the apathy of thirst and exhaustion. Beside them, squatting in the sand, was a woman, a young woman, her black headscarf smeared with dust. She must have possessed, once, a tenderly beautiful face. Now her face was drawn and pinched. In her hands she held an empty tin cup. She did not move at all, or ask for water. Despair keeps its own silence. Her brown robe swayed in the wind. She carried a baby slung across one hip. The child's face was quiet, too, its head lolling in the heavy heat of the sun. We had a little water left in our spare tank, and so we stopped. She did not say a word, but she did something then which I have never been able to forget.

She held the cup for the child to drink first.

She was careful not to spill a drop. Afterwards, she brushed a hand lightly across the child's mouth, then licked her palm so that no moisture would be wasted.

To her, I must have seemed meaningless, totally unrelated to herself. How could it be otherwise? I had never had to coax the lagging camels on, when they would have preferred to stop and rest and die. But what I felt, as I looked into her face, was undeniable and it was not pity. It was something entirely different, some sense of knowing in myself what her anguish had been and would be, as she watched her child's life seep away for lack of water to keep it alive. For her, this was the worst the *Jilal* could bring. In all of life there was nothing worse than this.

What we could do here was only slightly more than nothing. Maybe she would reach the wells. Maybe she would not. She might with good reason have looked at us with hatred as we began to speed easily away, but she did not. She was past all such emotions. She knew only that she must keep on or she would perish, and her child with her. As we drove away, we saw her rise slowly and call the burden camels. The beasts struggled up and began to follow her.

Across the great plains of the Haud, the wind swept the sand up into spinning dervishes of dust. The red termite-mounds stood like tall misshapen towers of the dead. On the carrion of camels the vultures screeched and gorged themselves. In the afternoons, the wisps of cloud formed raggedly in the sky.

"*In sha'Allah*," the Somalis said. "If Allah wills, it will rain."

We, too, said the same thing now. What else was there to say? All other words had ceased to have meaning in the *Jilal*.

CHAPTER FIVE

Flowering Desert

"VERY SHORTLY times," Hersi said, his words more a prayer than a prediction, "you will be hearing the voice of the *tug* in this land."

The *tugs* were dry river-beds for most of the year, but during the rains they flowed in spate, roaring briefly with their flood, hurling the water down to the sea, carrying it off where it could not be used. Hersi's expression had a biblical ring to it, almost like the Song of Songs.

> *The time of the singing of birds is come,*
> *And the voice of the turtle is heard in our land.*

If the rains ever came, perhaps even the Haud would be like Solomon's kingdom after the dry winter, when the flowers appeared on the earth and the vines were in blossom. It did not seem possible. The clouds had been gathering and thickening for so many weeks that we had ceased to expect anything of them. The rains would never come.

But at last they did come, and the violence of them matched the depth of the *Jilal* drought.

We had returned from camp and were temporarily based in Hargeisa. One afternoon we set off along the Wadda Gumerad road, Jack and Abdi and myself, on a short trip to a place in the Haud where Jack wanted to examine a possible *balleh* site. The road consisted only of the wheel marks of trade trucks, and even these had been obscured by the drifting sand. Somehow we took a wrong turning, and found that we were jouncing across the desert with not a trace of a road in sight. The Wadda Gumerad had completely vanished.

"We get lost, I think, sahib," Abdi admitted, furious at himself, for usually he could find his way unerringly through any portion of the Haud.

We were still wondering how to find the road when a sudden wind shuddered across the red sand. The sky turned greyish yellow, and the thunder began to growl. Then we heard a slow plok-plok-plok and saw the first drops of water unbelievably falling and being swallowed by the dust.

"Rain!" Abdi stopped the Land-Rover and jumped out, turning his face up to the sky. He let the quickening rain course over him – he held out his hands to it.

"Praise be to Allah, Lord of the worlds!" He spoke the Arabic words aloud, a mighty shout of thanksgiving. As we drove on, he talked excitedly.

"All thing come fine, this time. Sheep get fat, camel get strong now. You will see. Plenty meat, plenty milk –"

We, too, were excited, jubilant, thankful. Only gradually did our present situation dawn upon us. The storm was gathering force, and we were still lost. Because we had expected to be back before dinner time, we had brought no food and only one bottle of water. Even our customary spare water tank was empty today. Abdi's face grew sombre once more. He felt responsible for the fact that we had wandered off the Wadda Gumerad, but he reminded us, as well, that he did warn us not to venture out this afternoon in case the rains chose this day.

"You've been saying the same thing for weeks," Jack pointed out. "I could hardly wait around forever."

We shared the blame. There was no use in thinking about it. We were here, not there – what did it matter why? The rain became denser, and the sound of the thunder grew closer. Then the lightning burst like a gigantic roman candle, and the following thunder was like a cannon fired inside our skulls. The rain was a solid mass of water now, some ocean in the sky tilting and pouring out its contents all at once. The sky was black, illuminated momentarily by the explosive lightning. The deluge beat and battered at the canvas top of the

Land-Rover, saturating it. We were chilled and shivering, and we had no idea where we were going. All sense of direction was gone, for around us the desert had been transformed into a sea.

Thud! We hit a pothole. The muddy water splashed up around us. Abdi put his foot down hard on the accelerator, and the engine roared and strained, but it was no use. The Land-Rover was mired up to the axles. We were stuck like a bug in a pool of glue.

As suddenly as it began, the rain stopped. But this was only a breathing space. Soon the downpour would start again. In the meantime, Abdi got out and set to work feverishly. Jack joined him, but not hopefully.

"No stones around here. Nothing to block the wheels with. Well, let's try branches, Abdi."

We gathered flimsy thorn boughs, but these only snapped off or disappeared in the well of mud. I climbed tiredly back into the car. Jack and Abdi continued their efforts, but without success.

"I don't see how we can get out of here by ourselves," Jack said finally. "We'll just have to wait until a truck comes along."

Abdi's old eyes narrowed.

"If we wait, sahib," he said, "we wait one month. No truck pass this way when rain come."

Considering the fact that we had no food, this prospect did not seem hopeful. We sat huddled in the car, smoking thoughtfully, racking our brains but not emerging with any useful ideas. Then in the distance we saw a herd moving towards us, the camels looking like dinosaurs as they squelched through the mud, their long necks swaying, bending frequently to drink the water for which they had waited so long. As they drew closer we heard the cry of the herders, their voices guiding the animals and keeping the herd together.

"Ei! Ei! Ei! Hu-hu-hu-hu-hu!"

The tribesmen approached and eyed us warily. Abdi spoke with them, and their faces, as they realized our helplessness, took on a kind of avaricious joy. There were eight of them, tall young men with their spears slung across their shoulders. They were not of Abdi's tribe. In fact, their tribe and Abdi's had been on exceedingly bad terms during the *Jilal*. Slyly, one of them poked his head inside the Land-Rover and stared covetously at the rifle. Abdi immediately launched into a long and impassioned speech, his eyes glinting with menace. The tribesmen looked at me questioningly, shuffled their feet on the slimy ground, and drew away slightly from the vehicle. Over his shoulder Abdi hissed at me in English, not taking his eyes off the herders.

"You never move, memsahib. Stay there with rifle. I tell them we have plenty ammunition, and I say the officer's woman, she know how to shoot very well."

What presence of mind! Jack and I could not resist grinning at one another as we recalled my one unsuccessful attempt to fire the rifle.

"If they agree to help us," Jack said, "we'll not only have to give them what money we have – they'll expect the cigarettes as well. While they're busy, see if you can salvage a few, eh?"

The bargain was struck, and the young men set down their spears and began to work. I remained in the Land-Rover while it was being heaved at. The tribesmen shouted and shoved. The mud splattered like thick brown rain. The placid camels drank and gazed. Surreptitiously I managed to conceal a few cigarettes in my pocket. Finally, with a bellow of triumph, the tribesmen got the vehicle unstuck.

We paid them gratefully – it was little enough for what they had done for us. The bulk of our cigarettes, however, we parted with much more reluctantly. The tribesmen retrieved their spears and again regarded the rifle longingly. My hand remained firmly on the gun. I could not really take the situation seriously. I could not imagine our being attacked, perhaps murdered for the sake of a rifle. Abdi was wiser. He kept his eyes fixed on the men and never for an instant turned his back.

They were not all certain that Abdi had spoken truthfully about my excellent marksmanship, but neither were they certain he had not. We were held for an instant, all of us, in a state of suspended animation, no one wanting to be the first to make any kind of move. At last, as though they were able to communicate among themselves without words, they appeared to make the same decision simultaneously. Shrugging, they shouldered their spears, called the camels and went off. Across the plain we could hear their voices for some time, growing thin and reed-like in the wet and silent air.

"Ei! Ei! Ei! Hu-hu-hu-hu-hu!"

Night had come, so we left the car, which was now perched on solid ground, and made a fire. We sat around it on a damp hillock, smoking and looking up at the sky, a rich deep blue now that the moon had come out. Around us we heard the cackle of the hyenas. We were desperately cold, and the small fire did little to warm us, but we were glad of this respite. Then the moon and stars went out, and the rain began again.

"Must be we go on," Abdi said.

We trusted him absolutely. He was the one who knew what to do. We climbed back into the car and set off again. At last we managed to find our way back to the Wadda Gumerad, but the road had become a river. We were forced to follow the path pointed by this swift torrent of water, for it became impossible for us to see anything. There could be no darkness anywhere to compare with this darkness, unless in caverns under the sea where the light never reaches. The rain was a black wall of water before our eyes. Abdi hunched forward, glaring at the streaming windscreen as though hoping by sheer force of will to penetrate the dark rain. The Wadda Gumerad was full of small waterfalls, where the flood had gouged chunks out of the road and burrowed channels into the clay. The Land-Rover moved slowly, straining against the mud and rain, against the wild wind. It seemed a marvel that we were able to move at all.

Two days before, men and animals were dying of thirst here. Now some of them would drown. Every year, Abdi told us, a few sheep and goats, a few children, were swept away by the *tugs* when they flowed in spate. This must be the ultimate irony, surely – to drown in the desert.

Then we were on a vast plain, no trees or bushes anywhere. Our car was the highest object for miles, and all around us the lightning pierced down in pink shafts, a bright shocking pink that illuminated the entire plain in its flare, showing us the flat and open land, revealing to us our own faces. It was so close that we could not see how it could avoid striking us.

"You all right?" Jack enquired, not really a question – a reassurance, rather.

Yes, I told him. Quite all right. Probably I would have said so in any case, but as I spoke the words I realized with surprise that they were true. I would not have chosen to be anywhere else. If anything happened, at least it would happen to both of us at the same time. Perhaps some of the Muslim fatalism was rubbing off on me. We could not wish ourselves out of here, so there was no use in worrying about it. We would get out if we could – *In sha' Allah*.

The car bogged down again, and we decided to stay where we were until dawn. After an hour or so, the rain stopped and the lightning mercifully withdrew. The canvas of our roof was sodden and dripping, and all around us we could hear the voice of the *tug*, just as Hersi promised we would. When he spoke of it, however, we did not imagine we would be listening from this vantage point. The moaning of the *tug* was low and ominous, and we could feel the water sweeping and pushing against our uncertain fortress. But we were too tired to wonder whether the car would hold against the flood or not. Abdi crawled into the back, Jack and I settled ourselves in the front, and soon all three of us had fallen into a deep exhausted sleep.

In the morning, the situation had altered. The flood had abated, and we could see stones close by with which we could block the wheels. Externally, things had improved. Internally, they had worsened. We were stiff and cramped, damp, hungry, and without cigarettes. We were also extremely thirsty, for our one bottle of water had long since gone. We

would not perish of thirst with all this rain, but we would
have to be thirstier than we were at the moment, before we
would drink mud. I glanced at myself in the Land-Rover
mirror and immediately looked away again. I was covered
with clay and grime, my clothes filthy and dishevelled. I had
never felt more demoralized and miserable in my life. Last
night we were keyed up, tense, ready for anything, but now
that feeling was gone. We were depressed, wondering how
long it would take us to get back to Hargeisa, or if we would
get back at all. The thought of slogging through the mud
again filled us with weariness.

· We read these thoughts in each other's faces, but we did
not express them. We had developed, all at once, a reluctance
to say anything discouraging. It was better not to talk at all.
We began to gather stones, and finally got the Land-Rover
out of the gumbo and into action once more. We struggled
along the Wadda Gumerad, feeling the road slippery and
treacherous underneath us. We had only gone without food
and water for twenty-four hours. Compared to the tribesmen
in the *Jilal* drought, this was nothing. But it was quite
enough. My mouth tasted of bile, and I began to feel the
nausea of emptiness.

· "We try to pass Wadda Beris way," Abdi said.

"All right." We were in his hands. We had faith that he
would do the best thing possible. We travelled quietly, talking
very little, trying to reconcile ourselves to the idea of another
day without food, wondering how soon we would have to
drink the water from the dank puddles along the road.

But luck was with us. The rain held off, and in the afternoon we sighted Wadda Beris, the brown rain-soaked huts
and the clay-and-wattle tea shop of Haji Elmi, the old man
who had once shown Jack the tattered letter received twenty
years before from the Englishman who had hunted in Somaliland long ago. And here was Haji Elmi himself.

"*Salaam aleikum –*"

He was flustered at the sight of us, so bedraggled, but he
did not forget his manners. Because he was old, and given to
formalities, he used the Arabic greeting rather than the

Somali, for we were foreigners. He was thin and stooped, with a white beard. His frayed green and black robe and ancient khaki jacket hung lankly on his withered body. Abdi explained our plight, and Haji Elmi clucked his tongue like a mother hen and ushered us in to his tea shop.

A small square building, it was, clay plastered over branches, roofed with flattened paraffin tins. Inside, the roof was supported by gnarled *galol* branches, and the floor was earthen. A fire glowed in one corner, and into this fire a slender log was being fed, the bulk of the wood jutting out across the room. The air was heavy and pungent with wood-smoke. A few wooden benches were set around the room, and some coarse straw mats.

Haji Elmi's two boys, grandsons perhaps, bustled around and made sweet spiced tea for us, and soon the old man was handing us plates of dried dates and bowls of steamed rice moistened with *ghee*, clarified butter made from goat's milk. It had been a long drought, and there was not much food in any of the encampments throughout the Haud. But whatever he had, Haji Elmi gave to us. We crammed the rice and dates into our mouths – we had never eaten a meal as good as this one. When we had finished, we saw that the old man was searching through his treasure chest, a large tin box with a brass padlock.

"One still left – yes, I think so –"

Finally he found what he had been looking for. He held it up – a slightly mouldy pack of Player's cigarettes. We could hardly believe it. This man was a wonder.

Next he brought a blanket and pillow, both embroidered in the Somali traditional designs, birds and stiff-petalled flowers in brilliant red and green and yellow. These he placed in an alcove for me, so I could rest before we continued our journey. While I was lying down, Haji Elmi talked with Jack, displaying the ceremonial sword he once received for saving the life of a district commissioner during a riot.

"I take the stones on my own body," he said, "on my own body."

In my alcove, I listened and wished he had not spoken in

this way, sanctimoniously. But I recognized that the thought was foolish. He was not perfectly designed and lifeless like a cardboard cut-out figure.

We were not surprised when he came to us, many months later, with a flowery petition requesting Jack's help in obtaining government payment for a small *balleh* which Haji Elmi had got his grandsons to dig and from which he had been selling the water at a profit quite handsome enough to have made his enterprise worth while without any attempt at procuring a completely unwarranted subsidy. Haji Elmi was not surprised, either, when Jack said he had no power to help the old man in such a request. He had not really expected Jack to plead the unlikely case with the government. But it might have worked – it was worth a try, anyway. Haji Elmi had a sharp eye for a shilling, and he was addicted to intrigue and oratory. The petition was as much a part of his nature as the proud display of the ceremonial sword or the much-folded letter, and neither aspect of him was in fundamental disagreement with the generosity he showed us in his tea shop the first day of the rains.

That day at Wadda Beris, when we rose to leave, he refused to take from us a chit for money in payment of the meal and cigarettes. No, he told us – he could not take payment for such a thing. If he met us in Hargeisa or if we came out to Wadda Beris under different circumstances, that would be another matter. But this time we were travellers in need, and a basic tenet of Islam was that the hungry wayfarer must be fed.

We could only thank him and drive away. But afterwards, whenever we recalled the drenched desert, the dripping thorn trees and threatening sky, we thought of this hospitality, compared to which our own, given out of a state of plenty, would always seem poor.

Aleikum salaam, Haji Elmi.

Back in Hargeisa, Mohamed and Hersi and the others greeted us as though we had returned from the dead.

"*Wallahi!* You are here! We think we never see you, never no more!" Mohamed shook hands with us vigorously, then rushed off to heat buckets of much-needed bath-water.

Hersi raised his arms as though in benediction. "I giving thanks to Allah this day, for He is saving you from bloody terrible death."

Mohamedyero, Mohamed's small helper, beat loudly and joyfully on an improvised saucepan drum.

"Hey, Abdi!" Arabetto cried in amazement. "How you get back, eh? You fly? I try to go find you, but my lorry can never pass that way."

Arabetto was the good-natured and slightly jazzy youth from Mogadisciou, half Arabian and half Somali, who drove our Bedford truck. He had gone out, together with another driver and truck from P.W.D., to search for us, but had been forced to turn back. Now we realized how fortunate we had been. If we had been driving a heavy truck, we would never have got it out. The nature of our vehicle, the chance encounter with the tribesmen – these were strokes of luck. But if it had not been for Abdi's tenacity, we would probably not have made it. We felt a new bond with him, the sense of having lived through something together, and the awareness that we might owe our lives to him.

We were forced to wait in Hargeisa until the *Gu* rains were over. Our house was close to the *tug*, and in the darkness, through the steady hammering of the rain, we could hear the deep voice of the night river. When we walked out early in the morning, however, the rain had stopped and the *tug* was almost dry. Huge piles of sand had been deposited in the river-bed, like brown snowdrifts with fantastic contours, and Somali children were already playing there, in the same spot where only a few hours earlier the spate of water had foamed.

When the rains were reckoned to be nearly over, we went back out to camp in the Haud. The change in one month was unbelievable. We could scarcely recognize it as the same land. On that portion of the plain where once only the red termite-mounds stood, now the grass grew several feet tall, ruffled by the wind and swaying greenly. The thorn trees were thick with new leaves and the country seemed to have filled in, the grey skeleton no longer visible. The whole land was laced with flowers. White blossoms like clover were sprinkled through the short grass under the acacias. There were pale yellow flowers the colour of rich cream, and small mauve *wahharowallis*, and the scarlet flowers of the aloes spreading out on slender branches like some mythical tree. The air was full of the songs of birds and the high-pitched whine of insects. The swallows flew at such speed that they could be seen only as a blur of blue. The vultures were no longer in evidence – life had come back, and the birds of death had hidden themselves. Along the road, clumps of butterflies gathered around pools of water. They were small and light green, these butterflies, and clustered together they looked like a gigantic flower with innumerable fluttering petals. As the car approached, they swarmed into flight. The flower broke, and all the petals were scattered, only to form again into the living green water-lily when we had passed by.

We saw remainders of the *Jilal*, the skeletons of camels that had died in the drought. Now the grass and wildflowers twisted around the bare bleached ribs. But we had not yet been here long enough to realize, as the Somalis did, that the *Jilal* would come again.

The Somali tribes were walking out into the interior with their flocks and herds. Now the people smiled and waved as we drove past. The women were wearing new clothes, the red and blue and gold of their robes looking appropriate in a land suddenly grown to colour again. Some of the girls walking across the Haud, leading the burden camels, were so striking in appearance and moved with such an easy grace that they would have made the polished products of Mayfair look clumsy in comparison. They were voluptuous looking women, with coppery brown skin and softly rounded faces. Their eyes were large and dark, with long lashes. They seemed to glide along, almost like ballet dancers, with a perfection of balance that may have been gained from carrying jars and baskets on their heads. Many men of the desert were extremely handsome as well, tall and lean, with straight sharp features and keen eyes. The young herders had new robes, a flashing white, which they wore jauntily, the cloth draped around them in the manner of a toga and flung across one shoulder. What a contrast the people were, to themselves of a few months back. The season of new grass and plentiful water would not last long, so they made the most of it while they could. In the evenings, we could hear the sound of singing and the rhythmic clapping of hands from the nearby encampments.

"We are happy now," Hersi said, "for meat and milk have come back to our land."

The sheep and goats were lively, and the camels had their humps back again. Soon there were new flocks, too, composed entirely of lambs and baby goats, and these were invariably tended by a Somali child, a little boy or girl who pranced along as lightly as the young animals.

All was not paradise in camp, however, despite the season. We had taken up residence in the back of the Bedford truck, mainly because I felt more secure when sleeping at some slight distance from the ground. We had draped a mosquito-net across the open end of the canvas-covered structure, and had placed inside this makeshift caravan our camp chairs and table, and our bed, a new one complete with airfoam mattress. Let hardier souls sleep on canvas cots – they were not for me. I have never seen any reason for being more uncomfortable than necessary. Our truck-home would have been perfect had it not been for one thing. The renewal of life in the desert naturally did not exclude the renewal of insect life. Nightly, we waged a battle of the bugs. Mohamed would rush from the cook-tent to the truck with our dinner, hoping that not too many flying-ant wings would land in the food en route.

"Quick, quick!" He would shove the plates in under the net, but never quickly enough. "Oh-oh, I think some small something fall in –"

A dozen detached ant-wings and several frantic beetles would be floating like croutons on the surface of the venison soup. If this invasion had occurred when we first arrived in this country, I would probably have starved out of sheer repugnance. Not any more. Stoically, I spooned the bugs out and began to eat. The soup was easy – it was the rice which presented a problem. Mohamed cooked rice with snippets of fried onions in it, and in the half-light of our dining hall it was not easy to distinguish insects from onions. To Mohamed, the situation presented limitless possibilities for laughter.

"I get dinner with no light in the cook-tent tonight," he announced, grinning broadly. "Everything very dark. I can no see nothing. I think maybe no bugs come, that way."

No bugs, perhaps, but goodness knows what he had put in the dinner, groping his way around the cook-tent in the darkness. The mosquito net on our truck-house was alive, a crawling mass of wings, and Mohamed was fond of making comments on them.

"*Ei, wallahi!* Look here! Must be we call in the Locust Control men!"

Sometimes he would classify the creeping tangle of wings and antennae.

"Many different tribes here. See this small one? Plenty this kind – I think this one Habr Yunis. Plenty, plenty – but very small."

He himself was Habr Awal, and could not resist this dig at a rival and larger tribe.

"What about that big beetle there?" Jack asked him. "Which tribe is he?"

"That one is Ogaden," Mohamed said without hesitation, "Ogaden who get lost from his tribe."

We set our pressure lamp at a distance from the truck, in order to attract the bugs away from us, and although the method did not appear to work very well, we had only to approach the lamp to see how much worse the insects might have been on our net. Around the lamp they were a grotesque sight. They battered their wings against the scalding glass and even managed to thrust themselves compulsively inside until they reached the bare flame. The lamp was clogged with them and the ground was littered with charred wings.

My *bête noire* was the *balanballis madow*, the black

butterfly. It was really a giant moth with a corpulent furry body and eyes that glowed red like a demon's in the darkness. Each night at least one of these moths insinuated itself into our truck, and flapped around like a panic-stricken bird.

I had grown used to all manner of crickets and cicadas, to stink-ants with an odour that verified their name, to hordes of fawn-winged moths, to the green praying mantis with its coral limb-joints and its piously uplifted arms, to zooming beetles the size of golfballs. But I could never become accustomed to the black *balanballis*. To me, they were like the bats of hell.

Our relations with the nearby Somali camps had improved. Tensions had eased now that the *Jilal* was over, and the tribesmen's tempers were not so strained. They visited our camp often, and usually talked quite amicably with us. But the old rumours persisted. They always mentioned that they had heard that the water in these new *ballehs* would be poisoned, or that the government planned to put a heavy tax on the use of the water. Occasionally we met with active opposition. One day when Hersi and Omar were out digging test holes near a proposed *balleh* site, some Eidagalla men came up and threatened them.

"You have no right to dig there." The words were emphasized with a brandishing of spears.

Hersi, however, knew precisely how to reply.

"Is this your country," he enquired haughtily, "or is it Allah's?"

He had them there. They remained surly, but they lowered their spears.

The nomads continued to seek medicine from us. This season, which at first appeared wholly good, had its own evils. With the rains came the anopheles mosquitos, laden with malaria. We had obtained large supplies of quinine from the Hargeisa hospital, and we distributed these pills as widely as possible, but they reached only a relatively small number of people.

These particular quinine tablets had been left behind by the Italians when they were driven out during the war, after their brief occupation of this country. For some unknown reason, the pills were coated with a thick scarlet waxen substance which did not dissolve in the stomach, and so the quinine had to be chewed in order to do any good. Carefully, I explained this fact to each tribesman as I handed over the pills. Then I questioned Hersi – was he sure the man had understood?

"Oh yes, memsahib. He is understanding completely all your instructions."

But did he really? I had no way of knowing. We heard from time to time of tribesmen spreading warnings against this quinine, maintaining it to be useless. I sometimes had the feeling that most of the quinine would be wasted because the tribesmen, although many of them seemed to have faith in its efficacy, did not comprehend at all why it should be necessary to chew the bitter-tasting pills. For all I knew, they might feel the same towards these impressive red disks as they would about a Yibir's amulet – the advantage of it was in the possession of a powerful thing rather than in any physical action such as that of chemicals upon disease parasites. It was not a matter of intelligence but of viewing the whole of life through different eyes. How could I hope to explain the necessity, in my view, of rendering under Caesar the things which were Caesar's? If you are going to use the potions of science you must use them scientifically. But for the Somalis, nothing was Caesar's – everything, in effect, was God's. If the medicine had power, it was essentially a spiritual power. What could it possibly matter whether the pills were chewed or not? I was wasting my breath in explanations which simply did not strike home. We were looking at the same object, the tribesmen and I, this vial of red tablets. But I suspected that we were not seeing the same thing.

It was certainly not that they lacked the powers of observation. These were acute, a fact which was borne out by an odd item in an old book I had come across recently, written in the mid-1800's by an Englishman who was big-game hunting in Somaliland. The sahib had been troubled with malaria which, he said, was well known to emanate from the noxious night fumes around swamps and river-beds. The Somalis, he added with amusement, had a quaint belief that malaria was brought on by the bite of mosquitoes.

In some ways this story seemed to contradict my feeling that the tribesmen looked for spiritual causes and cures, but it did not really do so, for the insect had merely been observed as the agent or carrier, and what we termed disease germs might here be regarded as malignant djinn. But these were only theories, possibly quite unreliable. My difficulty was in discovering how the tribesmen actually looked at things, for without a knowledge of basic concepts, communication is impossibly confused.

Had they really understood? I asked Hersi again, seeking his reassurance – nonsensically, for I was by no means certain that he knew, himself, the reasons for the instructions he was conveying to them.

"They are hearing all," Hersi replied decisively.

Hearing, yes. We understood each other's words but not necessarily each other's meanings.

A great many people were ill with malaria throughout the Haud. Groups of women arrived at our camp carrying in their arms children who were so lethargic with fever that they could barely open their eyes. Malaria is the largest child-killer in all Africa. If a child manages to survive until the age of five or six, the chances are that he has developed quite a strong resistance to the disease. But it is the children under six who are most afflicted, and it was these young ones whom I found hardest to look at. Their small limbs burned to the touch, and they shuddered spasmodically with the fever's convulsive chills. Their eyes occasionally flickered open in a kind of bewilderment. And I turned away, unable to meet those eyes.

For many of the Haud women, the brief time of rejoicing after the rains was already over. They had managed somehow to keep their children alive during the season of drought, only to see them die of malaria in the season of plenty. I no longer marvelled that the Somalis believed in a God of ultimate mercy who at the Last Day would restore all things.

Who shall give life to bones when they are rotten? He shall give life to them who gave them being at first, for in all creation is He skilled: who even out of the green tree hath given you fire, and lo! ye kindle flame from it.

So the Qoran gives suffering a meaning and refuses the finality of death. I saw the necessity of this belief, without which life for these people would be intolerable. I would have shared such a faith, if it had been a matter of choice, but I could not. To me, it seemed that these children died point-lessly, and vanished as though they had never been, like pebbles thrown into a dark and infinite well.

The rains were not quite over yet. One evening a strong wind whirled up out of nowhere. The sky opened, and within minutes the entire camp was flooded. Everyone rushed around, trying to anchor things down. Under the pelting rain and wind, the big tent was on the point of collapse. Jack and Abdi hurriedly tied the guy-ropes from the tent to the Land-Rover, while Arabetto turned the Bedford truck around so that all our possessions would not get soaked. The camp was a shambles, six inches deep in water, like a big shallow *balleh*. Drenched to the skin, we ploughed through the water, gathering up ropes, buckets, shovels, before they could float away. Finally everything was more or less secure, and we all hastily took shelter in the big tent. The ferocity of the storm was something to behold – rain lashing like bursts of gunfire, the big wind beating at our canvas, the earth turned into a swamp, the flashes of sheet-lightning, the brooding sky.

In the tent, waiting for the rain to ease, we experienced that sense of companionship which sometimes occurs during even a minor crisis. Ourselves, Hersi, Mohamed, Abdi, Arabetto, young Omar the survey helper, the other drivers and labourers – we all talked together easily and lightly.

Could thunder ever kill a man, Mohamed wondered. Jack attempted to explain what thunder was, whereupon both Hersi and Arabetto maintained that they had known this all along. The exact same information, Hersi added with more piety than accuracy, was to be found in the Qoran.

After the storm, Jack and I returned to our truck, and the Somalis sat around the fire until nearly morning. Hersi led the singing, chanting the verse of a long narrative poem, while the others joined in the chorus. For a long time we listened to these strong voices singing in the African night. They blended with the rustle of water as the streams poured across the desert and emptied into the *tugs*. Occasionally we could hear the shrilling of still-wakeful birds in the thorn trees, and the mournful cry of the night-flying *ghelow*. All this was good, in ways we could not explain, better than anything we had ever known before.

Every day the Illaloes went through their drill. The corporal barked out orders, and I discovered that these bush police were trained in English. The drill commands were all the English that most of them knew. The words, therefore, had undergone a subtle transformation and were given a Somali intonation until they were scarcely recognizable to me.

"Ra – toor!" shouted the corporal, and the men turned right.

"Sho – hah!" And they shouldered arms.

"Ki – mah!" They understood him perfectly, and commenced a quick march.

They did not neglect their ancient skills, however. When they had time to spare, they practised spear throwing. One afternoon we had a spear-throwing contest, with the Somalis from our camp pitted against some visitors from a nearby *rer*. Our men won, much to their delight, although the local herdsmen appeared rather disgruntled at this unexpected reversal, for most of those in our camp were men of the *magala*, town-dwellers who were not reckoned to be as handy with a spear as the men of the desert. I waited until the visitors had gone, not wanting to embarrass our staff, and then I tried pitching a few spears myself. I did very poorly. The difficulty was not only one of strength – the chief skill to be mastered was balance. You must know exactly how to hold the spear and when to release it. A good spearman can kill a lion with what appears to be an exceedingly inadequate weapon to use against such a beast.

Somali boys are taught how to throw spears from an early age, and begin practising with miniature ones. Even when they join the police or the army, and learn to use other weapons, it often remains second nature with them to trust their spears most of all. One evening we heard low growls and snarls outside our camp, and the terrified cry of a young camel which was being attacked by a hyena. The Illaloes immediately dashed out. The first man was practically on top of the hyena when he suddenly realized that in the heat of the moment he had instinctively thrown down his rifle and picked up his spear instead. He came back to the camp for his gun, looking very sheepish, and the others teased him for days.

We packed up and prepared to move camp. A messy procedure, this, for we had had rain the night before and now everyone was slithering perilously through the mud. Our camp, usually in good order, now resembled a garbage dump. Tin charcoal burners, bedrolls, old vegetable peelings, boxes and tools – all were scattered about in wild disarray.

"We may as well have a quick lunch before we go," Jack said. "Tell Mohamed not to fuss – just a tin of beans."

The camp tables were already packed. We sat down to luke-warm baked beans with our plates balanced precariously on a baramile, a squarish metal water-container. We were a sorry looking sight, the pair of us. I was wearing canvas tennis shoes which were caked with wet mud, a pair of Jack's socks, a wrinkled old cotton skirt and blouse, and a kerchief wound around my head turban-style. Jack was clad in mud-splattered khaki shorts, a filthy bush-shirt and a fedora which looked as though it had been handed down through countless generations.

We heard the sound of a car approaching. Jack glanced up, stared and then gasped.

"Do you see whose car that is?"

Quickly I looked, and observed with horror the shiny black Humber. His Excellency the Governor of Somaliland had chosen this day to pay a visit to our camp.

We had met the Governor under formal conditions at Government House, and had been startled by the shrewdness of his questioning about Jack's work. He seemed to know all about everything – not a detail had escaped him. He had asked me, very directly, what I did with myself in camp. I had stammered over a reply, hesitating to tell him that I spent most of my time in attempting to translate Somali poems and folk-tales. Later I realized that I should have told him, for it was a subject which interested him.

This morning in camp, however, we could think of only one thing – he was a man who placed considerable emphasis upon formality. Only a short time before, we had read in a book about Kenya a description of him in his days there, when he used to don full-dress uniform to go and inspect a distant post where only four African policemen were stationed. We rose, shuffled through the mud, faced the splendid car and the tall white-clad man.

His Excellency remained calm and unperturbed. Never once did he refer to our disorganized state. He acted as though everything were in perfect order. He did not even lift an eyebrow in mild surprise.

There were no repercussions from this visit. Only indirectly did we later learn that His Excellency had made enquiries at P.W.D. to make sure that we had been issued with the proper camping equipment.

The night came when we saw the symbol of Islam plainly visible in the sky. The thin crescent moon, with the one star in startling symmetry above it, hung like a pendant of gold against the black throat of the sky. Ramadan had begun.

"There is no God but God," the muezzins called, and the People of the Book knelt in mosques of marble or mud, from Dakar to Kabul, from Ankara to Abadan, their faces turned towards the yearned-for city, receiver of pilgrims, holy Mecca.

In that assembly of wealth and want, of kings and *fellaheen*,

praying for strength in the month of fasting, the tribesmen in
the Somali desert also knelt, unaware that they were among
the least blessed of Allah's subjects. Their worship was as
bare and lacking in outward splendour as their lives. Their
mosques were circles of brushwood, their ritual ablution
waters the brackish dregs of mud pools or simply the sand,
their religious relics the memory of graves abandoned in the
desert. No minarets drew their eyes to the place of prayer.
Across the Haud, only the red termite-mounds stood higher
than a man, and the thorn trees where the vultures waited for
the next *Jilal.* The grandeur of Islam, the riches of Persia and
Arabia – these were only fables, heard, like the hope of
heaven, with a longing that could not conceive of its object.
Yet poverty gave them its compensations. The fasts of Ramadan held no unaccustomed terrors. Hunger and thirst they
knew as well as the faces of their kinsmen. They had no light
but the ash-coated embers of their campfires to rob the lumi-
nous star and crescent of its gold, and no intrusive doubts to
rob it of its meaning. Faith to them was as necessary as life,
inevitable as death. They looked up and knew the Word had
been made visible. The Lord of the Three Worlds, Creator of
men and djinn, had given a sign and a symbol to His people.

Muslim law forbids the taking of any liquid or food during
the daylight hours in Ramadan, and even forbids the swal-
lowing of saliva. In camp, only our meals were prepared
during the day. At sundown everyone prayed as usual, and
then they were allowed to break their fast. They had another
meal at two a.m., and prayers and discussions went on during
most of the night. It was therefore necessary for them to sleep
in the afternoon, and this they did for as long as possible in
order to lighten the fast, so the work was slowed down to a
maddening degree. It was a trying time. Tempers became
short; old grievances were brought forth; everyone went
around spitting profusely.

But in the evenings, after they had eaten, they had a sense
of well-being and sometimes they would gather to listen to
our small "saucepan" radio, so called because its round blue
metal case resembled a cooking pot. Jack fiddled with the

dial, and got dance music from Nairobi, sounding thin and far away and dreary. At times we managed to get a station in India, and listened to the high-pitched, nervous, syncopated music. Sometimes it was sensuous drum-filled music from Morocco, or snatches of melody from Ethiopia, a single flute with a high sweet sound, a rustling and rippling music like a mountain stream. One evening we achieved Radio Pakistan, and an argument arose between Hersi and Arabetto over what language was being spoken.

"I am hearing very plainly," Hersi said. "That is Arabic."

"No, Hersi, that's not Arabic." Arabetto, being half Arabian, had grown up speaking the language.

"Yes, it is," Hersi insisted. "You are not understanding it because it is grammatical Arabic."

Other issues arose in our evening sessions. Hersi explained to me about the "low" tribes, saying they used to be servants of the "higher" tribes.

"You know – the same way the black people in some parts of Africa are being servants to the Europeans."

He excluded the Somalis from this classification. They were men doing a job because they chose to, not because they had to. They passionately believed this, and in a way it was true. All of them had a few camels in the interior plains, somewhere, and could return to their tribes if they wanted. None of the men in our camp, with the single exception of Arabetto, had cut themselves off from their tribes. This was a good thing at the present time, for it enabled them to maintain their identity under the impact of an outside culture. But I wondered about the future. When this country had self-government, what then? How long would it take them to overcome inter-tribal bickering, or could it ever be overcome as long as the economic reasons for it still existed, the shortages of water and grazing? The tribal system might be anachronistic in some parts of Africa now, but despite its drawbacks, could it ever really be done away with here, where membership in a tribe was a nomad's only protection in a harsh environment? But against the likelihood or even inevitability of continued tribal disagreements must be set the

very real advantages which the Somalis had in comparison
with some other African countries. They had a common religion and a common language. With certain local variations
they possessed a common culture. Somalis from Mogadisciou
to Djibouti knew the stories of Arawailo the wicked queen,
or the legends of Darod or Sheikh Ishaak. The Esa around
Borama could speak with the Ogaden men, and be understood. The Habr Awal in the Guban and the Habr Yunis in
the Haud spoke the same words when they prayed.

Gradually we unearthed the presence of another irony, this
time one which struck us as amusing. In Hargeisa and Berbera we had heard a number of sahibs and memsahibs holding forth on the insensitivity of the Somalis, whom they
believed to be incapable of any emotion as subtle as tenderness or love. Now we discovered that the Somalis, for their
part, believed precisely the same about the English, whom
they regarded as utterly uninterested and indeed childishly
uninformed in matters of love.

Love was one of the two great subjects of Somali poetry,
the other being war. Love between men and women did not
here contain the dichotomy long ago imposed upon it in the
western world by the church, that of separating it, as though
it were oil and water, into elements labelled "spiritual" and
"physical." The Somalis recognized no such distinction.
Furthermore, love – like tribal war, in their view – was not
only a necessity and a pleasure, but a skill and an art. It was
discussed interminably among those of the same sex, but
men and women were not supposed to discuss love, even in
the abstract, unless they were married or belonged to one
another's taboo group. The system of marriage was highly
complex, and any blood relative, however distant, was taboo.
So repugnant was the idea of incest, which would of course
include any member of the taboo group, that talk could be
relatively free within this group, for it was assumed that such
talk would not under any circumstances lead to sexual con-
tact. Within the "possible" group, however, all talk of love

was banned, even between a boy of fourteen and a woman of eighty.

Marriages were usually arranged by the two families, with an eye to mutual financial advantage. Together with the tribal elders, the men in both families met to settle the essential questions, the sums to be paid by the young man for the bride-price (*yarad*), the token payment (*gabbati*) made at the time of betrothal, the percentage of the man's estate (*meher*) to be made out to his wife upon marriage, and the dowry (*dibad*) given by the bride's family.

But the choice was not entirely out of the young man's hands. His family would attempt to find a girl who pleased him, and he would usually make enquiries about the girl, through an aunt, and would ask all kinds of pertinent questions – what were her manners like, had she good legs and breasts, was she pleasant-tempered, had she wit and thrift? Standards of womanly beauty among Somalis were very specific. To be truly beautiful, a girl should be fairly tall, plump but not fat, with ample hips and breasts. A woman's buttocks should be well rounded – so important was this aspect of female appearance that Somali women often arranged their robes in a kind of bustle, to pad out their rumps in much the same way as women in our breast-conscious society assist nature with padded brassieres. Somalis placed great value upon a graceful walk and a proud bearing in a woman. The most favoured shade of skin was a light copper colour. Another mark of beauty was a brown or pinkish line across the teeth, a fairly common sight here. In one song the lover compares his beloved's teeth to a white vessel made of the pale inner bark of the *galol* tree and bound around with a string of pink Zeilah pearls – a reference to this beauty mark. Dark shining gums were also admired. In a well-known poem, in which the lover enumerates the features of his beloved, he places this one high on the list – "Her gums' dark gloss is like blackest ink –".

A young man saw his betrothed alone only once before marriage, when by custom he was allowed to spend a night with her. On this occasion he could undress her and do anything he wanted with her, short of actual intercourse. Should she prove a disappointment, however, practical considerations made it difficult for him to change his mind at this point, for if he did so, he forfeited the bride-price he had paid. With what care he scrutinized her, therefore, on the night of *dadabgal*, which means "to go behind a screen," and she, no doubt, scrutinized him with an equally sharp eye. True, he could divorce her easily by Muslim law, but this procedure would involve lengthy wrangling between his family and hers. He could also take three other wives besides her, but it was a rare man here who could afford more than one or two wives. Sometimes a woman would say that her *meher* was the penis of her husband, by which she meant that she received no legal portion of his estate, for he had agreed instead to take no other wife.

Love was an intense and highly emotional state – it was not expected to endure. Indeed, so much was it at variance with the starkness of usual life that no wonder love in this sense did not often survive for long after marriage. After marriage, Somali women, especially those of the desert, led lives of continual heavy work and drudgery. They cooked, cared for the flocks and children, wove the baskets and mats, fashioned and set up the huts, dismantled the camp when the tribe moved, and packed the household goods on the burden camels. They led the burden camels across the plains – but if they never rode the camels, neither did the men, for camels were almost never ridden in Somaliland. Not surprisingly, most women lost their beauty within a few years. Not surprisingly, also, they frequently became irritable and nagging. This was the chief complaint Somali men made about their wives.

"What a tongue she has, that woman – like flame."

But the status of women was low, according to both tribal and religious traditions, and a woman's wits and her sharp tongue were often her only protection. A husband who was unusually considerate of his wife would be thought weak and would be mocked at by his fellow tribesmen. Sexual fidelity was demanded of her, but not of him.

Like the flowering desert after the drought, love was of a

season, not for ever. While it flourished, therefore, let the songs be made and the beauty of young girls remarked upon, for soon enough they would enter their own *Jilal*.

Love as it appeared in Somali poetry was many things. It was the sensuous and lyrical *belwo*:

> *He who has lain between her breasts,*
> *Can call his life fulfilled.*
> *Oh God, may I never be denied*
> *The well of happiness.*

It was the sombre, almost macabre sense of mortality that ran through so many Somali love poems – take what today offers, for who can tell if there will be a tomorrow?

> *Your body is to Age and Death betrothed,*
> *And some day all its richness they will share –*

Or,

> *Turn not away in scorn.*
> *Some day a grave will prove*
> *The frailty of your face,*
> *And worms its grace enjoy.*
> *Let me enjoy you now –*
> *Turn not away in scorn.*

Some of the figures of speech in Somali love poetry might appear odd and even ludicrous to a European, for it was quite common for a poet to compare himself to a sick camel, when he was suffering from an unreturned love, or to boast that he was like the finest camel in his herd – strong, lithe, swift. But in order to appreciate what such comparisons meant to a Somali, it was necessary to understand what his camels meant to him. Camels were the mainstay of Somali life. They provided the tribesman with meat and milk, his staple foods, and they packed his goods across the desert. Their endurance in the drought was what saved him. Without his camels he would have been lost. They were not simply anonymous domestic animals to him. They were his livelihood, his wealth, his pride. He always knew each of his animals by name and could discern the footprints of each in the sand. He tended his camels not only with care but with affection. There were dozens of words in

Somali to describe every kind and condition of camel. It was no wonder that camels figured so largely in Somali poetry, even in love poetry, for they were as close to the Somali's heart as his own family.

> *Like a camel sick to the bone,*
> *Weakened and withering in strength,*
> *I, from love of you,*
> *Oh Dudi, grow wasted and gaunt.*

When a poet expressed his love in this way, one could be quite certain that, in North American parlance, he had been hit where he lived.

Another face of love was found in Elmi Bonderii's famous poem *Qaraumi* (Passionate), in which he described not only Baar's beauty but her domestic accomplishments as well, and ended with these lines:

> *When you behold my lovely, incomparable Baar,*
> *Your own wives, in your eyes, will all be old.*
> *Alas, alas, for ye who hear my song!*

Elmi Bonderii (Elmi the Borderman) was said to have died of love. He fell in love with a young girl named Hodan Abdillahi, but as he was not wealthy, she was married instead to Mohamed Shabel (Mohamed the Leopard). Elmi cherished his hopeless affection for five years.

"Then," Hersi said, "he died of love. Absolutely nothing else."

No one found this surprising at all. Love was a serious matter, a delight which could turn to disaster. But no Englishman ever died of love – of this fact the Somalis were quite positive. It seemed doubtful to them that the *Ingrese* had much need of love at all. Most Englishmen here were physically heavier than Somalis, owing to a better diet, and had greater muscular strength, although not as much endurance, for few Englishmen could have survived the hardships of the *Jilal*. This greater physical strength the Somalis attributed to sexual abstinence. Also, most English families had only one or two children, or else appeared to have none at all, for their school-age children were in England. Many Somalis therefore believed that sex was something practised only infrequently

by the English, who were indifferent where love was concerned, and probably inept as well.

We were very much entertained by the discovery of this
widespread belief, until we found that it was also, perforce,
applied to ourselves. This revelation placed it in a slightly
different light. When finally Hersi agreed to recite some of his
own *belwo*, he told us he would not do so before because he
did not think we would be capable of understanding or
appreciating love poems.

"You *Ingrese*," he said delicately, "are not so highly
acknowledgements as us in these considerations."

The month of Ramadan was not yet over when the *kharif*
began. The summer monsoon came up from the south-west,
over the Ethiopian mountains and across the plains of Somaliland, gathering heat as it travelled. The wind blew cool at
night in the Haud, but by the time it reached the coast, the
sands and the rocks would have imparted to it something of
their heat and its breath would be like fire day and night.

The *kharif* would blow until autumn, filling the days with
dust-devils and the nights with its moaning. On the great
plains, the camel herders' eyes would be sore with blown
sand. In the stations, tarpaulins would be whisked from lorries and secret files from office desks. Officers on trek, having
a sundowner outside their tents, would find their glasses of
gin and lime blown off the camp table. Young Englishmen in
outstations would wonder why they had not gone into com-
merce in London, as they lay awake at night listening to a
wind whose sound was like the distracted wailing of hysteri-
cal women. In the stifling town of Berbera, wooden shutters
on the old government houses would clatter all night, and hot
wind would rush in to half-strangle the angrily wakeful occu-
pants. On the Gulf of Aden the dhow traffic would slacken
off, and the dhow men who ventured out would pray mightily
to Allah to spare their fragile craft. The wind would be everywhere. It would ring in the ears, clog the nostrils, drive
breath from the throat. When it had spent itself it would

suddenly collapse, leaving the country to the hot season.

The *kharif* battered all night against our truck, making the canvas roof sound like the beating of giant wings. One night I imagined I had been wakened by the thudding of the canvas, until I glanced up and saw that it was something else that had roused me from sleep. There, outlined against the net at the end of the truck, was a large dark shape. I was frightened, but not unduly so, for I was groggy and not fully awake. I nudged Jack and told him that something was trying to get into our caravan. He heard me only dimly through his sleep and thought I meant my old enemy, the black moth.

"Shine your torch on it," he mumbled, "and it'll go away."

I groped for my flashlight, but by the time I had switched it on, the shape had disappeared. I turned over and went back to sleep. In the morning I was wakened by Jack's shocked yell.

"My God! Everything's been taken!"

Thieves had ransacked our truck-home, taking the type-writer, Jack's theodolite, the briefcase containing all his papers, the drawing instruments, slide-rule, our radio and innumerable smaller objects. It was not only the value of the haul that distressed us. Many of Jack's instruments could not be replaced in a hurry, and he could not work without them.

One of the thieves had dropped his spear, possibly when I wakened and shouted, and the Somalis in our camp picked it up and examined it with great interest. Mohamed, Hersi, Abdi, Arabetto and others – all lamented loudly.

"Never in my life I seeing such bloody thieving as contained in bloody this place –"

"Oh-oh – too bad, sahib, too too bad!"

Underneath, they were actually delighted with the excitement of the event. They darted hither and yon like swallows, gabbling at the top of their voices. I, too, could not help feeling the same secret excitement. The Somalis had hopes of tracing the thieves by the dropped spear, the shaft of which was splintered at the end – enough, they said, to make it clearly recognizable.

Jack, Abdi and Hersi set off in the Land-Rover for Selahleh, the nearest Somali settlement. At camp the rest of us waited nervously, unable to settle down to any work. The slow hours passed. At last in the distance we heard the furious honking of the Land-Rover horn – Abdi's invariable signal of a successful hunt. They roared into camp like three triumphant generals after a battle. With them they carried the typewriter, theodolite, briefcase and all the rest of the loot.

What happened? What happened? We could not wait to hear. Everyone shouted at once. Finally, piecemeal, the story emerged. They drove, they told us, to the tea shop at Selahleh and asked if anyone could identify the spear. The tea-shop owner disclaimed any knowledge of the weapon and refused to discuss the matter. At that moment a young Eidagalla man came into the tea shop. He took one look at the spear and nodded his head.

"Every man around here knows the owner of that spear," he said.

Where were the thieves, then? The tea-shop owner maintained a stubborn silence. At this point Hersi and Abdi applied their strongest methods. Glorying in the situation, they threatened the tea-shop man and the entire village of Selahleh with annihilation if the culprits were not yielded up. Abdi paced the room, waving the rifle and glaring in his fiercest manner while Hersi gesticulated, shrilled and bellowed, outlining in vivid detail the fate that awaited the inhabitants of this unfortunate settlement. The whole Army would descend, Hersi cried passionately, and would raze Selahleh to the ground. Camels would be looted. Huts would be burned. Nothing would remain. The desert would cover their dwelling-places and the hyenas would gnaw their bones.

His English version of it, to me, was only a pale imitation. In Somali, it would have been magnificent. He must have made it sound like the destruction of Sennacherib. The tea-shop owner began to have second thoughts, and finally his resolve to protect his fellow tribesmen, or perhaps to share in their haul, crumbled completely. He shrugged and signalled to his waiting kinsmen, who trooped out and returned a few minutes later with one of the thieves.

"Here is the man. He is yours."

The thief sweated and shook. His accomplice had fled, he said, but he agreed to take Jack to the place where the stuff was cached, provided Jack would promise not to go to the police. Jack's sense of British justice at that point was not nearly so strong as his desire to recover his theodolite and the invaluable papers which represented months of work. He readily agreed. They drove out across the Haud, and there, in a deserted *zareba*, they found everything hidden. Recalling it, Jack laughed.

"You won't believe this," he said, "but I swear it's true. After he showed us the *zareba*, the first thing he did was to ask me for a cigarette. I was so surprised that I gave it to him. I figured that any man who had that much brass neck deserved one."

The thief had revealed his disappointment in the theodolite. It was in a large wooden box, and when he stole it he thought it was a chest full of gold.

As we listened to the story, Mohamed brought around mugs of tea.

"No Ramadan today!"

They would make up the day of fasting later. Such days as this did not occur often. This was a victory, to be celebrated fittingly, with healths drunk in scalding tea and the story, embellished and embroidered, recounted again and again.

We discovered, a few days later, that people in nearby Somali camps were very upset about the theft, as they considered it a blot on their honour. Some of the Eidagalla pointed out that the thieves were members of the Arap tribe, and there were murmurings in the area to the effect that no one would feel safe until "spears have been raised against the Arap." Thus are tribal wars touched off. Fortunately the muttering died down after a while, and no spears were raised.

But the tale lived on, and was told many times around the fire at night, and lost nothing in the telling. For all we know, fifty years from now the Eidagalla in the Haud may be chanting a *gabei* called *The Thief of Selahleh* which tells how Abdi the warrior and Hersi the orator outwitted the enemy and vanquished him utterly, although by that time it will have been forgotten what was stolen and from whom. And so perhaps the theodolite case may be transformed, after all, into some rare carved chest laden with golden coins and necklaces like the sun.

CHAPTER SIX

Place of Exile

A T LAST the long-expected news – the tractors and scrapers for the job would be arriving soon. Berbera had no port facilities for unloading such heavy equipment, so the machines were being sent to Djibouti in French Somaliland. We set off for Djibouti to collect them.

Guś and Sheila and Musa travelled with us. Guś wanted to do some language research among the Esa people of Borama district and also among the Djibouti Somalis. When we arrived at Borama, however, a message was waiting – the ship had been delayed.

"I might have known something like this would happen," Jack said bitterly. "We may as well stay here until we hear from the shipping agent."

His patience was almost at an end. He had been waiting for this equipment for months, and now was beginning to wonder if it would somehow elude him for ever.

Guś and Musa decided to push on to Djibouti alone, while Sheila remained with us at Borama. They went on foot, hoping to catch a passing trade-truck. When they had departed, we were a dismal trio. The resthouse was bare and cheerless, and we had nothing to do. Jack was depressed, feeling he would never get started on the actual construction of the *ballehs*, the sites of which had been chosen and the plans completed for some time. Sheila was worried about Guś, who had set out with enthusiasm but hardly any money.

"What if they can't get a lift? They can't possibly walk –"

Already in her mind's eye she saw him lying dead of sun-stroke or dehydration on the scorching sands of the Guban. I would have felt exactly the same if it had been my husband who had gone, but as it was not, I had no doubt that Guś and Musa would make the trek in perfect safety. What I did feel, however, was a sharp sense of disappointment over their departure, for I had hoped we might continue at Borama the work begun at Sheikh, that of translating some of the Somali poems. Pessimistically, I felt they would arrive back at Borama just as we were leaving.

But one evening Guś and Musa returned. They were in poor condition, having been forced to walk a good part of the way back. Although they travelled at night when the sand was cooler, they had worn out their sandals and had almost worn out the soles of their feet as well. Plied with tea, food and questions, they made a rapid recovery and recounted some of their experiences.

"We were lucky to get a ride to Djibouti with that English doctor," Musa said, "but when we got started, we found he was taking along a young officer of the Somaliland Scouts, as well. Now this officer is a real sahib – you understand what I mean? We are driving along the road, you see, and an old man is crossing and does not get out of the way quickly, so the doctor slows down. The Army man says 'Shall I get out and shoot him?' A joke, yes, but as I am Somali, like the old man, I am not greatly amused. Next we stop at a well, where many Somalis are drawing their drinking water. Our officer gets out and washes his hands in the well. Now, you know, to Muslims this is a very offensive thing. Guś and the doctor try to explain, but no. What does he care? The people at the well begin to threaten, and finally we manage to drag him away. When we reach Djibouti, the doctor goes off to the hospital. Guś and I go to the town. The Army man goes somewhere – I don't know or care, and I think I will never see him again. But such good fortune is not to be. Later, we are walking along the shore when we see the doctor. He is very angry, and we soon see why. The Army man has got drunk and has taken the doctor's car away. He has left it on the beach while he went swimming. The tide has come up, and now the car is stuck. We help the doctor to get it out – what a business, wading in the sea, the water up to our knees. At last we get it going, and then the Army man comes floating in like a big fish, and says he does not see why the doctor is making such a fuss. The doctor then says some things which I shall not repeat to you. Next, we all go back to town. The doctor asks us to look after his car while he finishes his business. This we do, but the officer, who is still not very sober, stays also. The sellers in the marketplace begin to crowd around, offering melons for sale. These melons are not worth one rupee each, you understand, but I think if the officer wants to spend a whole rupee on a melon, why should I say anything? He becomes rather confused, and takes one melon, then another, then another and another – one rupee, one rupee, one rupee. Never have I seen such spending. He cannot stop – more melons, more rupees. I almost say 'Here is my head – one rupee'."

Musa's piratical moustache quivered with his deep laughter. To him, the poetic justice of this one episode was worth the whole wretched trip.

Now that Guś and Musa were back, we settled down to work on the poetry. It was a three-way process. Musa knew a great many *gabei* and *belwo*, and had a wide knowledge of the background and style of Somali poetry, but while his command of English was fluent, he had to discuss the subtler connotations of the words with Guś in Somali. Guś and I then discussed the lines in English, and I took notes on the literal meanings, the implications of words, the references to Somali traditions or customs. I would then be able to work on this material later, and attempt to put it into some form approximating a poem, while preserving as much as possible of the meaning and spirit of the original.

I had never before found Musa easy to talk with. I had been impressed by him – who would not be? He looked like a young sultan. But I had never felt at ease with him. For one thing, he was not accustomed to women who talked as much as I did, and sensing some constraint or disapproval in him, I tended to agree with him too often, mistakenly hoping to set the matter right in this way but in fact only making it more difficult for both of us. Now, one evening, discussing a long *gabei* by Salaan Arrabey, who was reckoned to be one of the best Somali poets, I was all at once aware of how easily we were talking and arguing. Tomorrow, probably, we would once again feel ill-at-ease with one another. But for a while, discussing this *gabei* which interested both of us greatly, the awkwardness was forgotten.

There were so many poems which could have been done, and we had such a limited time that we were able only to skim a little of the surface. Still, it was something. When Jack and I left Borama, I had a sheaf of notes to work on, several *gabei* and perhaps a dozen *belwo*.

Near Borama were the ruins of an ancient city, or perhaps several cities built on the same site. One might have been pre-Islamic, although nothing much seemed to be known about it. The more recent one, we were told, was believed to be about a thousands years old. It had been built originally by Arab traders, and why it was deserted was a mystery. In his book *Somaliland*, Drake-Brockman suggested that these ruined cities, which were to be found in several places in this country, were abandoned by the Arabs when they found the ivory and ostrich-feather trade was falling off, or when they discovered that the local Galla people would bring their goods to the coast and sell just as cheaply there. To what extent this theory would be supported nowadays by archaeologists, I do not know. Many of the walls of this particular city still stood, and where they had crumbled it appeared to be due to time and to the crowding in of foliage rather than any sudden devastation.

Amoud was the name the Somalis had given it. The word means "sand," and the name was apt, for the city had returned to the mountains and the desert. When it was alive, Amoud must have spread up the hillside, the brown-yellow houses mellow in the sunlight, among the stiff acacias and the candelabra trees. In the marketplace, the donkeys and camels would have been laden with the sacks of aromatic gums and ivory, the bundles of ostrich plumes, and would have set out for the coast, where the goods would be taken by dhow to Arabia. The young Arab traders would have brought back to Amoud their dark-skinned Galla brides, those women from whom came the beginning of the Somali race. The town would have been a babble of noise, shouting and haggling, the scuffing of feet along the rough stone roads, the uproar of camels.

But now, as we walked through it, Amoud had been dead a long time. The walls were falling away, and the mosque was desecrated by birds and small wild animals. The candelabra trees had grown inside the houses, their bright green tapers looking as though they had been here always. Generations of the *galol* tree had grown old and fallen, and their boughs were strewn around the ground. Blue flowers the colour of kingfishers grew in the tangled grasses, and the trees cast long shadows on the skeleton of Amoud.

On the way down the shale-littered hillside, we saw three young Somali girls on their way back to their huts at the foot of the hill. The girls paused and stared at us, calmly, disinterestedly. Looking at them, I felt they had something of the same timeless quality as the hills and the sand. The Arabs came and went, and they left their religion and their sons. The British came and soon would go, too, leaving, for what they were worth, some ideas of an administration different from the tribal patterns, some knowledge of modern medicine, some ability to read and write in a European language. But the bulk of the Somali people were not greatly affected by these things. They still built their round grass huts, and herded the camels, and told tales around the fires at night, and scorned the settled life, just as they did before the Arabs came, a thousand years ago or more. Change had been slow here. Maybe it would quicken its pace soon. Perhaps their own leaders would be able to think what to do with a country that was so largely sand and thorn trees. Within the next few generations, the nomadic tribal ways might splinter and break, and from their breaking a new thing might grow. Or perhaps their leaders would wrangle interminably, unable to discover a way of overcoming the desert. But whatever happened, for a long time the people would go on as they always had, herding their camels between the wells and the grazing, the grazing and the wells.

Looking at Amoud, and then at the nomads' huts crouched at the bottom of the hills, I could not help thinking of the western world with its power and its glory, its skyscrapers and its atom bombs, and wondering if these desert men would not after all survive longer than we did, and remain to seed the human race again, after our cities lay as dead as Amoud, the city of the sands.

At Abdul Qadr, a very small village, the only one between Borama and Zeilah, the hills were completely bald. A heat haze shimmered glassily from the black rock, and the village coiled around the hillside like something out of a science-fiction story, an earth settlement with a precarious foothold on a hot and empty asteroid. When we drew closer, however, we were astonished to see a procession of women and girls coming to meet us, all of them carrying vessels filled with fresh camel milk. Where did they feed their herds? Milk was always a problem for us. Our staff, like all Somalis, craved it, and in the Haud, the best grazing area in the land, even after the *Gu* rains we had difficulty in obtaining enough. How was it that at Abdul Qadr we found plenty? Mohamed expressed the belief that the Abdul Qadr people left vessels of water in some magic place and when they returned they found the water turned to milk.

"The dry thorns in this place," Omar suggested, "give better milk than the finest camel."

They were joking, but only half. We were all in agreement – the people of Abdul Qadr must be the personal friends of Allah.

Our lightheartedness disappeared as we left the hills behind and crawled in convoy, Land-Rover and trucks, out onto the

Guban. Our map of Somaliland classified the roads as "Roads, principal; Roads, other; Tracks (motorable in some cases)," but in fact there were no "Roads, principal" in our sense of the words, no smooth highways where driving was easy. Most of the roads were "other," and a good many of them fell into the third category. When we emerged onto the coastal plain, the track meandered through the sand and frequently disappeared altogether. All we could do was head in the right direction and hope for the best. The Land-Rover bumped over the rough desert, and we were shaken like seeds in a gourd rattle. The heat was so intense that I breathed raspingly, gulping at the air. Whenever we stopped the Land-Rover and got out, the sun was like a hammer blow on my head and the nape of my neck. Headache trammelled like hooves through my skull. We drove on and on and on, seeing around us only the rusty sand and occasional clumps of coarse grass.

Then I saw, dancing in the air just ahead of us, a dozen pairs of yellow wings. Sun-drugged and dizzied by heat, I nonetheless took particular note, for these birds were the first pleasant sight since we came down onto the Guban. I pointed them out to Jack and Abdi. Look – yellow canaries!

Jack and Abdi, whose eyes were better than mine, said nothing. I would discover my error soon enough. The dozen pairs of wings became two and three dozen, a multitude, and I saw that the creatures were not little yellow canaries but large yellow locusts. They were in the middle stage of their growth. When they were fully mature, their wings would be scarlet, with a span as wide as a man's hand. Soon we were driving through a swarm of them. They fluttered blindly in through the Land-Rover windows, and launched themselves like bullets at our heads. They were armoured, their bodies having the horny texture of sea-shells. Their fan-like wings were fantastically strong. We closed the windows hastily, even at the risk of stifling, and managed to rid ourselves of the insects inside the car. Outside, they clattered like rain against the canvas roof. The radiator became clogged with them. The windscreen was so splattered with their dead and oozing bodies that Abdi could hardly see.

Somaliland was one of the countries in which the Desert Locust Control operated. Bait was set mainly, we had been told, for the young hoppers, in the hope that these might be poisoned before they grew wings. Some day, if sufficient control work could be done, locusts might no longer be a threat throughout the entire East. But that day was a long way off.

The swarming locusts moved like the surge and flow of a tidal wave. Nothing could stop them. Their wings were a shadow all around us, and they even darkened and obscured the sun. In the land where they passed, no leaf or blade of grass would remain – they would devour everything. They were a plague, a scourge. Burdening the air with their thrusting flight, their terrible wings of gold, they seemed like the giant locusts of the Apocalypse – *the sound of their wings was as the sound of chariots of many horses running to battle*.

Stunned by this onslaught, half suffocated in our airless enclosure, we drove grimly on. After an eternity of battering our way through the battalion of wings, we overtook their front ranks and passed them. We flung open the windows and breathed freely at last, and now the scalding breeze across the Guban seemed cool and wonderful.

At the extreme western edge of the country, close to French Somaliland, Zeilah stood, almost with its feet in the sea. We sighted it from a long way off, and it had the quality of a mirage, a shining city, the mosque minarets white in the sun, and the tomb of the local saint appearing to be a dome of pure and scintillating ice. The yellow sand gleamed all around, and beyond the city one could see the long silver ribbon that was the Gulf of Aden.

Close by, the view altered. Zeilah was not a city but a small and almost deserted town. The tomb of the Hazrami saint was made of whitewashed mudbrick, stained by rain and goat dung. The shops and houses were decaying, the soiled plaster falling away in shreds and chunks. Many dwellings had been abandoned entirely. The streets were narrow, the houses jammed in together, their walls sinking into the sand and their grey bone-dry doors askew. They had a sad and rakish appearance, as of dead bones not decently buried but left exposed to the plain view and curious stare of alien onlookers. Around the flat sunbaked roofs the seabirds screamed. The Somali huts at the edge of the town had a neater appearance than the crumbling shops and tea houses. Made of woven branches and twigs, the huts had a thorny and thatched look. A few children played in the cobbled streets, and sometimes a donkey ambled into the town, bearing water vessels to be filled at the Zeilah wells. Over the whole place clung the reek of the sea, a warm salt smell mingled with seaweed and rotting fish.

Zeilah was once a great city, although nothing of the opulence it then knew remained here now. It was known to the ancient Greeks, who called it Aualites. According to Drake-Brockman, this coast was known at the beginning of the Christian era as Barbaria, from which the name Berbera may have been derived. Zeilah at that time was one of the most flourishing ports in East Africa. Like Babylon, that mighty city, its trade was in gold and silver, cinnamon, frankincense, pearls, beasts and sheep, and the souls of men. It was a slave port, for many centuries one of the largest. According to legend, Sheikh Ibrahim Abu Zarbay, one of the Hazrami proselytizers who came to this land with Sheikh Ishaak (the "ancestor" from whom the Ishaak tribes traced their descent), preached at Zeilah and was buried here. Zeilah reached its zenith in the sixteenth century with the rule of the Somali king Mohamed Granye, and after his defeat by the Portuguese, the city was for several centuries in the hands of the Arabs, until the country came under the administration of the British.

Once there was a pearl industry at Zeilah. The pearls were small and pink, highly valued in Arabia and along the Persian Gulf. But the pearl beds were all depleted now.

We saw the mosque where Sir Richard Burton, in his Arab merchant's disguise, preached so skilfully. A small mosque, it was, the disintegrating walls repaired with bunched-up thorn twigs. It might not even have been the same mosque. It was the oldest one in Zeilah – that was all we were able to discover. No one here had ever heard of Burton. Perhaps an old man dozing in one of the huts had heard the tale, but he did not emerge to talk with strangers like ourselves.

The Zeilah people had always been a mixture of races – Somali, Galla, Danakil, Arab. Political and religious prisoners used to be brought here from Arabia, and the town's name in the original Arabic meant "a place of exile." The present inhabitants were the last clingers-on, descendants of the Arab traders, the slavers, the pearl-divers. They sauntered the sandy uncluttered streets, seemingly indifferent to their fate. I recalled what an educated Somali friend in Hargeisa had told us about his experiences in Zeilah, when he was here for a time on a government administrative job. The Zeilah people, he said, could talk of nothing except the sea – the hazards of taking a dhow across to Arabia, how to deal with a shark when you were diving, the art of handling a dhow in the mad *kharif* wind. These things they still knew, but all else seemed to have vanished. They did something which he felt had a subtle horror about it – they chanted songs whose meanings they had forgotten. The words were Galla, or Danakil, mixed with Arabic or archaic Somali, all so blended and changed that they were unrecognizable. They would chant them over and over, the mysterious words and phrases of a dead past, possibly imbued now with a magical significance. Our friend said he could hardly believe it at first, and thought maybe it was only the young people who did not know the meaning of the songs. He asked the elders of the town. They smiled gently and said no, they didn't know the meaning of the words in the old songs, either. These were just the songs their people had always sung, that was all.

The town was quiet. The coastal tribes came here for water, but few people lived here permanently any more. When we attempted to find some of the famed Zeilah mats, small circular grass mats beaded in marvellous designs and edged with cowrie shells, we could find no one who made them nowadays. The old skill seemed to be lost. Everything here had been shrunken by time and the sun, grown pale, faded to shadows. It was harder here than it was at Amoud to imagine the way the city must once have been, hard to believe that the caravans had ever poured in here, the camels bellowing and complaining, the wooden bells around the beasts' necks clanking in the hot briny air. Hard to believe, too, that here the slaves boarded the dhows and said their last farewell to Africa and to everything they knew, or that once the bazaars and streets echoed to the shouts of Mohamed Granye's armies. All gone now. On one side of Zeilah the still and tepid salt water lay, and on the other, the sands of the Guban stretched away and were lost in the heat haze.

We resided at the Residency. Heaven only knows how old this place was. Possibly it was built when the British first took over the administration of this country. It was in constant use as long as a district commissioner lived here, but now there was no D.C. at Zeilah and the Residency served only as an occasional resthouse for travellers such as ourselves. Reputed to be the only three-storey dwelling in Somaliland, it was enormous, built of rough stone blocks of brownish coral colour, with grey wooden verandas around the middle tier. Many years ago it might have been luxurious, but now it resembled a mausoleum with a view. It faced onto the sea, so we could sit on the long shuttered veranda and watch the tides come and go, which they did silently, for the water here did not lap or murmur or beat in waves against the shore. The sea was sluggish, eerily quiet. The garden contained only a few dwarfed palm trees, dwelt in at the moment by locusts who chewed clickingly at the leaves all night.

The inner portion of our apartment consisted of a main room, a bathroom and a wide hall. The builder obviously had some deep obsession with doors, of which there seemed to be hundreds. Sitting inside the main room, a person could not face all these doors at the same time. There was no solid wall for one to get one's back up against. Always a door was there, behind you. Above us were the empty rooms and the blank windows of the top storey. An open stairway led up, but we never went to look there.

The floor boards in our apartment were bare and dusty,

and cobwebs hung like grey ferns on the walls. The furniture was bizarre – a long table which was oddly covered with green felt, now frayed and stained; a sideboard in which none of the doors or drawers would close; a corner cabinet with swirls of wood at the bottom, elegant in its youth, possibly, but now looking like an aged tart grubbily furbelowed in the finery of another era; a curious little cupboard with two sections, the top portion glassed-in and looking as though it had been designed for false teeth in a tumbler of water at night, the lower shelf looking as though it were meant to harbour a china chamber pot, no doubt one that bore a crest or coat-of-arms in gilt. The slightest noise echoed. When a piece of paper was blown across the floor, it sounded like the rattling of sabres. The bathroom boasted a galvanized tub which had evidently for some time been a favourite nesting place of spiders and scorpions.

The second tier of the Residency had two apartments. The other was occupied by Ugo, the Italian foreman who was accompanying us to Djibouti and whose special responsibility was Alfie, the great lumbering diesel truck which would be used to transport the tractors back. Alfie was something of a curiosity, for the Italian mechanics in Hargeisa had ingeniously built it out of discarded pieces of Italian wartime trucks. Jack had explained to me what a remarkable creation it was, with its Alfa-Romeo chassis and gearbox, a Fiat engine with its own gearbox (the combination of the two sets of gears giving a great range of speeds), and a Lancia front axle and steering gear. Ugo was sturdy, staunch-hearted and cheerful, and would have been an excellent companion except for the fact that he spoke practically no English and we spoke practically no Italian. On the veranda we chatted with him, after a fashion, over an evening drink.

"Somaliland – *fenomenale*," he said. This was his favourite phrase. He believed that all Somalis were incomprehensible and probably insane, and they in turn believed the same about him. Ugo offered to teach us Italian, but for some reason, possibly the climate, we managed to pick up only two words, *rampicanti* and *piroscafo*, neither of which was much use to us, there being neither vines nor steamships at Zeilah.

We sat in the darkness, for if we brought a lamp onto the veranda, the locusts would immediately begin an invasion. We finally said goodnight to Ugo, but then we found that we could not bring ourselves to sleep in that huge dusty stifling room with all the doors. We moved our bed out onto the veranda and tried to sleep there. Now that the human voices were quiet, the house could be heard. Everything creaked, like the timbers on an old ship. The doors could not have been oiled in decades. The salt wind had corroded the hinges and locks, and in a sudden gust of wind every door in the place would open and slam shut. Through the veranda the wide-winged bats hovered and swooped, from rafters to eaves, down across our bed and over to a niche in the wall. Small unseen creatures of the night made mild rustlings in the woodwork and around the decrepit furniture. The heat was relentless. We lay wearily open-eyed in our sweat-soaked sheets, and at last, uneasily, we slept.

We kept our thoughts secret for a while, feeling apologetic and faintly ridiculous at having apparently yielded to the place. Only after several days here did Jack and I discover that we both had the same strong impression that the Residency was occupied by something other than ourselves and the bats, mice and insects. We did not believe in ghosts. Yet here and now, in this place and at this time, we could not even in broad daylight rid ourselves of an overpowering conviction that something existed here which we were unable to explain, some residue of anguish. We did not expect to see a long-dead Englishman walking through one of the many doors. This was no horrific ghost, nor did it threaten us at all. This occupancy was quite different – a sense of mourning, of inexpressible sadness. Whoever it was whose sorrow still clung around this place, he must have been English, we were certain, and young and – what was the right word to describe him? – bewildered.

We were vaguely ashamed of our feeling. We would not have dreamed of mentioning it to anyone else, but we began to notice how the others were reacting. Mohamed was always glancing back over his shoulder. Mohamedyero refused to sleep inside the building — he took his sleeping mat outside.

"I am thinking we should proceeding Djibouti right away and awaiting there for this ship," Hersi said. "This Zeilah place no good for us."

But when we asked him why, he would not say.

Weeks later, when Jack returned to Zeilah to collect the last of the tractors which had been stored there, he chose to stay in the cramped and airless P.W.D. shack rather than the Residency.

"I know it's crazy," he told me afterwards. "I've never felt like that before, but I just couldn't force myself to spend a night alone in that place."

Then one evening in Hargeisa, we got talking about Zeilah with the wife of an administrator. Her husband was stationed there many years before, and they had lived in the Residency.

"A rather peculiar thing occurred to me there," she said. "My husband was out on trek and I was alone in the house. I heard footsteps very clearly on the stairs, but when I went to look, no one was there. This happened several times during the evening. When my husband came back, I told him about it, and he informed me, rather reluctantly, that there was a legend about the place being haunted by a Somali policeman who had been murdered there."

She laughed a little. "Believe it or not, just as you choose. I hardly believe it myself, now. But when you're there —"

We could see perfectly well what she meant, for we had felt the same way, there. Obviously we must have been mistaken, however, to have felt that the occupancy of the house was connected with an Englishman. We thought no more about it until a few years later, in London, when we chanced to meet a man who had been stationed for a time in Somaliland after the war, doing investigations for the War Graves Commission. He had been at Zeilah, and knew the old Residency. In the course of our reminiscing, we mentioned the story of the murdered Somali policeman.

"Yes, that was the legend devised for local purposes," he said, "but when I was investigating there, I turned up a good deal of information from the past. What actually happened was that a British administrative officer killed his wife there and then shot himself."

How implausible such a tale seems, at a distance. How hackneyed, even. Nevertheless, there it is. I cannot entirely dismiss it, nor deny the overwhelming sense of occupation we felt in the tall grey house at the edge of the leaden sea, where the locusts flew with the silken wings of destruction, while out on the shore the whorled and fluted sea-shells, pearl white or gaudy as paints, inhabited by living claws, scuttled across the wet sands like creatures of fantasy which only in that one place could exist.

A message was brought to us at Zeilah – the ship had docked. It hardly seemed possible, after so many delays. Thankfully, we left the Residency and drove to Djibouti, thirty miles away.

In camp I had often felt I would not care if I never saw a city again. Yet I was delighted to see Djibouti, overjoyed at the sight of pavements and paved roads and office buildings of contemporary design. For one thing, Djibouti afforded an opportunity for me to change from my trek clothes, old dirndl skirt and blouse and the necessary but unflattering headscarf, and put on my best cotton dress and my broad-brimmed straw hat with the velvet ribbon. Thus attired, and strolling as gaily as the man who broke the bank at Monte Carlo, I discovered that I was the object of quizzical and disapproving stares. Finally I perceived the reason – all the French women in Djibouti were wearing mushroom-like topees, and seemed to have the impression that I in my flimsy straw might drop at any moment from sunstroke. It took me less than five minutes to decide I would rather risk sunstroke than wear a topee.

On the Djibouti streets we saw a wide variety of people. Small stunted Arabs in rags, begging. Indian merchants in white linen suits. Young Frenchmen with sunburnt skins, clad in open-necked shirts and attractively short shorts. Older

Frenchmen, stout and red as Santa Claus, with bulging thighs, clad in open-necked shirts and very unattractively short shorts. Somali and Danakil women wearing mission-style dresses with clumsy bodices and hideous puffed sleeves, a contrast to the women who wore traditional Somali dress, graceful robes of scarlet and blue and gold, and the long *kool*, necklace of amber. A scrawny yellow-skinned Arab sprawled on top of a cart loaded with wood and charcoal, beating his thin grey donkey languorously with a stick. The short wiry Yemeni dockers looked as though they could be knocked over with a feather, but they had the reputation of being very tough. Italian mechanics in blue denim overalls shouted at one another. The many priests all wore long beards and white robes tied with a black cord at the waist. Some of them rode bicycles and looked like sails in the wind, their robes flapping around them as they veered down the crowded street.

The Somali *magala* was a shantytown, hovels of flattened paraffin tins and wooden boxes. The stench and the hordes of flies were indescribable. Europeans were not encouraged to come here, as it gave an unfavourable impression of the city. The French residential sections were what one was supposed to look at – comfortable bungalows and apartment blocks, in both contemporary and Eastern styles. The contrasts between the African and European standards of living were the same as those found in Hargeisa, but here they seemed slightly sharper, more emphasized. The *magala* was a worse slum, the European cantonments more polished and sophisticated.

Djibouti was surrounded and almost overpowered by the strong glare of the sun. The buildings and the dark green palms seemed to waver before our eyes. The colours blurred and glowed – the turquoise sea, the buildings of soft ripe yellow like the melons that grew in the salt flats outside the city. A really incongruous note was the famous railway, the only one in this part of the world, that chugged between Djibouti and Addis Ababa three times a week.

We had iced German lager at a bar called *Le Palmier En Zinc*, where the metal palm was said to have been the first tree in Djibouti. One difference from British Somaliland struck us as refreshing – here, French people worked as shop clerks, waiters, barmaids. The barmaid in *Le Palmier* looked young, old, very pale. Her hair by nature was brown, and this shade showed at the roots, but it grew progressively more blonde until at the ends it was nearly colourless – it resembled those paint-colour charts the hardware stores had at home, showing how many variations of yellow it was possible to obtain.

Most of the shops were Greek, with a few French and Indian ones. The Italians sold excellent ice cream. One of the buildings in the central square looked like an illustration from a book of sorcery, a design for a warlock's residence. Its basic shape was indiscernible, for it was covered all over with gables and pagoda-like protruberances, and verandas flowered from it in clusters. Its walls were robin's egg blue, its roof a bright orange slate. Grey shutters, latticed in a crude wooden filigree, were tacked onto windows the shape of mosque windows, tapering gracefully upward. The eyes of many women in purdah seemed to be peering from behind these shutters, or so we imagined, peering out at a world which they were never allowed to touch. Was it an old-style eastern brothel, or the house of a sultan whose fifty concubines were kept in strict seclusion, or a Chinese establishment that sold potted lilies in the front and opium in the back? More likely it was an importing firm that dealt in paraffin or soap, but we never found out, and I was not sorry.

A striking feature of Djibouti was the large number of churches and missions. Only one state school existed, we were told, and many Somalis sent their children to mission schools. The Somalis with us were deeply shocked by this situation, for in the Protectorate no missionaries were allowed. They referred to the mission priests as "child stealers," and Hersi told us why this name was used. In times of famine, here and in Italian Somaliland, many Somalis took their children to the missions, where they were fed – at the price of relinquishing Islam. Whether or not this was actually ever made a condition of receiving help, I do not know. The significant thing was that the Somalis believed it.

The police in Djibouti were among the most magnificent men I have ever seen anywhere. They were Senegalese, huge men with muscular necks and legs which resembled carvings of the ancient Assyrians. They wore crimson fezzes and smart khaki uniforms, and were tall, broad, handsome, completely self-assured. Hersi, Abdi, Mohamed, Arabetto and the others did not share my admiration of these Senegalese. They were extremely apprehensive about them, and I soon realized why. The French administrators here followed a stunningly simple policy – if the police were recruited from another colony, and did not have tribal or family connections in the country where they worked, they would have no objections to strong-arm tactics in dealing with the locals. The Somalis and Senegalese were completely alien to one another, and their mutual mistrust could easily turn to hatred. Divide and rule. Whatever one could say against the British administration in colonies, this was one gimmick they did not use.

"I am fearing we getting into some trouble here," Hersi said. "If so, who will believing us in this place?"

Hersi relied, always, on his verbal skill, for he was of a slight and slender build. Here his oratory would not serve him, for the Senegalese did not speak Somali or English, and Hersi did not speak Senegalese or French. Jack and I shared his nervousness. The trouble could be real, or it could be trumped up. We did not want any difficulty with the authorities at this point. We could see ourselves flung out of the country, going back without the tractors for which we had been waiting so long.

"For God's sake, be careful," Jack cautioned everyone. "And whatever you do, stay away from those Senegalese."

Yes, yes, of course – they would be extremely careful, they promised.

"I go softly-softly," Mohamed said fervently. "I swear it."

His idea of going softly-softly was to raise a thunderous howl – "Thief! Thief!" – when my purse strap was neatly cut away with a razor blade one day and Mohamed managed to snatch it back. We narrowly escaped a riot. The hefty police glowered but providentially did not pounce. On another occasion, Abdi reckoned some Djibouti Somalis were speaking derisively about him, and once again we avoided disaster by a hair's breadth. The old warrior was quite prepared to take them all on at once, all two hundred of them, and only through the concentrated efforts of Jack and Arabetto, one on each side of him, did we manage to drag him away.

None of the Somalis with us had ever seen Djibouti before, and their feelings were very mixed. For one thing, the openness of the love game here was both shocking and exciting to them. In Djibouti there was a belief that it pays to advertise. Outside doorways were large signs – *Club Des Jeunes Femmes Somalis et Dankali* and *Club Des Jeunes Femmes Arabiques*. One place, especially anxious to impress, said "Established 1935," but failed to state whether or not the same *jeunes femmes* had frequented the establishment since that date. Collections of postcards sold in the shops were entitled "Views of Djibouti," but the title was not entirely accurate, as the views were mainly concerned with unclad Somali womanhood. We received a variety of reactions to the city from the Somalis who had accompanied us. Abdi virtuously maintained that the young men could not work as hard as he, an old man, and the reason was quite plain.

"Man he get woman too much, he no get strength," Abdi said, flexing his biceps.

Mohamed refrained from mentioning this aspect of Djibouti, at least directly. But he, too, claimed to dislike the city.

"Djibouti too cost," he said with a regretful sigh. "All thing cost too much."

Hersi, always conscious of his status as a *mullah*, had yet another point of view.

"People in this place, they are not proper Somalis," he said. "They never showing us proper hospitality, as the *Kitab* commanding. They are thieves, these people, and also bloody poor Muslims as well."

Only Arabetto, less divided or more frank than the others, admitted he liked the city.

"Just like Mogadisciou," he said with a grin. "Plenty girls."

All were united in one respect, however. They believed that great wealth could be obtained by buying goods cheaply here and selling at an enormous profit when they returned to Hargeisa. Mohamed, Abdi and Arabetto purchased large quantities of cheap perfume, which they subsequently disposed of at a small profit. Hersi, inexplicably, decided to go into the sweater business. He bought a dozen thick wool sweaters and later could not sell them at all, for by the time we returned to Hargeisa it was the height of the hot season.

The British consul, who was also the manager of an export-import firm here, kindly offered to put us up. His wife and child were away during the hot season, he told us, so he would be glad of the company. We accepted gratefully, and moved in. The bungalow had electric ceiling fans in every room, and the blades whirred night and day but seemed only to whip the air into an invisible froth without ever cooling it. The heat felt worse here than it had on the exposed Guban. The house thermometer read 115 one day, and after that I refused to look at it. The consul was at his office all day, and Jack was down at the docks, getting the tractors unloaded, so I was alone in the bungalow. I wanted to work on the Somali translations, but all I could think of was the oppressive heat. Finally I discovered a way to escape it. The consul's bathroom was enormous, with a sunken blue-tiled tub like a small swimming pool, and great flagons of eau-de-cologne standing invitingly around. Each morning I filled the tub with cold water and perfume, and spent most of the day there, emerging at intervals to re-fill my pint glass of orange squash. I felt a few qualms, true, as I sat in the cool depths of the consul's bathtub and worked on translations of desert poetry. But these misgivings were never sufficient to make me seriously consider moving to more uncomfortable surroundings for the sake of atmosphere.

In the evenings we went out, often for dinner and then on to a nightclub. No one in Djibouti attempted to sleep before two or three in the morning. The nightclub we visited most often was on the sea front, hemmed in with potted palms and surrounded with an air of gloomy nostalgia. The orchestra was composed of Italians, and as the night wore on, they became fed up with the dreary waltzes and foxtrots. Abruptly they would leave the dance floor and go out on the veranda, where they would sing Italian songs, slow and sad ones. The same people came to the nightclub every evening. There was a kind of *esprit de corps* in Djibouti at night – the misfits, traitors, outcasts, smugglers, wan middle-ageing prostitutes, the colonial service men in their immaculate whites, the perspiring commercial men whose sallow faces were pimpled with prickly heat – they were all the same here in the nightclub. No difference existed between any of them now. There was no feverish gaiety, no pretence. A few of the younger dancers asked for jazz, and the orchestra obliged, but half-heartedly. Most people preferred to dance more languidly. Conversation over the drinks was low, subdued. The evening was too hot to permit raised voices. Life was an existing from one whisky-and-soda to the next, and home was a place you would never see again.

Once when we got back to the consul's bungalow, we found the livingroom filled with locusts. The entire front of the house was like concrete lace, open to the air in geometrical patterns, a design which ensured a maximum of insects. The locusts were everywhere – the sound of their wings was louder than the steady chunking of the ceiling fans. But we, exhausted and full of gin-and-lime, couldn't have cared less. Jack and the consul got out rackets and used the locusts as tennis balls.

"How many do you make it?" the consul puffed cheerily, swiping away at the locusts.

"I haven't a clue – I lost count after the first couple of dozen."

Victory was achieved at last. The livingroom floor was strewn with locust corpses, and we retired and slept fitfully under the eternally whirling fans.

For Jack, the days were a nightmare. The equipment consisted of two Caterpillar D-4 tractors with scrapers, and a D-4 bulldozer. When he first went to the docks to supervise the unloading, he discovered that the machinery was packed down under everything else in the ship's hold, crated in gigantic wooden boxes, one of which was jammed solidly behind a pillar. No one had the remotest idea how to get them out. In the port, there were no cranes heavy enough, so the job had to be done mainly with the ship's limited equipment. Jack toiled like a coolie on the docks all day and every day. When the boxes were finally lifted out, the task of uncrating the tractors remained, and then loading them one at a time onto the old diesel truck, Alfie, and getting them back to Zeilah, where they would be temporarily left until they could be transported one by one back to Hargeisa. Ugo and Jack, in a situation filled with all kinds of technical difficulties, were forced to communicate in a tortuous manner. When Jack wanted to say something to Ugo, he gave Hersi the message in English. Hersi told Arabetto in Somali, and Arabetto passed the information on to Ugo in Italian. The reply came back in the same way. Considering that Hersi and Arabetto knew nothing about tractors, and that the words for various parts of the machines did not exist in the Somali language, it was little wonder that Jack and Ugo frequently had to make wild guesses about what the other was trying to say. As if these difficulties were not enough, the crane operator at the port spoke only French, which none of our party could speak.

"I know now," Jack said heavily, "exactly what the tower of Babel must have been like."

The sun blazed down on the docks, and the harsh glare of light never let up for an instant. One afternoon Jack arrived back at the bungalow and hesitated in the doorway.

"Peg – give me a hand, will you?"

I was immediately alarmed. What was the matter?

"I can't seem to see," he said, his voice tight with anxiety.

He had suddenly gone blind. He had a splitting headache and everything had turned to darkness. I was frantic with worry, but the consul remained unperturbed.

"Sunstroke," he said calmly. "Bound to happen sooner or later, working out in the sun all day. It'll probably pass off after an hour or so."

What if it didn't? I had the momentary unreasonable conviction that every doctor in Djibouti was incompetent, irresponsible and probably alcoholic. Later, when all was well, I recalled this feeling with some shame, and could no longer maintain the same comfortable scorn at the Hargeisa memsahibs' delusions about the country, the host of dangers they conjured up to frighten or entertain themselves.

After a few hours, just as the consul predicted, the mist lifted from Jack's eyes, and the next morning he was back at the docks again.

We were as glad to leave Djibouti as we had been to arrive. When the last piece of machinery was unloaded and ready to be taken to Zeilah, everyone climbed aboard and we were off. The Land-Rover and trucks drove for the last time through the paved streets, past the misshapen old buildings, past the slickly shining new apartments, past shuttered mysterious dwellings, past the clean whitewashed walls of the *Pharmacie de la Mer Route*, past *Le Palmier En Zinc*, past the Italian *gialotto* shop, past the rotting shanties of the *magala*, past the date palms with their bunches of orange-brown fruit, past white-robed priests on bicycles and chalk-faced women looking forlorn under the small umbrellas of their topees.

Farewell to the homesick city, the shabby Paris of the Gulf of Aden. *Nabad gelyo*, Djibouti – may we never see you again.

From Zeilah, we set out onto the Guban in the late afternoon, when the heat was not quite so severe. As usual, we moved in convoy – first, the Land-Rover with Jack and myself and Abdi; next, Ugo driving Alfie, which was loaded with a tractor and was towing a scraper; then the Bedford truck, driven by Arabetto and carrying Mohamed and Hersi as well as the gang of labourers; and finally the old P.W.D. tractor from Zeilah, which we had borrowed to go part of the way with us, through the worst of the sand, in case the heavily loaded diesel got stuck. Jack did not want the new tractors driven back to Hargeisa under their own power, as the trek might wreck them and would in any event take too long.

Seven miles out of Zeilah, the diesel got bogged down in the sand. Everyone piled out and began digging, poking thorn boughs under the wheels, shoving. The P.W.D. tractor finally hauled Alfie out, but at that moment the diesel's steering broke. Ugo and Jack ingeniously managed to fix the steering with bits of wire, a job which took two hours. When we got going once more, it was growing dark. We forged ahead and reached a dry river-bed where the loose sand lay thick and treacherous. The diesel sank down once more and almost turned over. This time it was seriously stuck. Even the old tractor could not budge it. Alfie's wheels spun furiously, unable to grip in the slithering sand. Even if the diesel could be dragged across the river-bed, the danger area extended for several miles ahead, the sand lying soft and crumbly as brown sugar.

Then, all at once, the night arrived and with it a sand storm. We were on the flat treeless Guban, with only a few clumps of grass to stop the blowing sand, and the wind was careering across the desert. Arabetto shifted the Bedford so that work could be done by its lights, and Abdi did the same with the Land-Rover. Fortunately, Jack had insisted upon bringing the boards from the tractor crate, thinking they might possibly come in useful.

"We'll try making a portable road," he decided.

Everyone seized a board. These were thrown down in front of the diesel's wheels, and as Alfie began to heave out of the sand, towed by the old tractor, the wheels gripped on the boards and crunched slowly ahead. For some distance the moving road of boards continued. As the wheels came grinding forward, someone would pick up the last board and run with it to the front of the diesel. All the time the sand was whipping against us, peppering our limbs as though with buckshot, filling our eyes and mouths with grit. The wind howled and shrieked.

"*Wallahi!*" Mohamed gasped. "I think this wind is some *shaitan*, some devil."

By midnight we had been travelling for eight hours and we had gone exactly twenty-five miles. Jack and I slept at last in the Land-Rover, while the Somalis and Ugo went to sleep in the trucks. We were all so tired we hardly cared whether we lived or died.

But something had been changed by this tussle with the desert. After this night, when Jack managed somehow to devise ways of getting our unwieldy caravan across the shifting sands of the Guban, the attitude of the Somalis was subtly different. They began speaking, for the first time, of "the *balleh* camp" or "we belong to the *balleh* job," as though the work now possessed an entity. And they began to call Jack *odei-gi rer-ki*, the old man of the tribe.

CHAPTER SEVEN

The Ballehs

THE GREEN of the good season had faded from the Haud, and the Somalis were wondering if the *Dhair* rains, which sometimes fell in autumn, would come this year. If the *Dhair* rains failed, there would be trouble here when the winter drought set in, for the Habr Awal from the Guban were moving up into the Haud plateau this year. Every morning we saw families of Habr Awal trekking past our camp, the women and girls leading the heavily loaded burden camels, the children and old people shouting at the flocks that trooped dustily along, and in the distance, the men whistling and singing, or blowing on the wooden flutes which were used to keep the shambling camel herds together.

"These people having bloody poor brains," said Hersi, who was Habr Yunis. "They should not coming this place."

Mohamed, being Habr Awal, naturally took a somewhat different view.

"Many Habr Awal camels come too much sick this time," he said. "I hear it – Habr Awal people all saying must be they find some different-different grass, for make their camels get some healthy. Must be they come here. They never make trouble this place."

The young camels were being weaned now. The Somalis had a sharply effective way of accomplishing this separation. They placed a forked stick over the small camel's nose, and when the infant tried to get milk from its mother, the prong of the stick jabbed the she-camel, and she moved rapidly

Faces of Somaliland
C.J. Martin

Hargeisa town
C.J. Martin

Hargeisa wells
C.J. Martin

A Sergeant – Somaliland Scouts
C.J. Martin

A Somali nomad
C.J. Martin

Basket weaving
C.J. Martin

Making sandals
C.J. Martin

The Haud
C.J. Martin

The Haud before
and after the rains
C.J. Martin

Mohamed
Margaret Laurence

Hersi, Jack, Abdi
Margaret Laurence

Arabetto
Margaret Laurence

Isman Shirreh
C.J. Martin

Jack, author and Gino
Margaret Laurence

The bungalow at Sheikh
Margaret Laurence

Working on a Balleh
C.J. Martin

A Burden camel carrying portable hut
C.J. Martin

A Nomadic encampment
C.J. Martin

A Qadi
C.J. Martin

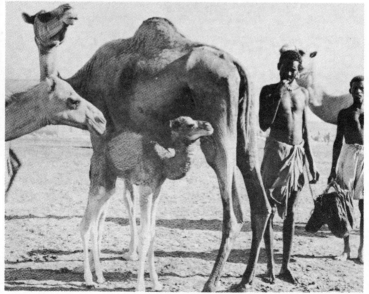

Herders with camels
C.J. Martin

away, no doubt leaving the bewildered young one, who was unaware that it had a spear on its snout, to wonder why it had been rejected so peremptorily. Could it be that the foul tempers of full-grown camels dated back to this early traumatic experience? The Somalis remained unaware of any such interesting possibility. Cast into abrupt independence, the young camels nibbled sadly at the coarse grass, and the milk was saved for the people.

Happy to be back in camp, I pottered around our truck-home, arranging our meagre furniture – bed here, table there, camp chairs next to the table, cases of tinned food stowed under the bed. Re-acquainting myself with the desert, I had a feeling of homecoming. Here at Balleh Gehli was the shallow pool, now only a shiny skin of cracked mud, where one morning just after the rains I walked down early and saw a child filling a water-vessel, and she, surprised, turned suddenly and gave me a smile of such radiance I could scarcely believe it was meant for a stranger. And here were the *myrrah* trees which a few months ago were covered with small yellow blossoms, the fragrance of which was subtler and sweeter than any bottled perfume. I was glad to see everything. Even the ember-eyed *balanballis*, haunting the truck at night with its black wings, seemed almost an old acquaintance.

Our camp had expanded to fairly large proportions. As well as Hersi, Mohamed, Abdi, Arabetto, Omar, Mohamed-yero and the labourers, we now had the tractor drivers. Also, this time Gino was with us, for now that the construction of the *ballehs* was about to begin, Jack needed a foreman on the job. A middle-aged Italian, Gino was built like a wrestler, a man of enormous strength, but very gently spoken. He lived in a caravan which he had built for himself, a marvellous structure complete with screened windows. He had promised to bequeath it to us when he went on leave, and although I did not wish him to be gone, I could not help eyeing the caravan enviously from time to time. Only those who have never experienced anything except comfort think that physical comfort is unimportant.

But we, too, had a luxury now – a separate diningroom

which the Somali labourers had built for us. It was a brushwood hut made of twined acacia branches and filled in with
clumps of a plant called *gedhamar*, a kind of herb with a
pleasant smell similar to summer savoury. The woven
branches allowed just enough sunlight to filter in, but the
heat was kept out. Our water bottles, stored here, became
chilled at night and remained cool until noon. When the sun
was shining across the top of the hut, the bunches of *gedhamar* looked silvery grey, as though the ceiling had been
hung with tinsel. During the days I worked in the hut, and it
was the most agreeable place for work which I have ever had.
I had finished with the translations of the Somali poems I
obtained from Guś and Musa, and now I was collecting
Somali tales, which were told to me by Hersi and Arabetto in
their spare time.

The main cause for jubilation in our return to the Haud
was that the excavation of the first *balleh* was about to begin.
For us, this was a landmark, a historic occasion. The Somalis
in camp, however, did not entirely share our excitement.
They tended to be blasé about the whole thing. Having
become accustomed to the sight of the heavy machinery
while the tractor drivers were being trained, Hersi and Abdi
and the others now felt that these roaring giants held no
mysteries. With a fine sense of onomatopoeia, they called the
tractors *agaf-agaf*, and because they had no basic understanding of machinery, they took the earth-moving equipment completely for granted. Although they swanked a little
when they showed it off to visiting tribesmen, they were not
amazed at its performance. It was just one of those things. A
balleh, after all, was only a hole in the ground – digging one
should be a simple matter. They did not doubt that the *agaf-
agaf* would accomplish this task easily, but they saw nothing
to marvel at when the steel-clawed ripper successfully
attacked the red Haud soil, which was almost as hard as
concrete, and broke it so that the scrapers could follow and
scoop it up. Jack was wryly amused.

"They don't know how difficult it is, nor how many problems we've had in actually getting to this point, so it doesn't seem wonderful to them in the slightest."

I could understand their naïve sophistication, for I had no comprehension of machinery, either, but at least I had shared some of the headaches involved in reaching this stage of operations.

The project, as originally conceived, was to have provided a chain of reservoirs to catch and hold rainwater along most the southern boundary of the Protectorate. On paper the scheme had appeared relatively straightforward, but Jack's initial reconnaissance over the west and central stretches of the area showed clearly that, like so many projects in Africa, this one would be anything but simple. The Haud was virtually featureless and such slopes as existed were generally long and gentle, particularly in the vicinity of the boundary. There were not even the rudiments of streams, stream channels or defined water-courses, however seasonal. Dams were definitely out, because there was nothing to dam. Some form of pond would have to be produced which, while basically nothing more than a large hole in the ground, would be scientifically designed and sited.

After miles of driving and tramping, working with compass and hand-level, after boring test-holes and digging test-pits, after examining rock and soil, after looking at the region's few existing *ballehs* – the hand-dug shallow water holes of the Somalis, after pondering morosely on the possible and dreaming of the impossible, Jack at last got the pattern set. Each reservoir would be a large rectangular hole dug at the foot of a carefully selected slope. The earth which was removed would be banked up around the sides and lower end, making a huge U with the arms pointing uphill, although the slopes were so gradual that "uphill" was really too extreme a word. In order to reach out and gather the water that perhaps once a year, for a few brief hours, might come coursing down this slope in a thousand little rivulets, long walls would stretch out from the top of the U. Low banks of earth a thousand feet long or more, these wing-walls would check the water and deflect it very slowly towards the reservoir so that as little silt as possible would be carried with it. Beyond the ends of these walls, ploughed furrows would stretch further out and very slightly up, and would divert and channel the annual bounty on a front of over half a mile.

Rock too hard for a plough or a ripper existed no more than six or eight feet down, and so the reservoirs would be disproportionately shallow and evaporation would be more serious than one would wish. Ironically enough, although the rock was impervious to the attack of our equipment, it was not at all impervious to water, and no clay deposits were present here which could make the bottom of the *ballehs* water-tight. Fortunately there was some clay mixed with the silt and sand, and Jack knew from observation that the Somalis would drive their camels into the water when it had become shallow, so little by little the animals' feet would pack a natural cement bottom as the years went by.

Thirty *ballehs* were to be built, spaced about ten miles apart, along the waterless area three hundred miles long, just north of the Ethiopian border. Each *balleh* would have a capacity of about three million gallons and would provide water for approximately three months after being filled by rain.

The planning of the *ballehs* and the selection of sites had been a long and painstaking business, but although Jack had had a good deal of anxiety over it, he had also enjoyed it more than any other job he had ever done, for this was the first time he had ever been able to put his own ideas into practice. He had been impatient to get started on the excavation, but even after the equipment had finally been hauled here all the way from Djibouti, the actual construction of the *ballehs* could not begin until Somali drivers were trained to operate the machinery.

Easier said than done, this. Swarms of eager young men had applied for the jobs, and although a few of them had driven trucks, most had never even seen a tractor, and the scrapers were totally unfamiliar to them, for there had never been any scrapers in this country before. Six men were finally

selected. Being aware that the tractors were virtually irre-
placeable, and therefore having a strongly protective feeling
towards them, Jack was apprehensive about them in the
hands of the all-too-enthusiastic Somali novices. The Somali
boys, for their part, were terribly anxious to hold their jobs
and to do well, and so they would frequently demonstrate
their talent by attempting to perform some outlandish feat
which would strain even those machines, tough as they were.
Or, out of ignorance, they would zoom gaily along in the
wrong gear, and Jack would have to dash out to save the
precious machinery. With three tractors cavorting around in
this manner, it was not easy to keep an eye on all of them at
the same time. They reminded me of boys on bicycles at
home – *Look at me, Ma! No hands!*

But now, at last, the drivers were trained, in a manner of
speaking, and the great day was here. The first day's excavation went well. From the sidelines, Mohamed and Hersi and I
watched while the ripper chewed at the soil and the scrapers
began to shovel up the chunks of earth. The wilderness was
quiet no longer. The tractors whoomed unceasingly. Around
us, the dust was churned up and settled like red flour at our
feet.

In the evening, Gino brought a straw-covered bottle of
Chianti to the brushwood hut. This was the champagne with
which the job was launched.

"Here's to the *ballehs*!"

We were optimistic, re-charged with hope. All our troubles
were over, we felt, knowing full well they were not, but willing to believe for a moment that everything would go like a
song from now on.

The evenings were cold. After dinner we sat in the brushwood hut, shivering in our sweaters and jackets, and listening
to the squeaky trembling voice that issued from Arabetto's
old gramophone. He had a few well-worn Italian records, and
he and Gino would listen nostalgically to *Santa Lucia*, one of
them remembering Mogadisciou and the other remembering

Milan. Arabetto was the only Somali who had a taste for this foreign music – the others pronounced it an abomination to the ears. Arabetto told us with amusement about the reaction of one of the labourers to the gramophone.

"He never see such thing before. He say – is it some devil, or is some small man inside?"

Another evening entertainment, if it could be called that, was watching the insects grimly battling. The large black crickets, noisy as a calypso steel band, emerged at sundown from the ground. We saw them digging their way up – plop! plop! – and there they were, hundreds of them crawling around at our feet. Then the sausage flies began buzzing through the air, their plump bodies clumsy and hardly able to fly, looking exactly like miniature sausages. An English sahib of local legend was reputed to enjoy eating these creatures – at parties, he would pluck them from the air and pop them in his mouth, and all the ladies would bleat and shriek to see him chewing. It struck me that there must surely be easier ways to establish one's reputation as a character.

The next insects to put in an appearance at the evening battlefield were the killers, the black *jinna* or stink-ants, with their voracious jaws. When a sausage fly dropped bumbling to the ground, or a cricket faltered, the *jinna* would be upon it instantly, and within seconds it would have been devoured. We tried to avoid stepping on the *jinna*, for when we did, they gave off the most rank odour imaginable.

The Somalis had an enigmatic tale about the stink-ant. They said that if you went to the *jinna* and asked him why he was so thin in the waist, he would explain – "It is a result of riding a great deal on a fine horse. Anyone knows that riding draws in the waist." And if you asked him why he had such a foul stench, he would answer, "Because I once visited a woman who had a stinking birth." And if you asked him why his jaws were open so wide, he would reply, "Because I used to go with a group of boys from village to village, dancing, and I was the one who went in front, shouting that we did not come to beg food or money, but only came to dance." I do not pretend to understand this story, but the Somalis considered it uproariously funny.

The brushwood hut in the evening was a place of contentment. In the navy-coloured sky, the white clouds scudded silently across the moon. Outside the thorn-bough fence that enclosed our camp, we heard the low sullen moan of a hyena or the yapping of foxes. Many hyenas came snooping around our camp at night, and from the half-joking comments of the Somalis, I began to suspect that there was some magical significance attached to them. When I enquired if this was so, Hersi shook his head in emphatic denial.

"Our religion is forbidding such magical things absolutely," he said. "We are Muslims, memsahib, Muslims."

I begged his pardon and the matter was dropped. But one day Mohamed told me that the night before they had heard a scuffling out beyond the camp, where our hyena trap was always set, and when they went out to see, they found that the hyena had pushed a stick into the trap and in this way had avoided being caught itself.

"Hyena is very clever," Mohamed said, tapping his forehead. "He think just like a man."

Then he told me that the Esa people around Borama were reputed to be able to talk with hyenas. This idea, I recalled, was expressed in a *belwo*.

> *I ask the stealthy hyena*
> *That prowls past Dumbuluq's fires,*
> *If he in his wide wandering*
> *Brings back one word of you.*

Mohamed told me that many people believed that every so-many years the hyenas lost their cowardice and became man-eating. There was a basis in fact for this belief, for in the dry *Jilal* the hyenas roamed the streets of the towns at night, looking for water, or going to the meat market in search of offal, and when they came in packs they sometimes carried off a small child. The supernatural powers attributed to hyenas might have been some survival of the totem idea, identifying tribes with animals in order to obtain the benefit of the animal's powers. Perhaps the beliefs were also encouraged by the fact that hyenas always disappeared completely and mysteriously in the daytime.

I took a keen interest in these magical beliefs, and then one day I was paid back in full measure for my unintentional condescension. Gino had made a miniature wood stove of cast iron, complete with oven, a perfect replica of the kind of stove I remembered from my childhood, and he said I might use this intriguing toy. It took a whole morning for me to bake a cake, for the stove was so small that it had to be fed with chips and shavings, and the cake took twice the usual time in the oven. On the first occasion, Mohamed was gloomy and disapproving.

"I think you no bake today, memsahib."

Why not, I asked him.

"Today Friday," he said. If you make cake today, must be it will not come good."

I disagreed. Friday might be the Muslim sabbath, but it was not mine. Besides which, I was not superstitious.

I went ahead, and the carefully tended cake fell flat. Mohamed could not resist beaming broadly at this fulfilment of his prophecy. I never baked on a Friday again. And after that day, the cakes rose beautifully, just as Mohamed had known they would.

We drove out at twilight across the great plain, looking for *gerenuk* and *dero*, for we had a lot of men in camp now and they needed meat. All at once we saw an appealing sight – a huge she-ostrich, very fussily maternal, with no less than eighteen young ones, all traipsing solemnly behind her, single file. She craned her neck and looked back to inspect her little troop – yes, they were all there, and safe. We drew up the Land-Rover and waited quietly until they had marched past. Young ostriches were often snatched by hyenas, but a mother ostrich would stand up to a hyena and could deal it such a powerful blow with her feet that it would go off yelping across the desert. In Hargeisa, a neighbour of ours had a pet baby ostrich which was cared for by the stable boy, a tall Somali youth whose nickname was Aul and who was as graceful as the deer of that name. When we went back to our house for an occasional week-end, we saw Aul every morning leaping lightly into the ostrich's pen.

"*Gorayo! Is ka warran!*" He greeted it always in the same way. "Ostrich! Give news of yourself!"

But the small ostrich, who was exceedingly dowdy and draggle-feathered, did not utter a sound.

One day in the Haud we found an ostrich's nest, with its two layers of gigantic eggs carefully covered with sand. The Somalis were overjoyed, as they loved to eat the eggs, one of which would make an omelette sufficient for several hungry men. We took one of the eggs for ourselves, and Jack blew it out so that we could keep the shell. To do so, he had to drill into it with a hand-drill, for it was of the consistency of thick bone china. When we had it cleaned out, and on display in our truck-home, the Somalis began to make optimistic remarks.

"I think you get small boy now, memsahib," Mohamed said confidently.

What was this? What did he mean? Hersi obligingly explained.

"Soon you will be conceiving," he said gravely. "This ostrich egg is very helpful for such considerations."

This was the same Hersi who did not believe in magic. The ostrich egg, it appeared, was a powerful fertility charm. The Somalis had been concerned for some time about my child-less state, and they knew quite well that I was concerned about it, too. They regarded the ostrich egg hopefully – aid had arrived. Only Abdi did not have sufficient faith in this object. Perhaps he felt that, being *Ingrese*, I would require double the usual quantity of helpful magic.

"Lion fat," he informed us. "I think you needing this thing. If woman eating fat from the *libahh*, soon she get child."

When he was out hunting *gerenuk*, he searched in the thickets and thorn bushes, but alas for my unborn children, he found no lion. Occasionally we heard their voices, rumbling and coughing in the night, and once or twice we saw pug-marks in the morning sand, but the beasts remained cannily hidden.

One day Abdi found something else, however, almost as good. Although of no magical use, this catch was a triumph. He returned to camp with the Land-Rover horn blaring, his victory music, and everyone dashed out to see. Springily as a boy, the old warrior leaped out and showed us what he had brought back – two cheetah.

It was against the law to shoot cheetah, and Abdi knew this as well as anyone. But he had seen four of them under a *qoda* tree. Old marksman that he was, he had been quite unable to resist the temptation. He shrugged and threw up his hands – how could anyone fail to comprehend his predicament?

"I never no think," he said. "I see them – one, two three, four *harimaad*. Quickly quickly, I taking rifle – bam! bam! I get two. You think sahib coming angry?"

"No, I don't think so, Abdi."

Who could be angry? He was a hunter. He simply could not help shooting. But I could see, nevertheless, that these cheetah would be an embarrassment to us. For all official purposes, they must be said to have been shot on the other side of the Ethiopian border. And who could prove they were not?

One of the beasts was still alive when Abdi hauled it out of the Land-Rover. With the Somalis' usual nonchalance about a wounded animal, all the men in cap stood around, poking at it, tormenting it, laughing. Beautiful and destroyed, it crouched on the ground. It was bleeding terribly, and its strength was almost gone, but its eyes still shone with menace. Jack and Gino were both out at the *balleh* site, and I could not cope with this situation. When I asked Abdi and the Illaloes to kill the cheetah, they paid no attention. They were enjoying this too much. Why cut short their pleasure?

The cheetah, panting and nearly dead, suddenly put every vestige of its remaining strength into one last effort. Incredibly rousing itself, it lashed out and tore a labourer's leg from knee to ankle.

Outraged shrieks all around. *Wallahi! Shaitan!* I stood aside, looking at the shocked and bleeding labourer, and could feel nothing but coldness. Fortunately, Jack arrived at this moment, fetched by the nimble Mohamedyero, who had raced out to the *balleh* with the news. He took one look, then fetched a crowbar and immediately killed the cheetah. I bandaged the labourer's leg, which was not seriously damaged, for the rip did not go deep, but I remained aloof.

Why should they have any mercy for the cheetah, who killed their sheep when it could? Life was too hard, here, for any such sentimentality. I knew this very well, but I could not help admiring the desperate courage of the animal. The Somalis thought I was foolish to want the cheetah put out of its pain at once, and I thought they were cruel to want to prolong its agony. Neither of us would alter our viewpoints.

The labourers skinned the animals and pegged the skins out to dry in the sun. The Somalis had no way of curing animal hides, other than sun-drying them. Later, several labourers spent the entire day working the skins with their hands, as Eskimos do with their teeth, to soften them. One skin was sold in the Hargeisa market, and Abdi and the Illaloes who were with him shared the money. The other, Abdi gave to us. It was a light yellow pelt with well-defined black spots. The cheetah, we learned, was the fastest animal on four feet. It was considerably smaller than the leopard, and the leopard's tail always ended in black, whereas the tail of the cheetah ended with light fur. We kept the cheetah skin, and at last smuggled it out of the country. It stayed on the floor of livingrooms in many houses, for many years, in England and West Africa and Canada, a hazard to unwary feet, and a reminder to me of different points of view. Ultimately it became a legendary beast, for our two children, when they were old enough to enjoy stories of the "olden days" before they were born, somehow developed and would not relinquish the belief that it was their father who shot this cheetah as it charged at him in the wilds of distant lands.

When Gino went on leave, there was no one in the camp who could work with metals, so Jack hired a man of the Tomal, the traditional blacksmiths to the Somalis. Mohamed Tomal was a wisecracking but hardworking young man, full of arguments and always eager to prove his point. One day he and Jack got into a long discussion about *khat*, a leaf widely used throughout the Muslim world, where alcohol was forbidden, and chewed for its narcotic effects. In Somaliland it was against the law to sell *khat*, but truckloads of it were constantly smuggled in from Ethiopia. Mohamed Tomal put the old question to Jack.

"You *Ingrese* drink whisky and gin, but you say Somalis must no chew *khat*. How so?"

"I didn't make the laws," Jack said. "Personally, I don't care whether you chew *khat* or not, except that it would probably make you sleepy and you wouldn't be able to work as well."

"Oh, no!" Mohamed Tomal was shocked. "*Khat* never make man sleep. It helping he for work. A man which chewing *khat*, he work all night. All night – I swear it. And he never feel tired."

"Oh?" Jack was sceptical.

Mohamed Tomal gave him an offended glance, but said no more. The following day, however, the blacksmith came to Jack with two gifts – a short spear, double-barbed like a fish hook, the shaft gracefully bound with brass wire, and a long knife with a wooden handle decorated with burned patterns. He had fashioned both these weapons during the night.

"I work all night," Mohamed Tomal said triumphantly, "and I chew *khat* all night – you see, sahib? You see now?"

Jack, laughing, had to concede the point. But he still had to forbid *khat* in the camp, not that this edict ever stopped anyone.

We were becoming acquainted with the new men in our camp. Apart from Mohamed Tomal, there were the six tractor drivers. One of the two men who had had some previous experience on tractors was Mohamed Magan. In his late twenties, he had a bulky, almost chubby appearance. His round face was impish and confident. When he walked, he had a swaggering sailor-like gait. He had never held any one job for long, for he was decidedly temperamental. Once, he told Jack, he suddenly felt fed up with his job, so he simply stopped his tractor and walked away. In the beginning, he was much the best operator of the crew, but the others began to catch up with him, for he tended to be too sure of himself and was often careless. Nevertheless, he had more feeling for machinery than the others, more dexterity and a better sense of timing in handling the Cat and scraper. But he hated to be told off about anything. One morning he was late for work, and Jack called him down about it. Mohamed Magan did not say anything, not a word. But that night we were wakened by a sudden noise.

Jack sat up, jerked into consciousness. "That's one of the Cat's starting engines!"

He had a shrewd suspicion of what was going on, so he did not hurry unduly to go and have a look. By the time he reached the *balleh* site, there was Mohamed Magan, beginning work. It was exactly four a.m.

"You tell me not to be late," he said.

Jack did not know whether to be angry or amused, especially when Mohamed Magan put on an elaborate pantomime to show how he had to get off the tractor and feel the scraper with his hands to determine whether or not it was fully loaded, for he could see nothing in the enveloping darkness.

A complete contrast to Mohamed Magan was Ismail Ahmed. An extremely handsome boy with straight well-cut features, he had attended Qoranic school in Hargeisa, and could read and write in Arabic. He was unusually serious about his religion, and this, in a country where everyone took religion seriously, meant that he had almost a sense of vocation. He seemed cut out for the religious life, and perhaps should have been an *imam*, a priest.

"Ismail Ahmed is not like other people," Hersi said of him, and this was true. There was about him a quietness and a reserve which the others did not have. But he was always the first to offer to help Jack if anything needed fixing on a tractor. As a driver, he was not as good as some of the others, for he worked almost too carefully.

The one whom Jack thought would ultimately become the best driver of all was Isman Shirreh. He was an Arap, which was a tribe looked down upon by most of the others, but despite this handicap, Isman was one of the most popular men in camp. He was friendly to everyone, quick on the uptake and yet not over-confident. He and Arabetto became close friends, and in some ways they were similar. Both were, in a sense, outcasts, and both had an irrepressible laughter. Sometimes at dusk, when the Illaloes were going through their drill routine, Arabetto and Isman would march up and down nearby, burlesquing the whole performance.

Does every group, inevitably, choose a clown for itself? Ours was Ali Wys, who looked more like a Frenchman than a Somali. Slender, almost delicate, with a thin face and a long mournful nose, he wore always a quizzically humorous expression. He had a high hoarse voice which many times a day rose above the drone of the engines, as Ali shouted his comical complaints. He walked in a slow, loose, ambling fashion, and seemed to take pleasure in his role as jester. And yet there was something sad in his subtly expressive face. He had to endure a good deal of mockery from the others, because he was neither deft nor strong enough to shift the Cat gears without apparent effort, and when he struggled at it, the others were quick to notice and taunt.

The tallest man in our camp was Omar Farah, who was called *Omar Wein* – Big Omar. Lank, gangling, rather awkward, slightly hunch-back, Omar looked like a country boy astounded to find himself in a mechanized society. He was not a boy, actually, at all, being older than most of the others and having a wife and children in Hargeisa. He was the steadiest of the drivers, solid, plodding in his work, conscientious. He had none of Ismail Ahmed's other-worldliness, and yet he was always one of the first to go out to the brushwood mosque as sundown approached and the time for evening prayers arrived.

Jama Koshin had worked on tractors before, and this was why Jack had picked him. But he wore a dull expression and seemed unresponsive to explanations about the work. The others made fun of him mercilessly, calling him stupid, and he tended, perhaps not unnaturally, to be sullen and unsociable. We were never able to penetrate his mask at all.

The Cat operators worked in two-hour shifts, spelling each other off, for the work was heavy, the sun was hot, and the dust was hard on the lungs. Jack, however, like the Cats, was at the site most of the day, from six in the morning until six at night. Even after dinner, his work was not finished, for it was a rare evening that did not bring at least one dispute to be settled. Men out in camp, cut off from their families and thrown constantly into one another's company, disagree violently and often.

"Some small trouble, sahib – I think you must listening to these informations."

Hersi's familiar voice, and there they would be, a dozen men grouped and ready for a *shir*, the traditional Somali meeting at which the two opposing men stated their cases at fiery length, and everyone else then gave his own version of the case, holding forth with all the passionate appeals and detailed verbal reconstructions of a skilled lawyer.

A labourer had lost a purple cotton robe, and swore he had seen another labourer wearing the identical garment. The accused swore by Allah, by his entire tribe and by his mother's life that he was innocent. Did Nuur Ahmed imagine this was the only purple *lunghi* in the whole of Somaliland? But Nuur Ahmed maintained his cloth had a tear in one corner, and when Hersi Jama, acting as mediator, examined the cloth worn by Yusuf Farah, lo and behold – there was the torn place, plain as dawn. Terrific shouting followed, as the assembled company took sides. The evidence of each side was always diametrically opposed, and it was never possible to obtain any clear picture of what had actually happened.

"You know, I really wonder," Jack said after one of these sessions, "whether they hold these *shirs* with any intention of settling the matter at all, or if it isn't merely a form of entertainment."

But as they expected him to participate in the *shirs*, he could not very well refuse. He was concerned mainly with keeping some kind of equilibrium in camp. If these disputes were not settled in some fashion, they grew and assumed grotesque proportions.

With Gino gone, Jack was now the only one in camp who knew how to fix anything that went wrong on a tractor, so he often had this type of work to do in the evenings as well. Only gradually did I realize what a strain he was working under, and how difficult it was for him, sometimes, to maintain an even temper. Occasionally it was impossible.

One late afternoon, Jack dropped into the brushwood hut for a quick cup of tea before going back to see about changing the oil in the tractors. All at once he dropped his cup and shot out of the hut like a man gone berserk. What on earth had happened? I stared out, but all I could see was Ali Wys, driving a tractor and scraper to its usual night-time place in the camp.

"Stop that engine!" Jack bellowed. "My God, man, what do you think you're doing?"

Stunned, Ali stopped and looked at Jack with blank incomprehension.

"I think you want the *agaf-agaf* over there, sahib –"

For a moment Jack could not trust himself to speak. Then he nodded brusquely and began to explain. When he came back to the hut, he gave me a wan grin.

"That was a narrow escape."

"What did he do?"

"The oil was drained out," Jack said. "If he'd run it any longer that way, the motor would have been ruined. He didn't realize. The oil pressure gauge still doesn't mean anything to him. He wasn't there when I told the others not to move the Cats. He thought he was being helpful. But damn it all, he might have wrecked it."

The blunders made by the Somali drivers were not done on purpose, as many Englishmen here believed, nor did they indicate any lack of intelligence – another belief common among *Ingrese*. They were simply the actions of men who had virtually no mechanical experience. How would we have fared, if we had been given a dozen camels and told to wrest a living from the desert?

"I remember, as a kid, taking an old Model-T apart and putting it together again," Jack said. "I was always tinkering with radios – all kinds of things like that. But men like Ali Wys and Omar Farah learned as kids how to throw a spear and how to recognize the tracks of their camels in the sand."

We realized, more and more, the complications caused by this difference in accumulated knowledge. Yet, under the tensions and demands of the moment, it was not easy to remain patient. Sometimes Jack would explain a point at great length, and the drivers would all nod and say "Oh yes, we understand," and immediately go and do the opposite. In the evenings, Jack would go over these difficulties endlessly, trying to puzzle out reasons for them, trying to discover ways of communicating with men who spoke his language only slightly and who had none of his technical and mechanical background.

"I was explaining the design of the *ballehs* to some of them today," he said, "the fact that the wing walls will have to jut out in a straight line, and I realized from what they said that they don't have any real concept of what a straight line is. Why should they? There aren't any straight lines here. There isn't a tree that doesn't grow crookedly."

Every culture in the world passes on knowledge to the next generation, but the nature of that knowledge suits the survival requirements of each particular place. The significance of this difference was borne in upon us one morning when we heard a flock of birds crying nearby. Jack and I paid no attention, for the sound had no meaning to us. But every Somali in the camp dropped what he was doing and rushed out, shouting.

"*Wa mas!* Snake!"

Sure enough, there it was, a big diamonded Russell's Viper, its thick body raised and tense, its flat evil-eyed head swaying, holding the birds horribly enchanted. Abdi killed it with a stick, and Jack asked him how he knew a snake was here. The old warrior looked surprised at our ignorance.

"When the *shimbir* speak that way," he said, "the snake is there."

So, piece by piece, both ourselves and the Somalis accumulated a little of this new knowledge, this knowledge not our own, the things that had not been handed down to us.

But the difference in the heritage of facts was not the only reason for a disparity in outlooks. We looked at the whole of life through different eyes. Our basic outlook came from science; theirs, from faith. We put our confidence in technical knowledge. They appeared to put their confidence in ritual.

One evening, doing some repairs, Jack told Isman Shirreh to clean a pipe on a tractor, for a lump of dirt was clinging to the outside, and if it fell in it would clog the pipe. Isman obligingly snatched up a rag and cleaned vigorously – holding the pipe so that the dirt fell straight in. To him, it was the act of cleaning which was important. The concept of keeping dirt out of motors was meaningless. The same was true of greasing the tractors – the important thing seemed to them to be the faithful application of grease almost anywhere, not the fact that the grease had to be forced into bearings, however difficult to get at, for it to do any good.

A few snatches of mechanical information, imparted as the need arose, could never be sufficient to change a man's total outlook. The drivers maintained their belief that there was a mysterious virtue in the repetition of certain acts. They cleaned the tractors conscientiously, following the same procedure each evening, and as long as nothing altered in the situation, all was well. But if one factor was different, they did not adjust their actions to meet the changed requirements.

Even if they were told to do something differently, they often seemed compelled to continue ritualistically in the same way as before.

The soil of the Haud was so hard that the ripper's steel teeth became bent and twisted. Jack found it necessary to borrow a heavier ripper from P.W.D. and to use it with additional weights attached. Every day something occurred to tax the ingenuity. But the technical problems, however many or however tricky, were much more easily solved than the human ones.

Whatever the day's difficulties, the arrival of dusk brought a feeling of peace to the camp. The tractors and scrapers came lumbering in, big dusty yellow machines, driven by dust-covered men. At one side of the camp, the Illaloes were going through their drill, with much slapping of rifles and snapping to attention. On the other side, the rest of the Somalis were facing Mecca and chanting the evening prayers. Above the shouts of the corporal and the low roar of the tractors could be heard the chorus of *Amiin* – Amen.

To guard, to work and to pray – in these ways our camp was related, after all, to the camps of the Somali tribesmen throughout the whole land.

When the first *balleh* was completed, we moved to Balleh Gedid. For the Somalis this process – packing up, heading off, re-settling – was one which involved a great deal of excitement. The camp was like a circus, with its air of noisy festivity, its songs, its tents, its crowd so busily exuberant.

"*Helleyoy – helleyoy –*"

None of the songs were sad today; all were eager and elated. The Somali equivalent of the English "Hey!" was *warya*, and the camp was loud with this reiterated cry, as the tents were dismantled and the equipment gathered.

"*Warya*, Abdi-o! *Warya*, Mohamed-o!"

Everyone yelled at everyone else. Come and give a hand with this tent-pole! Who has seen the other baramile? Where does this water drum go?

Finally the parade moved off, an imposing array of vehicles and shouting men. The small speedy Land-Rover led the way, followed by the yellow Bedford three-ton, with its brown canvas canopy mumbling in the wind. Next came the water truck, a three-ton fitted with a big tank, and towed behind it was the diesel-fuel trailer. Then the bulldozer chugged along with majestic slowness as it pulled the heavy workshop trailer containing the tools and spare parts and the generator which we now used to supply the camp with electric light. Next in line was Gino's caravan, now our home, towed by a tractor with scraper. Finally, at the end of the parade came the other Caterpillar and scraper, pulling the ripper and plough. The scrapers were piled high with tents and petrol drums. Our numerous water drums were wedged onto every vehicle where any space could be found. Men were perched all over, some on the trucks, some on the scrapers.

Jack and I could not help wondering what the Somali herdsmen thought as they watched our crawling but thunderous trek. We knew very well what the Somalis in our camp thought about it, however, and we were in complete accord, for this was one feeling we shared spontaneously with them – an upswinging of the heart for no reason other than merely to be going somewhere, to be on our way.

At Balleh Gedid, we found ourselves with some camp followers. The camp of one Somali family travelling by itself was known as a *jes*. Jack and I became aware of the nearby presence of such a *jes*, in which dwelt one rather disreputable looking man, an attractive girl of about sixteen, an old woman and a little girl. New licences for desert tea shops were not being issued by the government at this time, but when we questioned the Somalis in our camp about this *jes*, they told us blandly that it was "just a small tea shop," or else they pretended complete ignorance of it.

In the evenings, the drivers and labourers drifted over in that direction in ones and twos. When they returned, the next batch ambled over. If the *jes* was a tea-shop-cum-brothel, we did not mind. But one thing we had to be concerned about –

the *jes* was using water from our drums. We had a camp of thirty men, and although the water truck went into Hargeisa once a week, we always had to be careful.

"What is happening," Jack said in annoyance, "is that they are taking water on the sly, to give to the *jes*. I'm not going to have it that way. I'd rather give an understood daily ration. I suppose it's fair enough. The *jes* provides amenities of one kind and another.

So the *jes* received its allotment. The old woman sometimes visited our camp. She had a high and whining voice, and whenever she saw me she began her monotonous plea for alms.

"*Baksheesh! Baksheesh!*"

Asha, the little girl, who was about eight years old, had a curiously vacant and withdrawn look. Then, from Arabetto, who was more frank than the others, I learned that she was a child prostitute. There was a special name for such children, which meant literally "a small opening."

Asha sometimes came alone to see me in camp. She wanted me to give her a comb, which I did. This comb was the only thing she ever asked from me. Her hair was unkempt, and her face was unwashed, an unusual sight here, where children were normally well cared for. We did not talk much, Asha and I, for I did not know what to say to her. I never asked her about her life. My knowledge of Somali was too limited, and who would I get to translate? She sat quietly in the brushwood hut, and when the afternoon shadows began to lengthen, she went away.

"*Nabad gelyo*," she said. "May you enter peace."

But I did not reply, for I found myself unable to say *nabad diino* to her – the peace of faith.

I did not know what to do. If we forbade the *jes* to stay near the camp, the crone would only move her trade elsewhere, so the child would be no better off. Here at least Asha got enough water. Possibly many Somalis felt the same as I did about children such as Asha, but how would they feel about my meddling? I had the strong suspicion that I might easily make Asha's life worse by interfering. I could not take her away from the situation entirely, and what else would do any good?

So, whether out of wisdom or cowardice, I did nothing. The *jes* remained with us for several months. Then, in the *Jilal* drought, it vanished one day and we heard no more about it. But Asha's half-wild half-timid face with its ancient eyes will remain with me always, a reproach and a question.

The *Dhair* rains failed, and the *Jilal* began again. The dry winter months crawled by, slow as the giant tortoises that outlived the droughts of a century. On the great plain, what was left of the grass lay wind-flattened and white. The vultures could be seen again, on the thorn trees, waiting.

Each year it was the same. In the *Jilal*, the Somalis were a dying people in a dying land. The dust filled their nostrils like a constant reminder of mortality. The wind whistled through the dried seed pods on the thorn trees, and the aloes plants dwindled and wilted, their shrunken brown flesh stinking in the sun. But neither the people nor the land would die, although the weakest of every species would not feel the rains of spring. There was a toughness deep in these people, like the fibre of desert cactus, the ability to eke out life, the refusal to die easily. At the times of prayer they knelt, for they were the People of the Book, the People of the Right Hand. They were not forsaken but judged by the Lord of men and djinn. They did not understand His will, but they bowed before it. Though the rains of compassion would not fall for a long time, yet was He the Compassionate. When He willed it, the land would be reborn out of the dry womb of death. Fresh water would be sweet in the mouth again, and there would sound once more the songs of men and the laughter of young girls. But nothing could make it happen sooner, nothing could hasten the day, neither rage nor tears, neither curse nor prayer. It would happen when Allah willed it, and not a moment before.

With the onset of the *Jilal*, we expected an upsurge of

rumours about the *ballehs*, but these appeared to have tapered off permanently. We no longer heard that the tribesmen were saying the *ballehs* would contain poisoned water, or that the water would be sold by the government at enormous prices. Now that the actual construction was going on, the tribesmen might be reassured by the sight of what was being done. Or more likely, their attention was diverted from us by the fact that so many Habr Awal were still in the Haud, and the other tribes were complaining about their presence.

Sometimes a group of nomads came to watch the work. Usually, they did not say anything. They stood at a distance, and watched the noisy tractors snorting through the dust, and then they went away. We did not know what they were thinking, nor whether they realized that next year these *ballehs* would be of some use to them.

Then one day Ahmed Abdillahi, the young Eidagalla chieftain, came to visit our camp. He was as handsome and deep-voiced as ever, and had it not been for the drought he would have been perfectly happy, for his wife had just borne him his first son. Through Hersi, he questioned Jack about the almost-completed *balleh*.

"When the rains come, this *balleh* will be full of water? So large a thing?"

"We hope so," Jack said. "We think it will be."

Ahmed Abdillahi nodded approval and then produced an outsize camel bell, which he had made himself, out of *galol* wood, and presented it to Jack.

"Some of my people are too proud to say now they think the *ballehs* will be a good thing," he said. "But after the rains, *In sha' Allah*, they will say so."

This camel bell ranked as Jack's first, last and only presentation. It was a strange and unwieldy creation, with a hank of handwoven rope at the top. But we valued it greatly, for it signified the first real acceptance of the *ballehs*.

Almost imperceptibly, the work changed, became less a matter of perpetual crises. The tractor drivers were growing more accustomed to the machines, more adept in operation and maintenance, less liable to make the mistakes which plagued the first months of excavation. Also, where Jack once felt he was constantly talking at cross-purposes with them, now some kind of understanding had grown between them and himself. They seemed to feel themselves part of the camp now, and in their work they operated as a crew a great deal more smoothly than they once had. The misunderstandings and the immediate problems presented by the desert terrain – these did not cease. But they were settled somehow. The work was getting done.

Balleh Gehli. Balleh Gedid. Balleh Hersi Jama. Slowly, the line of reservoirs was emerging across the waterless Haud.

CHAPTER EIGHT

Arrivederci, Italia

THE ITALIANS lived apart, in a separate community, more truly exiled than any of the English here. Most of them had come out to Ethiopia as settlers, after the Italian take-over, when there was nothing for them in Italy. They were overwhelmingly non-political. They had come to Africa hoping to own their own land or their own business. Things hadn't worked out that way. They were taken prisoners-of-war by the British, and after the war they were offered jobs by the Protectorate government, for they were excellent mechanics and road-builders. Now they lived in Hargeisa in a settlement of men, for none of their wives were with them. But by Italian standards the pay was high – enough to justify this unnatural life. They lived frugally and sent most of their pay back to their families in Italy. They went back on leave, but they had really said a final goodbye to their own land. They spoke of home often, and lovingly, but with a shrug and a cynical grin. Sure, life was rotten – who didn't know that? They had been kicked around by history, but when had ordinary people not been? There was the music, the *vino* – they took what they could, and lived from day to day.

They had built a church for themselves, each man contributing whatever skills he possessed towards the fashioning of the carved benches, the altar, the wrought-iron candelabra and lamps. This church had great simplicity and beauty, and it stood amidst their cramped and ugly bungalows like a small cathedral in the slums of a medieval town. For an obscure reason known only to itself, Rome had sent them an Irish priest.

We did not much like the Hargeisa Club, the sanctuary of the English, for it was so often filled with dreary complaining, especially from the memsahibs. *It wasn't just diarrhoea, my dear, it was enteric dysentry – the cramps were simply unbelievable, worse than labour pains. I'm certain Ali's got away with more than five pounds of butter this month – what on earth can one do? If I sack him, the next one will be exactly the same. We've had the new "boy" a week and he's impossible – doesn't know a carving knife from a teaspoon.* For our taste, a little of this went a long way. More and more we found ourselves going to the Italian Club instead, where there was a warmth of laughter, and where, if people had problems with their innards or their cooks, at least they did not talk about them all the time.

Compared with the Hargeisa Club, the Italian Club was very shabby in appearance. A zinc-covered bar stood at one end of the long narrow room, and at the other a stone fireplace was crowned with a framed picture of a blonde glamour girl. Around the room were hung discoloured paper lanterns and streamers, permanent relics of Christmases past. A rasping gramophone played incessantly – lively Italian melodies, usually, or *Jezebel*, currently popular. On Saturday nights the gramophone was turned off and the Italians provided their own music – an accordion, a guitar, and Ugo's frenetic drums.

Aldo, short and stocky, never stopped shouting. To hear him discuss the slightest thing, you would think he was going to burst a blood vessel. Banditto was given his nickname because he looked like a Sicilian bandit – a slit-eyed and devious look, combined with a jazzy manner, a swarthy skin, black and slicked-down hair. Dolpho was slim, with a sharply handsome face, and eyes that gave the impression of knowing a great deal more than he ever said. Jobless in the thirties, he had gone out to Ethiopia and got into the trucking business, at first driving for someone else and then managing to buy his own truck. He lost everything, of course, in the war. He spoke to us of wars in general.

"We are the people who always lose – the people like us in every country. The leaders – they don't fight. Some of them make money, most of them lose nothing. But we always lose, no matter which side wins."

Between the Italians and the Somalis there was an uneasy truce. They did not really like each other, and yet there was a kind of understanding between them, for in some ways they were similar. Both were emotional; neither comprehended the British restraint. To the Somalis, the Italians were more recognizably human than the English, for at least they openly acknowledged the need of men for women.

Feruccio was the barber. He carried on his business in his bungalow, which he shared with Umberto. Jack went one Saturday afternoon for a haircut, and found Umberto on the stoep, sipping a mixture of Chianti and bottled lemonade. Sit down, sit down, Umberto urged hospitably. Perhaps the *signor* would not mind waiting? Would he have some *vino*? Very refreshing with lemonade – a drink to make you sweat properly. Feruccio could not give a haircut for a few minutes.

"He ees focking. Soon he finish."

Jack and Umberto sat on the stoep in the sunlight, amicably passing the time of day, and after a while a Somali girl stepped out of the bungalow and walked quietly away, and then Feruccio emerged briskly, with scissors and clippers in his hand.

"So – okay. Now we get to work."

The others always referred to *il Capitano* by his now nonexistent rank, for he had been in the Italian army before the Ethiopian war, before the days of the *Duce*. He was the old style of Army officer, a gentleman adventurer, but one would never have guessed it from his appearance. He was in his fifties, I suppose, a slender and dapper man who now worked as an accountant in P.W.D. Stores. He looked like a scholar and spoke like an aristocrat. Meeting him, one would have imagined he had spent his life in libraries and drawingrooms. But not so.

Il Capitano, who had learned surveying in Kenya many years ago, had been the first man to do a general survey of the Danakil country, a remote portion of Ethiopia, and the seventh white man who had crossed that territory and emerged alive. A number of explorers had met their deaths there. The Danakil country was a fabled place, still inhabited by warrior tribesmen who had long had a reputation for ferocity and hostility to strangers, and who collected as souvenirs the genitals of their dead enemies.

Shortly after the Italian administration began in Ethiopia, the government had decided that the Danakil country should be surveyed. Understandably, no one wanted the job. When the Captain said he would do it, he was unable to find Ethiopians who would go with him. The government in Addis Ababa told him they would find staff for him. And they did. They opened the Addis jail and released every political prisoner, every thief, murderer and cut-throat. These were the men who were to accompany *il Capitano* on his trek into the Danakil country. He was given twenty-four hours to get his uncertain army out of town, and in the meantime all the citizens of Addis, European and African alike, firmly barred their doors.

So out he went. With him he carried a whole year's pay for his entire crew. He had only one man whom he felt he might possibly be able to trust, but with that amount of money, he could not really be sure of anyone.

"That first night," he told us with a faint smile, "I did not sleep so well."

But the straggling brigade proceeded, and the Captain began to train and drill them, for he had the feeling that his only hope lay in welding them into some sort of organized company. There were fights and conspiracies and stabbings, but he persisted and gradually his strange corps took on a kind of unit. They succeeded in surveying the area, and they even managed to recruit a few wild Danakil into their ranks. When they returned to Addis, more than a year later, they were a vastly different force from the one that had started out.

The Danakil knew some remarkable things, *il Capitano*

told us. They made use of a certain plant to drug poisonous snakes, which the tribesmen could then handle. They were fond of leaving these snakes around in unexpected places. Once an Italian truck driver, going near Danakil country, rashly parked his vehicle at night and went to sleep inside. When he wakened, he sensed something wrong. Looking down he saw, perched on one of his feet, a snake curled up on a puff of local cotton fibre. The snake, a small and deadly one, was beginning to waken from its drugged sleep. The driver did not have much choice. Quietly he drew his revolver and shot the snake, shooting his own foot off as well.

The Captain's greatest treasure was his pet cheetah. The beast was kept chained outside his bungalow, but when he returned in the evening he would unchain it and wrestle playfully with it. Quite a sight, this – the man so delicate in appearance, and the huge tawny spotted cat. He had acquired this cheetah when it was a small cub, so it had never had to hunt for its food. The result was that it had grown to a much larger size than any cheetah we ever saw in the Haud. It was the most graceful animal I have ever seen, with the possible exception of the desert gazelle, the *gerenuk*. But I would not have trusted it one inch. *Il Capitano* trusted it completely and had no fear of it.

He had recently come back, he told us, from his first leave in Italy in nearly twenty years. He was glad to be back in Africa. Things had changed too much at home, and he had been away too long.

There will be no niche for his kind in the new Africa, and that is probably as it should be. But I will always hope that this gallant and enigmatic man has not been forced to go back and live in a crowded European city, for he was a man of Africa, as much as any Somali or any Danakil.

Gino was the Italian we knew best, for he became the foreman on the *balleh* job. He had come out to Ethiopia seventeen years before, to farm. He had worked his land until the war came, and then he lost everything he thought he owned, including a good many of his teeth, for when the Italians began to lose the war, the Ethiopians attacked Gino's farm, and himself, and yanked out with pliers any teeth that had gold fillings.

He had only been home to Italy a few times in all these years. He had a son and a daughter, grown up now. He showed us a picture of his wife when she was young and pretty. She was growing old now, as he was, and they had been together very little.

Gino was a thickset bull-necked man, colossally strong. He was acknowledged as the finest mechanic in the country. He had done much of the work on Alfie, the giant diesel truck made out of scraps. When Jack needed a plough to make furrows at the sides of the *ballehs* in order to widen the catchment area, he discovered there was no proper plough in the whole country, so Gino made one for him, dredging the design from memory and the parts from old armoured cars.

Gino talked sparingly, even among the Italians, and with us hardly at all, for he spoke practically no English. Out in camp, he and Jack communicated in a curious way. When general subjects were discussed, language was a real difficulty, but when they were speaking about the work and the machinery, each spoke in his own tongue and somehow they understood one another – how they managed to do so was a mystery, even to themselves.

In the evenings in camp, Gino would come over from his caravan and sit in our brushwood hut for an hour or so. We used to pass around the Italian-English phrasebook, but it was not much help to us, for it consisted of such phrases as *Where is the key to my watch?* We wondered how many centuries had gone by since the book was revised. Jack and Gino tinkered with our "saucepan" radio, and Gino always tried to get music. Any kind of music was preferable to talk. As soon as he heard a spoken voice, he would switch to another station.

"*Troppo propaganda*," he said. He had had quite enough of that. Music was not so misleading.

He got along with the Somalis better than most Italians

did. Even Abdi, who for no apparent reason said of Ugo "*Wa fulley* – he is a coward," never made this comment about Gino. Arabetto, who grew up in Italian Somaliland and could speak Italian, was the one who most often helped Gino at the forge. Gino had fashioned this forge himself, so he could repair machinery on the spot.

The role of blacksmith always seemed a fitting one for Gino, for there was a massive quality about the man. But his powerful hands were made to forge ploughshares, not swords.

Only gradually did we come to realize how difficult was the Italians' position here, and how remarkable was their capacity for laughter. The government could scarcely have managed without them now – they were the reliable artisans, the men who repaired the machinery and kept the lorries in running order. And yet, apart from a few P.W.D. English who appreciated their work, they were given no recognition. In one sense, the administration could not be blamed – the fact was that there were hardly any Englishmen here who had sufficient knowledge of machinery to recognize how much the Italians were doing. Socially, they were non-existent as far as most English were concerned. They were not invited to English homes; they never appeared at the drinks parties. They were committed to Africa, and deeply. They did not want to risk losing their jobs. But always their jobs depended upon the whim of the English. They had to be deferential – they had to touch the forelock, in effect, and doff the cap to the lord of the manor. Sometimes the English whose goodwill they had to cultivate were men who were much less competent than themselves.

"How it must gall them," Jack said blackly. "I've never known more efficient mechanics anywhere, and yet they can't afford to argue with an Englishman, even if they know damn well they're in the right. The Somalis are more free, in a way – if they get really fed up, they can always go back to their camels. But the Italians have to be agreeable, no matter how they feel."

Probably one should not ever make generalizations about people, but we will always be disposed to like Italians because of these men in Somaliland, living out their isolated lives and refusing to mourn. Where have they gone now, with the country independent? I do not know. It is unlikely that most of them would stay on – the Somalis would not have the money to employ them, and they probably would not want to stay anyway, for the bitterness between themselves and the Somalis will not easily be eradicated. Some of them may have gone to Eritrea, perhaps, or Djibouti. Some may have gone back to Italy, to the families who are now strangers to them. And this may be the worst of all – after so many years, to find they are once again exiles, this time in their own land.

CHAPTER NINE

A Teller of Tales

ALLAH, WHO ordered all things and wrote each man's fate indelibly in the book of life, had not been generous to Hersi. In a land where a man was still judged on his capacities as a warrior, Hersi was small, punily muscled, almost flimsy. His wits were his protection, but Allah had been ironic even here, for although He had given Hersi the power to conjure up words and to conceive orations, He had also given him an impediment in his speech. The cruel nickname applied to him among his own people was Hersi Halftongue. But he met the name spiritedly.

"I may have only half a tongue, but I swear by the Prophet that I am a whole man in the most important way."

He made this remark to Guś, who was able to speak with him in Somali. He would never have said such a thing to me. Some deep sense of decorum or taboo forbade it. In fact, so careful was he in this respect that once when he and Guś were discussing Somali marriage customs, he became immediately silent as Sheila and I appeared. He had been speaking about dowry, we later learned, and had been quoting the proverb – *The daughter of a poor man has no vagina*. He looked at us with embarrassment.

"It's all right," Guś told him. "They can't understand. They don't speak that much Somali."

"You never know," said Hersi, and refused to say another word.

Unfortunately, he had picked up a number of English four-letter words, the meaning of which he did not appear to know, and even when he was talking with me, he sprinkled his conversation gaily and liberally with these.

"I believe he'd pass out," Jack said, "if he knew what he was saying."

We were careful never to let him know. But generally his half-tongue served him well. As our interpreter, he invested even the most trivial comment or request with an air of importance, and he made pronouncements like an oracle.

"It is growing dark," his voice could not have been more solemn if he had been announcing the end of the world, not merely the end of day, "and we cannot succeeding in shooting any game in bloody this place. Therefore I think we must returning to camp presently times."

His English had a grotesque lyricism about it. He specialized in high-flown phrases – *absolutely excellent* – *all our considerations* – which he scattered like hopefully sown wheat. His education in English had been brief, only a year at the government school, after which he had been forced to leave and get a job for his family's sake. But he practised reading and writing continually. Sometimes I would see him beside the camp fire at night, squinting, holding the book up close so he could see in the smoky orange light, or filling the pages of a scribbler with his laborious scrawl. He was neither educated nor uneducated, and so he was sensitive about his errors. Criticism and correction were hard for him to take, for he was aware of his vulnerability. He scoffed at the Sheikh schoolboys, their youth and inexperience, perhaps knowing that they with their firmer grasp of English would one day make it impossible for such as himself to hold an interpreter's job.

He had attended Qoranic school for a while, and he was able to read and write Arabic. But his true talent was with his own language. It was a regret to me that I could not follow him when he spoke Somali, for he was not only an orator but a poet. In his youth he had composed many love-songs, some of which were well known throughout the country. His feeling for poetry was strong. Once at Sheikh when Musa was reciting some of his own love poetry, Hersi came up to him afterwards.

"You have opened a wound that had healed," he said.

Hersi's mode of expression was unfailingly dramatic. Once when he and Jack and Abdi were driving past Mandeira, in the hills, Hersi pointed to the high rocks and the cliffs.

"There is the capital of the lions. When you are hearing their voice in the night, you will be shook."

He always called the Haud "this island place." It seemed to us that he intended to say "this isolated place," but his phrase was better. The Haud was an island place, so seemingly remote that one almost doubted the existence of the rest of the world.

Each day in camp, Hersi taught Somali to me for an hour, and when the lesson was over, we sat in the brushwood hut and chatted. Our favourite topic was religion. Hersi was a *mullah*, a kind of lay-priest, and he had read the Qoran four times. After I had read the Qoran in English, we were able to converse better, for the *Kitab*, The Book, was Hersi's constant frame of reference. It held, he believed, all truth, all the answers for everything. He was in this sense a fundamentalist, for he took the words of the *Kitab* literally at every point. And yet some of the Prophet's furious cries against the infidel seemed to have passed him by, for his tolerant outlook towards other religions was not commonly found among Muslims any more than it was among Christians.

"If a man is saying he is religious," Hersi maintained, "and is not having highly respects for all the mighty prophets, then I say that man is without religion."

And in the sand he drew a peak, an inverted V.

"This side here, it is the way of Esa," he said, using the Arabic name for Jesus, "and this side here, it is the way of Mohamed. Both paths leading to God."

I recalled a letter I had seen not long before in an English newspaper. It was from a Christian clergyman, who said that Jacob Epstein's statue of Christ made Him look as though He were a Syrian or an Arab or some other foreigner.

Squatting in the desert dust, wrapped in his faded pink

and black robe, and wearing his squashed and grimy old felt hat, Hersi elaborated on his beliefs.

"Each land must following their own prophet, but showing greatly considerations for other prophets, too, for all prophets being sent by God."

In the realm of politics he was on less certain ground.

"I wishing to ask you something," he said to Jack one day. "White-skin people – these I know. Black-skin people – these I know. I even am hearing of yellow-skin people. But these "Reds" which Radio Somali mentioning – can you tell me is such people truly having red skin?"

He spoke of his wife and children, who lived with his tribe. He had, alas, only daughters. If a girl was not beautiful, she would have difficulty in finding a husband, and if she did find one, you could be sure he would not be a man who owned many camels. To be beautiful, a woman should be tall and have copper-coloured skin. Both Hersi's daughters were still quite young, but he had begun to worry already.

"One is very shiny," he said, "but the other is small and black."

He knew, however, that there was no use in his worrying about anything, for all things were in the hands of Allah. His fatalism was total. Once when we were in Hargeisa to get supplies, Hersi bought a small bottle of *ghee*, the liquid butter that was eaten on rice and was regarded as a delicacy. He shoved the bottle in the back of the Land-Rover, and on the return trip to camp, it was joggled and the *ghee* was spilled.

"Why didn't you tell me it was there?" Jack demanded. "I could have put it some place where it wouldn't have spilled."

Hersi shook his head. "No. Such thing is not possible. If Allah was intending me to eating that *ghee*, it would not getting spilled."

Hersi came of a distinguished family. Risaldar-Major Haji Musa Farah had been his uncle. During the wars against Sultan Mohamed Abdullah Hassan at the beginning of this century, Musa Farah fought with the British and was the highest-ranking Somali in the Camel Corps. His exploits had become legends. Hersi spoke of him with reverence.

"He was a man. Such we are not having in these days."

Hersi himself toiled mightily, but he would never see himself in such a high position as that of Haji Musa Farah. He cherished his uncle's fame, and envied it, and yet it was a burden to him, too, not only as a personal reproach but as a heritage of community suspicion. For among the most anti-British of the Somalis, Hersi's tribal section, the Musa Arreh, was taunted for having long been too close to the government.

"Musa Arreh," they said, "*Ingrese* Arreh."

Hersi was the peacemaker of the camp, and he applied himself to this task with enthusiasm. The night-long discussions, the bizarre arguments, the complicated settlement of quarrels – these were meat and drink to him.

Arabetto overstayed his leave and arrived back in camp several days late, and Abdi, who was always gunning for him, tried to persuade Jack to fire him. Jack refused, and Abdi and Arabetto had a long and heated disagreement. Hersi acted as mediator, and later made a report to us, in which his own role as counsellor was emphasized to the full.

"I saying to him, 'Abdi dear, you are my sections. We are same tribe. But you ask me to tell the sahib to give discharge to Arabetto. I can't do it, Abdi dear, I can't do it, my cousin.' And I saying to him, 'Are we Muslims?' And he saying, 'We are Muslims.' And I saying to him, 'All right. If we are Muslims, must be we cannot sucking the blood of other Muslim peoples. This man is Arabian. Doesn't matter his mother was Midgertein. He is Arabian. But he is Muslim. Must be we cannot sucking his blood.'"

Then he told us of the advice he had given to Abdi regarding Europeans.

"I saying to him, 'Abdi, my cousin, you must keep from getting so hot. I am understanding the conditions of the Europeans better than you. You must giving the sahib a sweet answer. It is in their character. You must not shouting and getting so tempered.'"

This gave us something to ponder, we in whose character it lay to need a sweet answer.

One day Hersi received the news that his wife had just given birth to their third child. He was completely downcast, for it was another girl. Three girls – such bad luck no one should have. Shortly afterwards, he brought his family to see us, his wife Saqa and the two younger children, Amiina who was six years old, and the new baby, whose name was Fadima. I had imagined his wife would be older and more shrewish than she was, considering Hersi's woeful recounting of the demands made on his wages and the way in which his wife, as soon as she got to Hargeisa, always wanted to buy new clothes. Saqa, however, was only in her middle twenties, finely built and tall, with large dark eyes and long lashes. She was a magnificent woman, and possessed an extraordinary amount of poise. It seemed strange that she was married to a man as slight and nervous as Hersi.

Hersi took his family that day and put them on a trade-truck bound for Awareh. As they were leaving, Saqa said to him, "Give my salaams to the white woman." At this, the other passengers glared at both Saqa and Hersi, and several voices muttered the old mockery.

"Musa Arreh – *Ingrese* Arreh."

Hersi was caught, partly by the past, the memories and handed-down sagas of Haji Musa Farah's achievements, and partly by his own frail present-day. Only through jobs with the *Ingrese* could he utilize what accomplishments he had, those of reading and writing. Yet his education was so limited that his position could never be really secure. Nor was his education sufficient to enable him ever to break away from his tribe. He needed an established status in both worlds, but he achieved it in neither.

Only once, while he was working for us, did he gain a kind of fame, the recognition he yearned for. But the price he paid was a high one. At Balleh Gehli, the Balleh of the Camels, Hersi one day caught a ride on the back of a scraper, although everyone had been warned to stay away from the machinery when it was in operation. The driver, unaware that Hersi was there, let down the scraper apron and the heavy steel thudded back and jammed Hersi's hand. The drivers brought him back to camp. He was suffering with shock and was only half conscious. Three fingers had been crushed down to the middle joint, and were flat and limp like the fingers on a rag doll. On one, the bone was sticking out through the pulpy flesh.

For a moment we were all stunned, for this was the first serious accident on the job. Then everyone moved rapidly. Mohamed brought a bowl of camel milk – the Somalis' first remedy for all ills – and held it to Hersi's mouth. I put a temporary and loose dressing on the hand. Jack scribbled a note to the doctor. Abdi and Arabetto, who had warred so often, forgot their differences for the time being. Between them, they managed to get Hersi propped up in the Land-Rover, and then they drove him in to Hargeisa, two painful hours distant.

"It would have to be Hersi," Jack said morosely. "He always has such damn bad luck."

Slight consolation as it might be to Hersi, Jack decided to call the next *balleh* after him. When it was completed, it became Balleh Hersi Jama. Ultimately the name was announced over Radio Somali, and when Hersi went to visit his family at Awareh, he discovered that people there had heard of it, and he had become quite a personage.

But he would never have back the use of his hand.

Hersi really came into his own as a story-teller. When we first went out to camp, I realized he had this ability, for in the evenings we often heard his voice, chanting the *gabei* or rising excitedly in a lengthy recitation. But it took many months before he trusted me enough to tell me any tales at all. For a long time, whenever I mentioned the subject, he looked vague and pretended not to know what I was talking about. Stories? What on earth were those?

"We are not having such things presently times," he would murmur evasively.

I respected his reticence and was careful not to press the matter. After I had obtained literal translations of some *belwo* and *gabei* from Guś and Musa, together with a few folk-tales, I decided to try again with Hersi. I had heard an interesting story the other day, I told him. Perhaps he might know it.

"Oh?" he said distantly. "What is it?"

It happened to be one of the best-loved of Somali tales, the adventures of the outrageous 'Igaal Bowkahh. When Hersi discovered who had told it to me (for Musa was very highly regarded as a poet), he looked extremely thoughtful for a moment. Then he struck his forehead as though in utter astonishment.

"Why you are never telling me you wishing to hear such things?" he cried. "Stories – if we are speaking of stories, who is knowing more of these considerations than I? I know ten thousand!"

I told him I was sorry – it had certainly been remiss of me not to have brought up the question before.

From that day, we never looked back. Hersi not only told me the stories he knew himself – he also went to considerable trouble to gather tales from various elders in the town and in nearby camps in the Haud. He edited, of course, and would only tell me such tales as he considered suitable for my ears, but I realized that I could not expect the impossible, and I was grateful for whatever stories he could bring himself to tell me.

Every afternoon, when he was not needed at the work site, Hersi came to the brushwood hut. He told the stories to me in English, with an admixture of Somali and Arabic, for such English words as "saint" and "angel" were unknown to him, but I knew the Somali or Arabic equivalent. Although most of the labourers and drivers did not speak much English, there was always an audience. They drifted into the hut quietly, those who were off duty, and listened. They did not understand many of the words, but they recognized the familiar tales by the way in which Hersi acted them out.

For me, also, his acting had tremendous value. It compensated to some extent for the fact that I was not hearing the stories in Somali, in which he would have been able to express them with better style. Hersi belonged to that ancient brotherhood of born story-tellers. He played by turns the different roles in the tale, transforming himself by some alchemy of expression or stance into whatever he chose – a saint or a sultan, a thief craftily plotting how to outwit a naïve tribesman. He told me the story of the three wise counsellors – three hashish addicts whom a disgruntled sultan called in when his regular counsellors had all failed him. And for this moment, Hersi became the hashish addicts, dreamily twirling in their narcotic dance. When he told me of Arawailo, he made me see the barbaric splendour and the cruelty of that fabled queen. He told me of Deg-Der, the cannibal woman, and I could visualize her horrible countenance and her donkey's ear. He was not himself at these times. He was so carried away by his stories that he lived them, taking on the characters like cloaks. His timing was always exact – he never once spoiled a story by giving away the ending before the proper moment. When he finished, he would be exhausted and would have to be revived with a mug of strong spiced tea, for he was an artist and he gave to each performance the very best of which he was capable.

I do not know what has become of Hersi in the years since we last saw him. It is unlikely that he will ever find what he seeks. He is no longer a tribesman, but there is no real place for him in the realm of clerks and book-keepers, either, where he would so much have liked to establish himself.

But at least in Africa a good story-teller is never entirely without honour. Out in the Haud, when the tales are told around the fires, perhaps the thin unimpressive figure still rises and begins, with his flawed speech, to build in words the caliph's palace and the enchanter's tower, while around him the listeners sit, pulling their robes close against the chill of the night, and urging him on.

"What happened next? What did they do then?"

He warms, as always, to his audience. "It was like this –
listen, and I will tell you –"

And he becomes the people in the tales, the great Wiil
Waal who drove the last of the Galla kings from Jigjigga,
or Ahmed the miserable woodseller who – wondrously –
married a sultan's daughter.

CHAPTER TEN

Mohamed

"Helleyoy, helleyoy –"

MOHAMED was always singing *belwo*. He was fond of voice tricks – the song would rise weirdly to falsetto and plummet to bass within the space of a few notes, and the *yerki*, the small boy who was cook's helper, would applaud with a wooden spoon on a saucepan. Mohamed was not the quiet sort. He liked noise; he liked to make his presence known to the world. Whether he was preparing dinner for six, in town, or opening a tin of spaghetti in the Haud, he did it with dash and verve. He dressed vividly, favouring robes of royal purple, and when he visited the town for an evening, he put on his shoes of oxblood leather, tossed an embroidered kashmir shawl across one shoulder and tucked a small cane, like a swagger stick, under an elbow. He felt I was making a ridiculous fuss about nothing when I strongly objected to my brightly patterned linen tea-towels being used as turbans.

One might have imagined – as we did at first – that he was always like this, jaunty and cheerful, skimming on the surface of life like a beetle on a rain pool. But not so. He had times of melancholy, when some incommunicable despair took hold of him, and then he would sink into a silence so complete that he seemed to have gone elsewhere, to have vacated his shell which somehow moved around and worked without his being in it. Then some slight thing, some absurdity – the *yerki* chasing a chicken, to slaughter it, and being outdistanced by the ruffled and squawking bundle of feathers – would bring him back, and he would be garrulous and laughing once more.

Mohamed had never herded camels, but this was not to say that life had been less hard for him than for the desert men. It had been quite hard enough, but in a different way. He had been born in Berbera and had lived there all his life until he came with us to Sheikh and Hargeisa and the Haud. He had worked as a servant since he was ten, beginning as cook's helper and going on to become houseboy. He considered that he had been fortunate.

"I get lucky. Only few times I no get job –"

Now, at eighteen, he was a cook, and this appeared to be as far as he could go. He was quick-witted, intelligent, energetic – and illiterate. Easy enough to say, as many *Ingrese* did, that what a man has never known he cannot miss. But Mohamed had lived by his wits long enough to know that he had wits. He had a friend at Sheikh school, a boy whom he had known since childhood. Abdillahi's father had been in the army and was killed in the war; the government was paying for the boy's education. Mohamed brought Abdillahi over one day to meet us. Abdillahi, whose English was excellent, began to discuss the Gezira Scheme in the Sudan, a project about which he had been reading. Mohamed, who could not follow the conversation at all, and who had never heard of the Gezira Scheme, stood very much apart, his face vacant as sand. He never brought Abdillahi to see us again.

Mohamed's father, like a good many Somalis, had once been a seaman.

"He was going to Italy, and England, and – oh, many places, many many places."

He could not be more specific, for outside his own country, these two were the only ones whose names he knew. When his father returned to Somaliland, Mohamed told us, he bought camels with his savings. But most of them died one year during a severe drought. The ones that remained were taken, after the father's death, by Mohamed's older half-brother, who still kept them in the Guban.

"Seven belong for me," he said. "Seven camels, mine."

Perhaps some day he would be able to claim them, but it would not be easy, for the half-brother was determined not to give them up. This brother was Mohamed's only close relative. He did not remember his mother, for she died when he was very young. He clung to the thought of his elusive inheritance, the camels which were rightfully his. Unlike most Somalis, who could bring themselves to slaughter or sell one of their camels only under conditions of desperate need, Mohamed would have liked to raise what cash he could from his small herd. His ambition was that of a town-dweller – to buy one of the mud-and-wattle tea shops.

When the war came, Mohamed was thrown on his own resources and lived in any way he could, by thievery or begging – he was careful never to relate precisely how. When the Italians invaded Somaliland, the British retreat was attended by considerable confusion. Arms and equipment were left scattered and abandoned. In Berbera the Somalis foraged, gleaning what they could. On one occasion, some Somali families out in the Guban became alarmed when they received the news that heavily armed persons were approaching their camp. The tribesmen quickly gathered to meet these invaders, expecting a band of rival tribesmen, bent on attack. Instead, they saw a small boy who staggered as he walked, for he was weighted down with the three rifles he was carrying. Relating it, Mohamed rocked with laughter.

"I find them some place," he said. "I think maybe I can sell them."

Was he fortunate, to be able to laugh, or was his laughter a screen, a necessary protection? I do not know. All I know is that he was eight years old at the time, and he was alone. Those who grow up within a tribe are never alone, but Mohamed's father in becoming a seaman began the process of breaking away, and while Mohamed still prudently maintained some associations with his tribe, he had not lived within his clan for many years and he seemed uncertain how much they would stand beside him in time of need.

Shortly after he came to work for us, he asked us to leave the house unlocked when we went out in the evenings. Locking the bungalow was a reflection upon him, a seeming doubt of his capacity to guard our goods against outside thieves or his own temptation. He used small quantities of our tea and sugar, for this was one of the perquisites of a cook's job, but no one else was allowed to touch our possessions. We agreed to leave the house in his care, for we took his request as an indication of his sense of responsibility and also of his personal liking for us. This came as no surprise to us, for unconsciously we had fully expected ourselves to be more likeable as employers than the majority of English, known to us as "the sahib types." Were we not more democratic? What a good thing that Mohamed appreciated this quality.

In fact, of course, whatever we may or may not have been had nothing to do with the case. But only slowly did we come to see that Mohamed's identification of his own interests with those of his employer would have taken place whoever the employer happened to be. He acted not in response to what we were, but to what he himself was. But for a time we managed to ignore any indications to the contrary, and saw him mainly as happy and joking, self-reliant and responsible, because that was the way we wanted him to be.

We were all the more easily misled, however, because he was misleading, although he did not mean to be. He appeared so confident, so much his own master. He scorned to ask, when he did not know something. He would never admit ignorance. At Sheikh, once, we were given a cucumber – a rarity here, and not to be treated lightly. I told Mohamed we would have it for lunch, but it never occurred to me to tell him how to serve it.

"Fine," he said. "I fix it."

His manner indicated that he was completely familiar with this type of vegetable. Nobody could have guessed that he had never seen one before. And so the precious cucumber was duly served for lunch – boiled.

He was always at his best in times of crisis. The night of the big storm in camp, when everything was soaked and muddy, and the desert had become a lake, I went over to the cook-tent after the rain to tell Mohamed not to bother trying to cook anything. A tin of beans would be sufficient for dinner. To my astonishment, I discovered Mohamed calmly preparing dinner on several charcoal burners which the *yerki* was holding down so they would not float away. Mohamed himself, wading around in six inches of water, was not only unperturbed – he was positively triumphant. He appeared to be enjoying himself greatly.

"Dinner in five minutes," he promised briskly.

And in five minutes dinner appeared, complete with soup course.

Mohamed came to me one day with an exercise book and a pencil.

"Memsahib – you will teach me to read and write?"

No one had ever asked me to teach anything before. I was pleased by this request, and touched by his wish for self-improvement. Certainly, I told him, I would be only too glad to teach him. Why I should have thought myself qualified to teach anyone to read and write, especially in a language not his own, I do not know. But it seemed to me that it would be relatively easy, for Mohamed had a quick mind and a good memory.

I have read, in many books about Africa, of Europeans who taught their servants how to read and write. *Under my tutelage, Ali made very rapid progress and was soon able to write down his market accounts and to read the correspondence in The Times.* I wonder how they managed it. Mohamed was as clever as the next person, but he had never become accustomed to the discipline of constant practice. He soon grew tired of copying the same words over and over. As for myself, it became obvious that I did not have the faintest idea how to communicate a knowledge of reading and writing. One day he closed his exercise book and smiled ruefully.

"I think maybe not much use," he said.

The failure, I felt, was mine. Perhaps he felt it was his. Actually, we had both under-estimated the difficulties. But it was I who should have known better, simply because I was literate and ought to have had some comprehension of the fact that literacy is not acquired magically in a few days. What else had I under-estimated?

Ismail had been hired as houseboy, Mohamed as cook. Ismail was Habr Yunis, while Mohamed was Habr Awal, but this difference of tribe was only one of the troubles between them. Mohamed was the younger and least experienced of the two, yet we had made him cook, which was usually the senior post. Ismail had a brooding nature, and his resentment grew inwardly for some time without our being aware of it. He became more and more quiet; he barely spoke at all. Then, suddenly, touched by some trivial flame, the whole situation exploded. He and Mohamed had wrangled before, but never as vehemently as this. They screamed accusations at one another, and when we tried to sort it all out, we became hopelessly entangled.

Mohamed claimed that Ismail had frequently said, "Is the sahib your father, that you don't steal from him?" Ismail claimed that Mohamed had told everyone the sahib and memsahib liked him so much they could not refuse him anything.

Who to believe? We were angry at both of them. We resented everything that was implied in the conflicting statements. Had Ismail, so competent and so devoted to the formalities ("all sahibs have soup on trek"), merely been using this apparent concern as a mask for wholesale theft? Had Mohamed misconstrued what we intended as casual friendliness, and taken it instead as some magnetic attraction, some power over us? We felt ourselves to be misunderstood, and we knew that we had misunderstood both of them. More than anything, we felt confused. Only one thing was plain.

"We can't possibly discover which of them is telling the truth," Jack said. "Probably neither one is. All we can do is choose the one we want to keep, and fire the other."

Rightly or wrongly, we chose Mohamed. Ismail left us with bad feeling all around, having first handed us a letter written by a local scribe, in which his many grievances were set down in copious detail. We did not deceive ourselves that justice had been done. But what was justice, in this situation? We did not know.

Now Mohamed reigned supreme in the kitchen. He very much enjoyed having Mohamedyero, Little Mohamed, to command. He scolded the *yerki* unmercifully, but he protected him as well. Mohamedyero was ten, the same age Mohamed himself had been when he first went to work for the English in Berbera. Mohamedyero could never get rid of the idea that all his pay was to be sent home to his family, so he himself was constantly without funds. Mohamed lectured him sternly on this point, but then allowed the little boy to share his rice and jowari, so what the *yerki* learned, actually, was that if he was consistently helpless, Mohamed would provide for him.

"Mohamedyero, he has not much idea," Mohamed said patronizingly and often.

It was true that the *yerki* possessed a vast capacity for making errors. Even the fluent Mohamed was speechless one day when the little boy dumped out a large panful of fresh lime juice which Mohamed had just painstakingly squeezed, under the impression that it was dirty dishwater. Mohamed struck his forehead, turned up his palms beseechingly to the sky.

"I don'know – I think this boy, he no got nothing for brains –"

He hovered over the *yerki*, instructing him, haranguing him, but in the final analysis accepting the child's mistakes gladly enough, for the sake of having someone to take under his wing.

Whenever Abdi shot an *aul* or a *dero*, we divided the meat among everyone in the camp. One day when Mohamed wanted to show me something in the cook-tent, we entered and saw the *yerki* cutting slices off the cold venison intended as lunch for Jack and myself, and stuffing them into his mouth. With the other hand, he was busily turning on the charcoal stove a large *aul* steak for himself. So brazen was the child that both Mohamed and I burst out laughing.

"He like meat too much," Mohamed said.

The little boy looked up with a winning smile, believing that somehow he had miraculously escaped chastisement. Mohamed immediately caught him a swift blow to the ear and yelled at him that if he could not stop thieving he had better find himself another job. The *yerki's* jaw dropped open in surprise and so did mine. The only basic paradox was that of Mohamed himself, harsh and indulgent, blithe and despairing.

When we were at Sheikh, Mohamed asked if he could bring his wife there. Shugri, he told us, was fifteen, and they had been married only a few months.

"She is a little small person," he said, as though to guarantee that she would not be in the way.

We agreed readily, and so he sent for her. He told us about his wedding, which nearly caused a tribal war. Shugri's mother was Habr Yunis, and wanted her daughter to marry a man of that tribe. Shugri's father was Habr Awal, and was favourably disposed towards Mohamed, but the mother and father were divorced, and the father was living at Erigavo while the girl was with her mother in Berbera. Shugri's mother went on a visit to Burao, and while she was away Mohamed married Shugri. To marry without the full agreement of the two tribes – at first, this seemed to us to have been brave of Mohamed. Later, we realized it had been foolhardy as well, for the price of defiance can be ostracism. At the wedding celebrations, the Habr Yunis man who had been the candidate favoured by Shugri's mother, showed up and demanded the girl. With him he brought a group of Habr Yunis. Mohamed's wedding guests, however, included many stalwart Habr Awal, who swore that the girl would not be relinquished. Spears would be raised. Never let it be said of Habr Awal that they failed to defend – and so on. After much muttering, the entire company withdrew to the Qadi's court. As the marriage had already taken place, the Qadi's judgement was in Mohamed's favour. The battle was averted, and the H.Y. men went away.

In the meantime, however, Shugri's mother had heard the news and had caught the first trade-truck back to Berbera, furious at both her daughter and Mohamed. When she arrived, she screeched outside the huts where the festivities were still taking place, but no one heard her. Mohamed, telling of it, was almost convulsed with laughter.

"Too much shouting – too much singing – too much dancing. Nobody hear her at all!"

Another feature of the hubbub was the accidental breaking of the glass in the hurricane lamps through having perfume thrown profusely around – the hot glass, splashed with liquid, snapped as noisily as rifle shots. Finally, in desperation, Shugri's mother sent Mohamed a letter. When they met and conferred, he managed to pacify her. But she would not give up so easily, and he still expected trouble.

When I listened to this tale, it seemed to have only a ludicrous quality, a wild humour that appealed to me. But later, recalling Mohamed's hectic laughter, I wondered if it had not also been a kind of whistling in the dark.

Shugri arrived at Sheikh. She wore red sandals and a robe of indigo, and her headscarf was yellow silk. She was tall and slightly plump, and she carried herself beautifully. Her extreme youth imparted a softness to her face, but there was haughtiness in it as well. Mohamed was overjoyed to see her, and she was overjoyed to see him.

This undiluted joy lasted for less than a week. Then Shugri decided she must visit her mother, who was now living in Burao.

"I have to go there in a week's time," Jack said. "Tell her she can come along in the Land-Rover then."

Shugri tossed her head in refusal. Her mind was made up. She was going to Burao today. This meant that Mohamed had to pay her fare on the trade-truck. She would not ride in the back of the truck, either. She had to ride in the front beside the driver, which cost seven rupees extra. Jack and I were somewhat taken aback. Could this be the downtrodden

Muslim woman? She got this stubborn quality from her mother, Mohamed explained morosely. If only Shugri could get away from the old she-devil, she would be all right.

Shugri did not return to Sheikh. Mohamed asked us what we thought he should do. Should he send money? Should he go himself, to try to persuade her?

"I never want no other woman," he said. "Only her."

Who does not like to be asked for advice? I gave mine liberally. Certainly, he should go to Burao, but he should be much more firm. After all, she was his wife. What right had her mother to interfere? He should tell the old lady where to get off.

What I was assuming, of course, without realizing it, was that Mohamed's mother-in-law trouble was identical with the situations I had read about in the lovelorn columns of North American newspapers, and that his request for advice meant precisely the same as it would to a person at home. As it happened, I could not have been more mistaken.

Buoyed up by our encouragement, Mohamed went to Burao. When he returned, Shugri was not with him. He wore such a bleak expression that we hesitated to ask what had happened. Finally he told us.

"Finished," he said. "All finished with Shugri and me. Her section, they come very angry for me. My tribe come angry, too – I hear it. They say 'Mohamed, he don' know what he do. He no have much idea.' Everything finish."

Now we did not know what to say, for the problem was a much more complicated one than we had realized. These two had married without either tribe's consent, and now neither Mohamed nor Shugri was able to see it through. Shugri had told him she would like to return to him, but would do so only if her mother's people agreed. Mohamed, who had not lived in the dwellings of his people since he was a child, could not bear the thought that the members of his tribe were thinking ill of him.

When we went out to the Haud, Mohamed began to have trouble with Abdi. Mohamed was very protective where our possessions were concerned, and highly suspicious of anyone touching them. He was also tactless and did not trouble to hide his suspicions. Abdi came to us in a fury one evening and said Mohamed had accused him of stealing one of our spoons. Mohamed said he had not accused Abdi of stealing it – merely of having inexcusably borrowed and lost it. As usual, everyone denied everything, and the air was filled with maniacal shouting. Finally peace was restored. Mohamed grudgingly apologized to Abdi, who consented grudgingly to be placated.

Later that evening Mohamed came to us and tried to explain his position. His face was tense and anguished. He was speaking in a language not his own, and he was trying to express things he did not really comprehend himself. He hesitated, stammered, tried again.

"I work for you. I stay with you. Must be I care for your things. Must be you are like my mother and my father –"

He had used this phrase before, and we had shrugged it off, with some feeling of embarrassment, as an effort to consolidate his job by flattery. But now we could not dismiss it so lightly. No one could have, looking at his strained face, his beseeching eyes. There was something here that we had not seen before, and seeing it now we were appalled.

"Same like my mother and my father – same like my family –"

Almost everyone else in the camp was Habr Yunis. Mohamed was the only Habr Awal. But this was the least aspect of his severance from his tribe. The circumstances of his whole life had cut him off. His marriage had incurred the anger not only of his wife's tribe, but of his own as well, and now even his wife had left him. He had a deep need to belong somewhere, and so, without our knowing it, he had latched onto us. It was not a question of what sort of people we were, nor even of whether he liked us or not. It was merely any port in a storm. Unthinkingly, we had encouraged his feeling of our adoption of him. We had chosen him in preference to Ismail. We had been free with advice to him. We had certainly liked him – and perhaps we had needed him to like us, more than we knew. And now, to our dismay, we found we had apparently acquired responsibilities towards him of which we had no knowledge and with which we felt unable to cope.

"Listen, Mohamed," Jack began firmly, "you mustn't –"

Then he hesitated and glanced at me, but saw only his own uncertainty mirrored in my face. If we cast Mohamed off now, abruptly, how could we possibly explain our reasons and how could he possibly understand?

"Abdi, he is old man –" Mohamed struggled on. "I never come angry for him. I speak softly-softly. But must be he never no touch your things, never no more. Must be I look for your things. I no go somewhere. I swear it. Always, I stay here. Abdi, he don' know – nobody, he don' know –"

He felt that nobody understood. He did not understand himself. But he must try to express it, all the same. He must try to make us see.

We would never entirely see, for we had not worn his sandals nor looked through his eyes. But one thing we did see – his undeniable need, and our own inability to meet it. And yet we were trapped. What could we say, without making him feel worse than he already did? It seemed to us that whatever we said would be wrong. And so we did what people generally do in situations where they perceive some of the difficulties but none of the solutions – we evaded the issue. Peace had been reached with Abdi – everything was settled now, we told Mohamed falsely. Let us not worry about these things any more.

"All right." He shrugged and went away. For him, nothing was settled.

In his heart, however, he must have known one thing that sooner or later would have to be done, for he took the first step out of his dilemma himself. He came to Jack one day and asked for the rest of his month's pay in advance, for he had decided to call a *shir*, a meeting between members of his tribal section and those of Shugri's, and he had to supply tea and sugar for the elders. The dispute over Shugri had gone far beyond the question of the marriage now – he would never find any peace within himself until there was some general settlement of the trouble, some acceptance of him from his own tribe. And although he had lived away so long, he needed the elders now, to tell him what to do.

Our initial reaction was one of unqualified relief. Thank God, someone else could deal with the problem. Only later did we wonder about it – was it a step backwards, after all, for Mohamed to be forced at last to beg the approval of the elders? Perhaps it was, but it was necessary all the same. The *shir* could do for him what no stranger ever could – receive him into the only community which had any real meaning for him.

The *shir* lasted two days, and finally the elders on both sides were able to reach an agreement. Shugri would not live with her mother any longer. Instead, she would go to Erigavo to be with her father and his new wife, and after a while the elders would re-assess her attitude and decide whether she was to return to Mohamed or not. Mohamed was thoroughly scolded for his bravado in marrying her without all the proper arrangements, and a fine was levied against him, to be paid to the kinsmen of Shugri's mother.

Once more the *belwo* were chanted loudly in the kitchen, while the saucepans bubbled and snorted on the charcoal burners. Once more Mohamed joked with the *yerki* as he used to do. And we tried to forget that he had made an appeal to us for understanding when he needed it desperately, and we had drawn back because we simply had not known what else to do.

After Shugri had been at Erigavo for some time, Mohamed received word that she was returning to him. He bought new clothes for her – a grey skirt, a lime-green bodice, a headscarf of fuchsia silk. He had saved for her one of the bottles of perfume he got in Djibouti. There was about a gallon of it, and it was called *Etoile*. He asked Jack for an advance of a hundred rupees.

"Isn't that quite a lot for you to pay back?" Jack said dubiously.

"Oh true, true," said Mohamed airily, "but when a Somali send money to somebody, a hundred rupees is very nice."

So Shugri came back, and this time she stayed. When Mohamed learned we would be leaving Somaliland, he shook his head and said "I think you will stay," but it was a token expression, spoken out of courtesy.

Mohamed was the first person I saw in Somaliland, and he was the last. When we climbed on the plane he came with us and handed us a packet of sandwiches he had made. We had misinterpreted one another very often, Mohamed and ourselves, and if we had been staying on here, we still would do so. But we had come to know something of him, and he of us. We had been present during a significant couple of years in one another's lives. This must mean something, surely. We found it hard to say goodbye to him, and it seemed to us that he felt the same way.

A year or so later, when we were in West Africa, we heard from Mohamed. Through a local scribe, he wrote to tell us that Shugri had borne him a son, and he sent us a small pair of Somali sandals for our daughter. We heard one more thing about him. An English friend in Somaliland wrote to say that Mohamed was working now in a different field – he had become a union organizer for a newly formed domestic servants' union.

Mohamed was compelled to seek the elders' blessing, but it is too late for him ever to return completely to the old tribe. And yet he will never be entirely free of his need for it. I wonder if he may have found, at last, a new tribe now?

CHAPTER ELEVEN

Arabetto

WHEN ARABETTO was a child, his father once took him on a visit to Rome. One of the great regrets of his life was that he had been too young at the time to sample the Roman night life. What a terrible waste. Now he would probably never get to Rome again, for how could a truck driver ever save that much money? If he had his choice, though, he thought he might rather go to Paris.

"The Italians say *Paris – paradiso*."

His father, an Arab merchant, had owned a shop in Mogadisciou and had wanted Arabetto, the youngest son, to get an education. Time and again, Arabetto was sent to school, but he kept running away. He much preferred the life of the markets and docks. Finally his father gave up and let him do as he pleased. What his mother's attitude had been, he never said, for although he talked often about his father, he never once mentioned the Midgertein woman who was his mother. In any event, he had followed his own inclinations and had grown up on the streets. Now he was sorry for the chances thrown away.

"What I got, this time? Nothing. I don' know to read, I don' know to write. I know only my lorry."

This was something of an exaggeration. He knew a few other things as well, for he spoke Somali, Arabic, English, Italian and Swahili. He was a good mechanic, and although he was an incurably fast driver, he looked after the Bedford three-ton and handled it with care.

"He's got more feeling for machinery than the others," Jack said of him. "He's more at home with it."

Arabetto's father had died just before the war, and the shop and several trade-trucks were left to the older brothers in the family. Arabetto drove one of the trucks for a while, but his eldest brother never gave him enough spending money. Perhaps his brother was concerned about the jazzy kid who liked to go dancing every evening at the *Albergo*. They quarrelled, and Arabetto left home for good. He had worked as a driver in many different places – Jigjigga, Addis, Awareh, Borama, and now out in the Haud with us.

Arabetto was not actually handsome, being rather pock-marked on the face and having a deep scar on one cheek, but he gave the impression of being good looking. He was heavier in build than most Somalis, for he had never gone hungry as most of them had. His real name was Ahmed, but he was always known by his nickname, and the word itself signified his apartness from the others. There must have been, in places like Mogadisciou, many like Arabetto, but here he was unusual. Although he was half Somali, he was never accepted as one of them. He resented very much that they regarded him as an outsider, a foreigner, but in fact he was just that, for there was a vast gulf between the others and himself. The chief difference was that he had no tribe. He was the only one in the camp who had grown up entirely without any tribal connections. He was what the Somalis called *nin magala-di*, a man of the town, and in a way that even Mohamed, who had lived most of his life in a town, was not. For Arabetto did not appear to miss the tribal affiliations, or to need them. He neither gave advice nor asked for it. He went his own way. He had an air of tough and worldly humour, quite unlike any of the others in the camp, and he talked more freely than they did. His first week in camp he did something none of the others would ever do. Talking with us one evening, he lit a cigarette – and offered one to us, casually, hardly noticing that he was doing it. He spoke politely to Jack, always, but he called him "Mr. Laurence" or "sir." "Sahib" was a word Arabetto never used.

Not surprisingly, he was more politically minded than the others appeared to be. He sang for me dozens of verses of *Somaliyey Tosey* (Somalia, Awake) and he spoke of the future with certainty and openness.

"The Somali Youth League is saying ten more years and then independence."

This goal seemed impossible to me, considering the limited number of educated leaders. To him, it seemed not only possible but inevitable, a foregone conclusion. And time proved him right.

Arabetto felt closer to the Arabic culture than to the Somali, which he regarded as old fashioned and unsophisticated. He told me many Arabic stories, the old tales he had heard as a child, but even these, although they were preferable to the Somali tales, did not appeal to him much. He was somewhat amused by my interest in them. For himself, he preferred the modern Egyptian films which he used to see in Mogadisciou. These films were in Arabic, of course, and from his descriptions of them they must have been highly exciting, full of intrigues and fights and unrequited love.

One film concerned a young Egyptian girl who fell in love with an American soldier. Her brother commanded her to give the man up, saying that the G.I. was a Christian and she was a Muslim and such an alliance could never work. The girl refused, vowing that nothing in this world would part her from her lover. Her brother therefore took her for a ride in his car and drove straight into the Nile, drowning both of them.

"*Wallahi!*" Arabetto said. "What a film!"

The best film he ever saw was about a girl named Naduka, who had been lost as a child in the interior of the Sudan and had grown up as a "wild girl," protected and befriended by a band of gorillas. A good kind handsome cousin ultimately discovered her and fell in love with her, but a wicked old uncle simultaneously found her and attempted to poison her in order to get the money left to her by her father.

"But it is all right," Arabetto said. "This one gorilla, he find this uncle. Cri-i-ick! He break that man's neck, very easy.

Naduka, she marry the young man, and everything is very nice."

Arabetto's favourite song, which he had on a record, came from a film about a man who had been separated from his bride since the hour of their marriage, through the vile scheming of an older woman who wanted him for herself. Having finally escaped from the siren's clutches, he leaped into his little donkey cart and dashed away to his love. He sang to the donkey, pleading with it to go faster. Arabetto translated the Arabic words.

Hurry, hurry,
Fly like a bird –

The others in camp were scornful of Arabetto's music, but he paid no attention to their sarcasm. He would take his gramophone to the edge of the camp and sit there, cranking it and playing this one song over and over, clapping his hands to the rhythm, humming the tune.

But if Mohamed and Hersi and the rest did not appreciate his records, at least they laughed at his jokes. Someone was always telling me his latest. Once when a Midgan came along and offered to supply the camp with girls, for a substantial fee, Arabetto agreed immediately.

"Sure, you do that," he told the Midgan, "and I'll give you that little machine over there."

And he jerked a thumb towards the Land-Rover. Whether the Midgan fell for the offer or not, I was not informed.

The two hills outside Hargeisa, known as *Nasa Hablod*, the girl's breasts, called forth a good pun from Arabetto, whose surname was Nasir. *Nasa Hablod sidii Nasir hablod* – like Nasir's girl. He was married to an Arabian girl whose name was Safia Abdul.

"If I was Christian, she would be Mrs. Arabetto – what a name!"

He did not have a high opinion of Somali girls. They were beautiful, he admitted, but they tended to be spiteful and selfish. A Somali wife would rarely ask her husband how he was feeling or how his work was getting along. Of course, the men had only themselves to blame, for they treated their wives badly. It was all right for a man to hit his wife on the backside or the hands, but some Somalis would hit their wives on the face with a stick. That, Arabetto said, was not the right thing to do. He asked me curiously – did my husband ever beat me? When I said no, he shrugged cynically – never to beat a wife at all, that was carrying consideration too far.

One afternoon in Hargeisa, I went to Arabetto's house in the *magala* to meet his wife. Safia was an extremely lovely girl, with light olive skin and almost Semitic features. She wore a small gold ornament in the side of her nose, and a maroon silk robe with blue and white flowers printed on it. Her shawl was a thin and gauzy silk with gold embroidery, and she had a gold necklace and gold earrings. Arabetto, who never wore a Somali robe, had changed today from his usual khaki shorts and shirt to a cream linen suit.

Their house was one room, a mud-brick hut with earthern floors and cracked walls and no window. But Safia had fixed it up and made it clean and comfortable. There were two beds, in the Muslim manner, one large and high, a rope-webbing platform on stilts, the husband's bed, and the other much smaller and lower. Both were draped with embroidered coverlets. Safia had done all the needlework herself. The corpulent pillows, too, were covered with embroidered leaves and branches, birds and flowers, all done in rich colours, yellows and vivid reds and blues. In the midst of the traditional designs were two streamlined cars.

Whenever I think of Arabetto, I recall those embroidered cars, and the quick and syncopated song he played so often on the tinny old gramophone out in the desert.

> *Hurry, hurry,*
> *Fly like a bird –*

CHAPTER TWELVE

The Old Warrior

IN THE DAYS when the Somali riding camel was renowned throughout the East for its speed and endurance, the days when an English officer's advice to a newly arrived subaltern was that camel milk heavily laced with brandy formed a satisfactory and sustaining diet if one found oneself out in the Haud with the food supplies exhausted – in those distant days, Abdi was a young marksman in that now-legendary company, the Somaliland Camel Corps.

Men were warriors then. But those battles were over now, and many years had passed. Abdi must have been nearly sixty, but he carried himself as straight as a young man, and when he took a rifle into his hands, it became a part of him, his second self.

He had been a driver in government service for eighteen years. He liked to keep the same vehicle, and had driven one lorry until it was condemned to the scrap heap. This loss coincided with our arrival in the country, and so he was assigned to our Land-Rover. He was not pleased. Such a small vehicle – much too light – no good for anything. But after he had been driving it for a while, he admitted reluctantly that it had its points. Finally he became attached to it, and regarded it as his own.

In the beginning, when we drove with him, he was taciturn and uncommunicative. He answered our questions politely, but he did not make conversation. He seemed to feel it was not his place to do so. But he was not humble. On the contrary, he was extremely proud. Or – no. How to express such a combination of opposites? He was both humble and proud. He said "yes, sahib" and "no, sahib" with a meekness, almost a servility, that bothered us. And yet he carried himself haughtily, and would never admit there were gadgets on the Land-Rover that were unfamiliar to him. When he went out hunting with the rifle he would go on and on trying, even when game was scarce or the dusk was gathering, for he cherished his marksman's skill above all things and he hated to admit defeat by returning without meat.

Abdi never ran over a bird. A blue starling with an orange breast would saunter in front of the Land-Rover. Abdi would slow down and stop, and the bird like a tiny bright rajah would strut slowly off the road.

His life had been work and pain and little else. Some of his children had died in the seasons of drought. He had kept, always, a close tie with his tribe. His family lived in the Haud with the tribe and kept his sheep and camels. Most of his stock he had lost in the previous dry season. Now, this *Jilal*, as we drove across the desert and saw children in rags, begging for water, Abdi's face grew sombre and grim, and he lifted one hand towards heaven as though to say *Behold, O God, thy people*. In his tribal section, twenty-one people had already died this season. He said it was the worst year he remembered. Perhaps each year was the worst they all remembered. As he looked at the herdsmen struggling on with their camels to reach the wells, his eyes narrowed and his hands knotted – each tribesman was Abdi himself. Bitterness swelled in him, but he could not speak of it.

"Somali – very hard life." The few tense words were his only comment, and the hand lifted towards the sky. He was a devout Muslim. Could a man presume to question God? When I saw him this way, I always thought of a poem of Gerard Manley Hopkins.

> . . . *Wert Thou mine enemy, oh Thou my friend,*
> *How couldst Thou worst, I wonder, than Thou dost*
> *Defeat, thwart me?*

Abdi once brought his youngest son Adan to our camp for

a few days. The boy was five years old, a slender good-looking child with large alert eyes and long lashes. I talked with him in my broken Somali, and by the time Abdi got back from his hunting expedition that day, Adan had lost his shyness and was admiring the machinery in the camp. The Bedford truck caught his eye particularly – so big, such bright yellow paint. Abdi said he hoped Adan had not been a nuisance. I assured him that I liked talking with Adan, and said Abdi was fortunate to have such a son. Abdi nodded.

"Yes. He is a fine boy, this one." Then he glanced at me, and there was such a look of comprehension in his eyes that I was very much moved by his words. "I pray Allah send you a small boy, too."

When Abdi's eyes became sore with dust and wind, I told him I would bathe them with boracic. I waited for a long time outside our tent, and finally Abdi showed up. He had gone to put on his best red shirt and robe before he would appear for treatment. When I had finished swabbing out his eyes, he spoke the traditional blessing once again, so quietly and gently that I felt it was truly meant.

"Allah send you a son."

Later that day he spoke to Jack about me.

"Your memsahib – a queen," he said.

Abdi told Jack that he liked working for him because "you very strong – you always speaking true word – you always working hard" and also because "you never using wine." This latter statement was not true, but perhaps there was a relative truth about it, for Abdi no doubt had known some *Ingrese* who were heavy drinkers, and he had the true Muslim's fanatical feeling against liquor. Abdi liked me, he said, because I was "always kind." Both Jack and I felt he had judged us to be better than we were. We would hate to disillusion him – somehow we must try to live up to his opinion of us.

Is there a woman in this world who would not like to be told she is a queen, or a man who would not like to be told he is strong and just? In my diary, I recorded that it was surprising to find the ease with which "one gains their popularity" by showing friendliness and courtesy towards them. The Somalis, I went on to say, speaking generally but referring to Abdi, were good judges of character (naturally, they must be since they appeared to like me) and one of the chief ways in which they judged Europeans was whether or not the Europeans liked them. A later, much later, comment at the end of this paragraph bears in heavy lead pencil one word – *Bosh*. It was not all bosh, however – what I had really indicated by the initial statement was that I myself tended to judge people on whether or not I felt they liked me.

The night we were stranded on the Wadda Gumerad, in the storm, it was Abdi who kept us going. It was he who insisted that we must get the Land-Rover out of the mud and move on, or we would be lost once and for all. It was he who managed to get the passing tribesmen to help us, and who avoided their mobbing us to get the rifle. He had saved our lives, and we felt with him the bond of that gruelling night. We spoke our thanks, and told him we would like to give something to him, not payment, of course, for one cannot pay for one's life, but as a token. What did he want? A new *lunghi* and shirt, he said. So the trivial gift, a shirt and a length of cotton cloth, was bought and given. It never occurred to us that it might have a different meaning for him than it did for us.

Abdi's face was impassive most of the time, expressionless, difficult to read as a stone graven with ancient hieroglyphs. The exception was when he had been out hunting and was coming back to camp with an *aul* or a *dero*. At such times, he arrived with the Land-Rover horn sounding triumphantly, and his face was exultant.

He had a passion for hunting, not only hunting for meat but for anything. He fixed up looped-wire traps to catch foxes, and he was delighted when we brought steel traps out to camp, for with these he could catch hyenas. He baited the traps with deer entrails, and frequently in the middle of the night we would hear the hyena's shriek, and the cry "*Warabe!*" from all the Somalis. Within seconds everyone would be out, peering at the trapped beast, but from a cautious distance. Abdi was invariably the one who went up to the animal and killed it with a club.

"Bastard!" he would yell (always, strangely, in English). "Where my sheep you kill? You want to sleep? You sleep!"

Bash! And the hyena's skull would be broken. The hyenas were hideous mongrel-looking creatures, with powerful shoulders and teeth, their hair a dirty beige with brown spots, their bellies pale and bloated. In the trap, they snarled and lunged. Abdi appeared to have no fear of them. Seeing him approach those jaws, we were impressed by his cold nerve and courage. After a while we noticed, however, that he did not merely kill the hyenas. He continued to batter until the head was a red squashed mass. It was the same when he killed the Russell's viper which had been holding the birds captive with its eyes. No one else would go near, for this snake was a deadly one. Abdi walked up to it with his club and beat it to a pulp. When his stock died of thirst, or when his family became ill with malaria, or when his boys could not be sent to school because he did not have enough money, he could only say "It is Allah's will." But the snake and the hyena – these he could strike.

When Abdi hunted for meat, he adhered absolutely to the Muslim law forbidding the eating of meat which has not died by having its throat slit. Originally, no doubt, this law was devised as a means of preventing people from eating carrion. But now the effect of it was sometimes dreadful to see, for Abdi would never shoot a deer to kill it. He tried only to wound it, and would then pursue it across the desert until he caught it and could cut its throat. Once, when we were out with him, he shot an *aul* in the guts, and it ran about crazily for what seemed an eternity, bleeding thickly, half its stomach shot away. It came close enough for me to see the terror in its eyes. Abdi chased it, laughing proudly all the time. When finally he caught it by the horns, he was careful to say the required prayer as his knife slid into the deer's throat. I felt sickened, and yet I knew it was foolish to feel this way. The *aul* was meat to him – it had been meat to him even before he shot it, and the prospect of meat in this country was always a matter for rejoicing. If I had known starvation, I would not be much concerned, either, about the death throes of a deer.

Abdi began to clash with Mohamed. He resented Mohamed's position in the camp, for he felt that Mohamed had too much influence with us, too great a tendency to cast aspersions on others. If anyone influenced our opinions, Abdi would have preferred it to be himself. Also, he felt that Mohamed was questioning his honour by telling him not to borrow our spoons, for the implication was that he might steal them. On several occasions he became almost berserk, raving and shouting against Mohamed until the fire had burned itself out.

We were caught between the two. All we wanted to do was keep the peace. We could not see why either of them should be making so much fuss about so little. We came to see something of Mohamed's outlook, but Abdi's was more difficult to see, for it was more deeply hidden. To us, the old warrior appeared to be two men. One was gentle, compassionate, courageous, the man who stopped the car rather than run over a bird, the man who sorrowed for his destitute people, the man who would walk calmly up to a poisonous snake. The other was fierce, violent, raging, the man who struck again and again at the dead animal, the man whose anger had to run its course before it faded. The two men seemed in direct opposition. But were they?

When his fury had passed, he was at peace for a while, and then he came to the brushwood hut and talked to me, telling me about a strange bird, the *ghelow*. I had seen this bird only once. It was sleek and mottled brown, with a long neck and a little darting head like a snake's.

"If some man die," Abdi said, "always, we hear *ghelow* – crying, crying – all night."

If there had been no moonlight for fifteen nights, or if any bad trouble was threatening the area, the bird sang its dirge until morning. An occult bird, a bird of magical powers.

The old warrior had recently heard the *ghelow*. He spoke sadly, with resignation, as though the coming evil could not be averted. And so it proved.

Abdi made it plain to Jack that he disapproved of my chatting with Arabetto and Mohamed. Sahib and memsahib we were, and must remain so. The rules must be maintained, or chaos might descend upon everyone. He did not accept change of any sort.

"Young men no good," he told Jack frequently, speaking not only of Mohamed and Arabetto, but of all the young men whose changing views threatened his own.

Sometimes he asked us for things, and sometimes we gave him things he had not asked for. He asked Jack to go on his behalf to P.W.D. and get his pay raised, and Jack did so, for the old man worked hard and did his job well. I gave him old shirts of Jack's, to take to his numerous grown sons. He asked about getting some of his relatives hired on the *balleh* staff, and if the man in question seemed all right, Jack agreed. Three of the labourers and one driver were close relatives of Abdi's. Jack's outlook was that if Abdi's relatives in these cases were as good as anyone else, he might as well hire them rather than strangers. Unfortunately, as it turned out, this was not Abdi's interpretation at all.

Arabetto was the next object of Abdi's wrath. Arabetto's casual manner and his easy laughter seemed to infuriate the old man. When he was angry, he accused Arabetto of everything from theft to laziness, calling him a useless Arab, a diseased cur, and other even less acceptable names. Arabetto became, understandably, fed up with being nagged at and insulted all the time, and so he told Jack he would like to get a transfer to another job. Jack did not want to lose either man. He asked Arabetto to wait until the end of the month. We knew now that the crisis was coming, but we could not bring ourselves to face it yet.

Then Jack had to fire one of the labourers, who had proven no good on the job. It transpired that the man was one of Abdi's relatives.

"We will take that man back," Abdi said to Jack.

"Oh no, we damn well won't," Jack replied angrily.

We were disappointed in him. We felt he had let us down, in behaving so unreasonably, in not being what we thought he was. Oddly, his demands on us grew rapidly from this point on. There seemed to be no end to his requests, and we began to feel preyed upon. He asked to have more relatives hired, and Jack refused. He went to visit his tribe, and Jack allowed him to take the Land-Rover and half a drum of water. When Abdi was about to depart, he told Jack he intended to take a full drum of water. Jack told him he must not do so, for we did not have enough water to spare. Abdi said nothing, but later we learned he had told a great many people that the sahib was a *shaitan*, a devil, and an exceedingly stingy one at that.

We had admired and trusted him. We had believed that he liked and trusted us. What was happening now was so painful to us that we tried not to think of it. But it could not be ignored much longer. We received constant complaints from the others, for Abdi seemed to be growing suspicious of everyone and to imagine that all men's hands were against him. Hersi reported a night-long meeting.

"I tell him, 'Nothing is contained in bloody this place. Only suspicion. Nothing else. Who wanting to hurt you? Nobody. Abdi, dear cousin, you must not trying to run this camp.' For three hours, absolutely, he talking then, and no one understanding a word."

The *ghelow's* voice had certainly been heard. Now, when we drove with Abdi in the Land-Rover, he no longer said "God give you a son." He was silent, and his face was sullen. In a profound disillusionment, I felt he must have despised us all along. In my notebooks I tried to express it, perhaps in order to remove its sting. "You come to a country, and you think that if you regard people as people, everything will be all right. Not so. With the Somalis, the attitude towards the British goes too deep to be broken casually. I feel now that Abdi's sweet talk to us was in the main a method for achieving favours. I think he has always hated us, simply because we are *Ingrese*, and that he could never feel any differently.

He judges Europeans on what is given. He would rather be
treated shamefully, and left in peace to hate us, as long as he
is periodically given handouts of money and clothes, than he
would be treated as a man and not given so much. The
Somalis are proud, not grovelling, and in their own eyes they
are aristocrats and warriors. But they are also terribly poor,
their lives hounded by drought and disease. Many of them
cannot treat Europeans as people. If we are sahib and memsahib, Abdi can do his job, and be polite, and try with a clear
conscience to get as much as possible from us, secure in his
basic hatred of us. Why should we be surprised? But we are.
And hurt – for we trusted and in a way loved him. We can see
now why he dislikes Mohamed and Arabetto so much. They
are not so set in the mould. He considers them traitors. Jack
cannot reason with him any more. He can only say – if you
lose your temper, you lose your job. How strange it is to have
to say things like that."

Abdi's suspicions were ultimately directed against Hersi,
who, as interpreter, had Jack's ear, or so Abdi believed. Jack
was presented with a petition written by a town scribe at the
direction of some of the tractor drivers, and signed by them,
thumb-prints from those who could not write, and signatures
in Arabic from the others, for none were literate in English.

"Circumstances uprising from grounds of helplessness,"
the petition said, "compelled us to place our grievances
before your honour for necessary remedy. Originally, there
existed One fire which was burning inside the whole Camp,
but it is regretted to point out that the fire in question has
become widespread all over the Camp and the Staff. Such fire
can only be distinguished from the Top, or the Head, and the
Head is the Head of the Department. The cause of that fire
which rendered everybody helpless is ignited by the present
interpreter, Hersi –"

Abdi's name did not appear on the petition. Jack made
extensive enquiries, and the whole camp for several nights
was loud with the sounds of argument. The meetings went on
until dawn. It finally emerged that Abdi had persuaded the
drivers to write the petition. His own relatives, naturally, had

supported him, as they were all fearful of losing their jobs, and he had managed to convince the other drivers that they would all be fired unless Hersi was ousted.

So it had come at last. Now there was no way of avoiding it. Jack fired Abdi, and the old man left the camp. We saw him in Hargeisa several times after that, but he turned the other way and would not even look at us.

If there had been a fire in the camp, it was certainly Abdi, for after his departure the tensions eased immediately. Suspicions dwindled, and the Somalis were more relaxed, not only towards us but among themselves as well. Now it was songs that we heard around the fires at night, not the previous interminable bickering.

But it could not end here for us. Why had events moved so inexorably in this way? Could they have been dealt with in any other way? We did not know. All we knew was that we could not forget the man who drove through the blinding rain that night when we were lost on the desert, the man who was always the first to start work when we set up camp and whose work songs got the others going, the man who had wished us the blessing of a son. Trying, by writing it out, to unearth something of his meaning, I put in my notebook – "He is an exaggeration of all the qualities he possesses. He is courage and pride and anger writ large. Perhaps his is the face of Africa – inscrutable to the last." My feeling at this time was that I would never understand.

Probably I never will. But I no longer think it was a simple matter of his having hated us all along, as I thought in my first bitterness, although he certainly came to hate us eventually. He did have a deep resentment against the English, whose lives must have seemed so easy to him, but this readily understandable resentment was only one factor in the situation, and perhaps not even the determining factor at that. After a number of years, things do not look quite the same. I recognize now, as I did not dare to do then, how eagerly I listened to what I felt to be his admiration, but it was not merely a question of flattery falling upon ready ears, either. A possible clue to the puzzle was provided not long ago by

Mannoni's description of the dependence complex in *The Psychology of Colonisation*, a book which I read with the shock of recognition one sometimes feels when another's words have a specific significance in terms of one's own experiences. Seen from a distance, the details in my notebooks begin to take on a new meaning.

We felt that Abdi had let us down, but now I think that he must have felt, equally strongly, that we had let him down. I do not think his demands upon us were made callously or contemptuously, as I thought once, but with a feeling that it was his right to demand of us whatever he needed. Perhaps it all began with the night on the Wadda Gumerad. That event had significance for him, but not the same as it had for us. We cannot know with certainty how he thought of it, but my guess is that he felt a bond had indeed taken shape between us, but not the bond of friendship as it seemed to us. We acknowledged some bond, however, by our gratitude and by the gift. We even asked him what he would like, saying we would give him anything he wanted, within reason. Did we, then, in his eyes, agree to become his power at court? Did Jack, in firing one of Abdi's relatives, appear to negate a tacit agreement to act as a kind of protector to him and his family? I think so. We ourselves had established the bond. He was not to know that we did not see it in the same way as he did. His later and increased demands, which seemed so outrageous then, seem in retrospect to have been a frantic effort to prove that the bond still existed.

Abdi was a man of integrity, but in his own terms, not ours. He was also a man filled with rage against fate. But he was a faithful son of Islam and so he could not curse his fate, for that would be blasphemy against God. He fought, instead, where he could. He was a warrior, trained as a fighter both with the spear and with the rifle, and his heritage was that of a warrior. He was a Somali, and in his arid land life is uncertain and impoverished, and a man seeks help wherever he can find it. He was a tribal man, to whom the idea of gaining the support and aid of a sultan came naturally – and if not a sultan or a governor, then the closest ally at court that could be found, and the strongest. Even the words which we at first took as compliments and then as unscrupulous flattery, now seem to have been neither, to have been in fact almost totally unrelated to us as individuals. *You are a king. You are a queen.* If a man must seek a power at court, must he not also seek to reassure himself that the chosen official is indeed a strong one, capable of giving protection?

Everything moved inevitably to the conclusion. We did not comprehend his outlook, and he did not comprehend ours. He could not have acted in any way other than he did, and we could not have, either. And yet now I think that we would all have wished it otherwise.

In Paradise, the Qoran says, there are gardens where the fountains flow eternally and where the faithful may recline on divans and be attended by lovely women for ever and ever. A desert dweller's heaven, the heaven of Islam. But for some of the sons of the desert, I do not think this heaven will be quite enough. If I believed, I would wish there to be battles somewhere in Paradise, for an old warrior who never knew – and who probably could not have borne to know – that his truest and most terrible battle, like all men's, was with himself.

CHAPTER THIRTEEN

A Tree for Poverty

On the plain Ban-Aul there is a tree
For poverty to shelter under.

THIS PART of a Somali *gabei* always seemed to me to express Somali literature as a whole, which in its way was also a tree for poverty to shelter under, and so, when I had completed the translations, I took a title from these lines. Ultimately, the collection was published by the Somaliland government. It was the product of many people's work besides my own – Guś Andrzejewski and Musa Galaal, who gave me the literal translations of the poems, Hersi and Arabetto who told me the stories, and all those who talked with me about the subject. The following are excerpts from the introduction to this collection.

"Although they have no written language, the Somalis are a nation of poets. In the evenings, around the camp fires, the men sing and tell stories far into the night. And in the *magala*, or town, they gather in the tea shops and often several *gabei* poets will spend hours chanting their own poetry, listened to by a large audience. This country is lacking in almost all materials needed for painting or sculpture, and in any event the Somalis, being Muslims, are not in favour of making 'images'. But stories and poems require no special materials other than the talent of the person concerned. Folk literature is easily portable and costs nothing. Although the life of the Somali camel-herder is drab and harsh, in their poetry and stories one finds sensitivity, intelligence, earthy humour, and a delight in lovely clothes and lovely women.

"There are about ten different types of Somali poems, although some of these are not commonly used. The *belwo*, a fairly recent form, is a short lyric love-poem, and is easily recognizable both by its length and by the distinct tunes to which it is sung. The literal meaning of *belwo* is 'a trifle' or 'a bauble'. The same tune fits nearly any *belwo*. The verses are strung together, sometimes as many as fifteen or twenty, to make one long song, but the individual verses are not necessarily related.

"The composing of *belwo* is considered to be the normal literary activity of young men, and the general opinion seems to be that *belwo*-making is a relatively unskilled craft. The older men always hope that the young *belwo* poet will, as he grows older, desire to learn the vocabulary and style of the more complex *gabei*. The older men scorn the *belwo*, not because of its subject, love, but because of its shortness and 'lack of style'. They say it is frivolous and immature.

"The Somali *gabei* is considered to be the highest literary form. *Gabei* may be on any topic, but the rules of *gabei*-making are strict and difficult. A *gabei* poet must not only have an extensive vocabulary and an ability to express himself fluently, alliteratively and in terms of figures of speech. He must also possess considerable knowledge of the country, its geography and plant-life, Somali medicine and animal husbandry. The good *gabei* poet must know something about Muslim theology and religious history, for these subjects are often used in poetry.

"Love and war are among the most favoured themes for *gabei*. With the war *gabei*, the poetic form reaches considerable heights of drama and emotion. The Somali is a warrior by tradition and inclination as well as by necessity, and in the *gabei*, tribal war is painted as a man's proper occupation. The war *gabei* are composed with great spirit and with that feeling of recklessness and bravery that characterizes the Somali in tribal battles.

"Literary Somali is a superstructure erected on the foundation of everyday speech. A vast number of words are never used except in poetry, and these have a subtle and precise meaning. Often an amazing amount of information is compressed into one word.

"In the Somali *gabei* there is a wealth of material for future research. Many hundreds of *gabei*, of varying literary merit, exist in this country. At their best the *gabei* offer not only an interesting study of a highly disciplined and developed poetry, but also a great deal of information about Somaliland and the way of life of its people.

"A number of the stories found in Somaliland are Arabic in origin, and some of them must have come to this country many years ago. Arabia is the centre of the Muslim religion, and also has racial and cultural ties for the Somalis. The legendary founders of the Somali race – Darod and Ishaak – came from Arabia, and the majority of the Somali people still trace their ancestry back to these Arabian aristocrats.

"The modern Somali is portrayed in such tales as *'Igaal Bowkahh*. 'Igaal is a humorous character, and yet there is something in his essential toughness, his way of laughing in the face of disaster, his pride and jauntiness, even in the most discouraging of circumstances, that remind one very much of the pride, courage and humour of the ordinary Somali. It is this toughness and defiance that save 'Igaal from starvation and death.

"In a country as barren as this, where the population is almost entirely nomadic and where the actual process of survival demands so much effort and tenacity from each tribesman, it seems remarkable that there should be such a large body of unwritten literature, containing such a high degree of dramatic sense, vivid imagination and wit."

BELWO

When you die, delight
By earth's silence will be stilled.
So let not now the priest

Drive you from your song.

A man enchanted by the waking dream
That enters like a djinn, his heart to own,
Can never sleep, Amiina – I have been
Away, these nights, walking the clouds of heaven.
Woman, lovely as lightning at dawn,
Speak to me even once.

Your bright mouth and its loveliness,
Your fragrance, the look of you –
Ubah, flower-named, for these
My journey is forgotten.

All your young beauty is to me
Like a place where the new grass sways,
After the blessing of the rain,
When the sun unveils its light.

GABEI

To a Friend Going On A Journey

(extract from a *gabei* by Mohamed Abdullah Hassan)

Now you depart, and though your way may lead
Through airless forests thick with 'hhagar trees,
Places steeped in heat, stifling and dry,
Where breath comes hard, and no fresh breeze can
reach –
May Allah place a shield of coolest air
Between your body and the assailant sun.

And in a random scorching flame of wind
That parches the painful throat and sears the flesh,
May Allah, in His compassion, let you find
The great-boughed tree that will protect and shade.

On every side of you, I now would place
Prayers from the holy Qoran, to bless your path,
That ills may not descend, nor evils harm,
And you may travel in the peace of faith.

To all the blessings I bestow on you,
Friend, yourself now say a last Amen.

To A Faithless Friend

(extracts from a *gabei* by Salaan Arrabey)

Ye tribesmen gathered here, my song is of sorrow,
And of that man, the faithless, for whose sake
My lungs were parched with a desperate call to war –
'Awake and arm, oh Habar Habuush men!
The spear of vengeance is thrust at your kinsman's
heart!'
So strongly pulsed my cry that warriors, waking,
Took it for doom-knowing huur, *the fearful bird*
Whose eyes alone may see the angel of Death.

Oh ye who fought unflinching at my side,
Recall the tangled forest of Odaya Deerod,
Where the courage of men was tested in the fray,
And evil-tongued Olol swore by his wife
That we could never force him to surrender.
Then for my friend's sake, fiercely I flew at the foe,
Flashing my weapons like the winged huur.
For him in the war with strangers I yielded to no
man.

A woman in childbirth, fainting with cruel pain,
May swear this suffering never to forget,
But when her menstrual time has come again,
Birth's agony has faded from her mind.

My kinsman's memory is short as any woman's.

Now he forgets his anguish of the past,
Denies remembrance of the help I gave,
And in my dire need he turns from me –
Exceeding is the evil in such a man!

The slander of fools can injure honest men.
Friend, I gave you my trust, and you have repaid
By seeking to damage my name in the eyes of the
tribe.
If ever there was love in me for you,
Now, by Allah, it is strangled and destroyed.
This is the way of life, this bitter way –
Kindness towards men begets their secret hate.

If in this life our friendship we have failed,
Allah will decide our dispute in the other World.
Put someone else in my place among your kin,
As I sever the bonds of my loyalty to you.

Now do I hang your fate on the hem of your robe –
And the judgement, let it be left to Allah alone!

Somali Tales

'Igaal Bowkahh

'Igaal Bowkahh was the name he went by. He was a wizened little thing, with one crippled leg, and by no means handsome to look upon. One time 'Igaal Bowkahh decided to journey far away from the dwellings of his tribe, in order to get work and send home money to his family. After much travelling and many hardships, he found himself in the country of South Africa.

One day, in a town called Johannesburg, 'Igaal Bowkahh was seized by a reckless desire for gaiety and good food and the laughter of companions. And so, within the space of a single day and night he had flung away his savings. But 'Igaal did not mourn for his lost wealth. He was not that sort of man. Immediately, he began to make new plans, and very soon he decided to go to another town, which was a distance of four nights away. In his pocket only seven guineas remained. But 'Igaal was a stout-hearted man, and set out cheerily. Along the road he chanced to meet a man leading a fine dog. "Now, my good 'Igaal," he said to himself, "may Allah permit you to buy this animal and re-sell it at a handsome profit in some neighbouring village." So he offered the man seven guineas for the dog, which the man accepted gladly.

Then, with no money at all in his pockets, 'Igaal Bowkahh travelled for a short time with the dog, feeling very proud of himself for his good bargain, for dogs were expensive in that country. As he was walking along, however, he suddenly felt he would like a cigar. Ordinarily, he smoked a good deal, and now, as he thought of a cigar, the desire for one became stronger and stronger. Finally, arriving at a village, he made up his mind, and sold the seven-guinea dog for one cigar, and continued on his way in good spirits.

Just before the time of evening prayers, 'Igaal came to another small settlement. By this time he was faint and bleary-eyed from lack of food and water. There was no one in the village to whom he could go for help, and he felt very lonely. But he made the best of a bad lot, and settled himself as comfortably as possible in a sheltered little valley near the town. The village had many donkeys, and every day they were used for ploughing, but at night they grazed until dawn in the valley. Among them was a big mule, and 'Igaal gazed reflectively at the sturdy animal. While he stared, the moon rose and flooded the valley with soft light. It was the fifteenth night of the moon, by the order of Allah. 'Igaal began to have memories of home. He thought with nostalgia of the Somalis, and how they used to attack and loot each other's camel herds.

"Well, now, why not?" said he to himself, looking again at the donkeys.

Then, like a true man of action, 'Igaal rose and wrapped his cotton robe around his waist, in preparation for riding. He lost no time in cutting with his knife the ropes which tied the donkeys. He caught the mule with a bridle and halted the animal near a large stone. As he was a tiny man, he climbed the stone and from there mounted the mule. 'Igaal gathered his strength, then, and kicked the mule four times near the big vein along its belly. The mule bellowed in pain, and galloped away at an incredible speed, and the confused donkeys followed. Then 'Igaal flapped his arms like a bird and howled like a hyena, and the terrified donkeys ran and ran.

The people of the village came running out of their houses to see what had happened. But what could they do? They could not reach the stampeding donkeys on foot. They could only watch helplessly.

'Igaal drove and drove and drove all night. When the dawn came, he reached a village and took the donkeys to the marketplace. In that town, dogs and donkeys and mules fetched a good price. It was natural that these animals should be so expensive in that country, for the people were a poor lot who did not keep camels. 'Igaal, therefore, got the immense sum of thirty guineas for each donkey.

Thus the man who had been poverty-stricken five minutes before, now found himself with bulging pockets. He went to the village shops, where he gorged himself with food. Then he set out gaily on his mule. When he drew close to a place called Durban, he got off the mule.

"All right, my friend," he said. "You have served me well. Now you may go home."

'Igaal entered the town, and when he was passing the marketplace, he heard a group of men speaking Somali. 'Igaal greeted them in glad surprise, and they told him they were firemen on a ship. They said they would help 'Igaal to get a job. So 'Igaal found himself before the ship's captain, who looked him over and decided to put him on the crew list. The ship sailed that night, and 'Igaal with it. And so it was that the man who had done so much evil now found himself in a safe refuge and felt that his soul had entered into peace.

'Igaal Bowkahh came with the ship to Aden. When he had disembarked and was drinking tea in the town, he began to tell his story to some young Somalis of his tribe who were working there. When he had finished, they looked at him wryly.

"To tell the truth," they commented, "we think you must have been mad."

"And why?" asked 'Igaal indignantly.

"Well, why did you give seven guineas for a dog?" they enquired. "And why did you give the dog away for one cigar? These are surely the actions of a madman."

'Igaal Bowkahh laughed. "You are small children. I don't know why I bother to talk to you at all."

"What do you mean?" they asked.

"If you saw the world falling down," 'Igaal said, "what could you do, by yourself, to put it right?"

"Obviously, there is nothing anyone could do," the young men replied.

"Look here," 'Igaal said, "the best thing to do in that situation is to give the world a good hard kick and make it topple over properly! When I saw that my fortune was at a low ebb, I thought I might as well give it a shove and finish it off. But it turned out well for me, because, as the proverb says, a hard belly is the personal friend of Allah."

Ahmed The Woodseller

Many years and hundreds of years ago, there lived in the city of Sennah in the Yemen an insignificant little man called Ahmed Hatab. He was not greatly blessed by fate, having a squat ugly countenance and a shrunken and twisted body. He had a wife, but she could not be called a blessing, being a large shrewish creature who nagged at Ahmed because he was so poor.

Every morning, just before dawn, Ahmed went out beyond the city to gather firewood. In the evening, he drove his donkey-cart through the streets, selling the wood he had gathered. Each day Ahmed Hatab made three annas. Never any less, but never any more, either. There was never enough food in the house, and his wife was constantly complaining. Ahmed grew more and more weary with his life.

"Ahmed, you are a fool," he said to himself one day. "You spend years slaving to collect firewood, and what does it profit you? What does the pale fire of sunrise, or the cool dawn, or the singing of birds mean to you? Only another day to scrabble among the thorn bushes, picking up twigs. Why toil thus, to make three miserable annas a day? Better to die now, and get it over quickly, than to struggle and suffer, and die of starvation in the end."

And so it was that Ahmed Hatab determined to kill himself. The next morning he walked far beyond the city to a steep mountain and climbed to the top. Trembling a little, he approached the edge of the precipice, and after taking a last look at the world, he jumped.

Down and down Ahmed fell, and as he looked towards the bottom of the ravine and saw the pointed teeth of the rocks below, he shuddered and closed his eyes.

Crash! Ahmed lay there, motionless. Then he discovered that he could still think.

"I am dead," he thought. "But what happens now, in Allah's name? Where are the gardens and the fountains and the soft green couches that the Qoran promises?"

Then, moving himself gently, he stubbed his foot against a rock and shouted in pain. He was not dead after all, but very much alive.

"But this is strange!" he cried. "Here am I and there is the mountain, and certainly I was at the top a few minutes ago, and now am here, at the bottom. How is it that I am unhurt?"

Then Ahmed Hatab grew angry, and fury shook his small body.

"Cheated!" he gasped. "I have been cheated. Some devil has played a trick on me! But I have determined to die, and by all the saints and djinn, I will die!"

He walked and walked over the dusty roads and through the scorching sand until he came to the shore of the sea.

"Now, let us see who will die and who will live," he said to himself.

And so, with a flourish of his short arms, Ahmed plunged into the sea, and began splashing through the water in his haste to get out beyond his depth. But the further he went, the further the water seemed to retreat, and when he had waded along for a mile or more, the sea was still not above his skinny ankles. An enormous discouragement took possession of him, and slowly he plodded back to shore.

As he wandered along the road, pondering his bad luck, he saw something lying in the dust. It was a dead man. The fortunate fellow had evidently been murdered by thieves, for his purse was gone and a blood-stained club lay beside him. Ahmed picked up the club, and fondled it, and sat down to wait. Finally, as he had anticipated, the Sultan's soldiers came along the road.

"*Salaam aleikum!*" Ahmed Hatab shouted. "I have killed this man."

"You are obviously mad," the soldiers said, "to sit by the corpse and shout out your guilt so readily. But if you have killed him, then you shall be killed yourself, according to the law."

They took Ahmed to the Sultan, who commanded them to cut off the head of the little woodseller.

"The time has come at last!" Ahmed whispered to himself. "Nothing can stop your death now, my good Ahmed."

The soldiers took him to the prison courtyard and put his head on a block, and the executioner, who was a strong stout man, brought his huge scimitar down on the scrawny neck of Ahmed Hatab. But then a wonderful thing happened. The blade of the scimitar, tempered steel as it was, shattered into a thousand pieces, and the neck of Ahmed Hatab remained unscathed.

"This blade is faulty!" the executioner cried. "Bring me another, and a stronger, a blade of flawless steel!"

But again the scimitar broke, and Ahmed's neck did not. A third time a new blade was brought, and a third time the steel gave way. Then the executioner grew frightened.

"It is a miracle," he said. "Take this man back to the Sultan, for I will not touch him again."

The Sultan's face grew solemn when he heard of it, and he said he would not meddle with one whom Allah intended to live. So it was that Ahmed Hatab, still alive and still penniless, was turned free again. He thought he would walk to the next town and try his luck at dying there. Presently, he came to the place and his feet took him to the palace of the Sultan. Now, this Sultan's palace was rich and splendid, with many courtyards and fountains and gardens. The seven gates were guarded by armed soldiers and by massive dogs with formidable jaws.

Ahmed Hatab selected a gateway casually, and wandered in through it, dressed in his filthy rags. No one stopped him, and so he whistled and sang to draw attention to himself. But the guards only stood stiffly beside the gate, as though Ahmed were not there, and the watch-dogs did not even glance up. Ahmed grew angry again, and stamped into the palace itself, through long corridors hung with rich carpets, and into the throne room of the great Sultan.

The Sultan was there with all his advisers and wise men. As the door opened, and ragged Ahmed marched in, they all looked up in horrified surprise.

"Who are you," the Sultan demanded, "and how in the name of all the saints and djinn did you get in here?"

"May Allah preserve your Mightiness, oh pearl of Sultans," Ahmed replied humbly. "I walked in."

"What?" cried the Sultan. "With all my armed guards and my ferocious watch-dogs at the gates?"

"Indeed," said Ahmed, "that is how it happened."

"Go outside my palace and try to get in again," the Sultan commanded, "and we shall see if my guards and my dogs are so blind twice."

So for the second time Ahmed Hatab strolled in through the palace gates. And neither the guards nor the dogs stirred. Then the Sultan of that city was greatly amused, and admired Ahmed for his supposed cleverness in slipping past the guards. He decided to make Ahmed one of his advisers, and to bestow an estate upon him, and to give him one of the royal princesses as a wife.

The Sultan's youngest daughter was slim and bright-eyed, graceful as a flower. She came and combed the beard of Ahmed Hatab, and gave him fine clothes of embroidered brocade and spoke to him most gently and lovingly. Ahmed had never seen such a woman in all his life, and his heart flamed with love and desire for her. In a few days, the daughter of the Sultan was married to the little woodseller, and so it was that Ahmed Hatab, having found good fortune far beyond his dreams, decided that life was worth living after all.

"Now I shall not die," said he, "for life has turned marvellously prosperous. I will live until I am an old greybeard, and will grow more mighty and more rich every year."

But at that moment, a faint breeze came in through the window, and when Ahmed looked around, there stood an angel.

"It is your time to die now," the angel said, "and I have been sent for you."

"Ah, the unfairness of it!" Ahmed cried. "Where were you, I ask, when I wanted to die, and jumped off the precipice?"

"Your time had not yet come," the angel said.

"And where were you," Ahmed sobbed, "when I waded out into the sea, and the water would not come above my ankles, and when the executioner's blade broke, and when the watch-dogs did not flick an eyelash as I entered the Sultan's palace?"

"I have told you," the angel said patiently. "Your time of death was not then. But now it has arrived, and I am here to take you."

Then Ahmed stopped his weeping and moaning, and glanced up with a look of great craftiness.

"If I must die, so be it," he said. "But you would not have me die without saying my prayers once more?"

"Why, no," the angel said. "You are free to pray before you die."

"Then," Ahmed said, "promise me you won't touch me until I have been to the mosque once more."

The angel promised, and swore on the Qoran. Then Ahmed jumped up joyfully.

"Aha!" he laughed. "I didn't say when I would go to the mosque, and now, my good friend, I don't intend to go just yet!"

So the wicked Ahmed continued to live, and grew more wealthy, and enjoyed his wife, and had a fine house and many servants. But he never went inside the mosque.

Then it happened that the chief priest of the mosque died, and the Sultan called Ahmed Hatab to him to discuss the appointment of a new *imam*.

"You have been my faithful adviser," the Sultan said, "and my son-in-law, and now I intend to appoint you as *imam*."

At first Ahmed refused politely, saying that such an honour was too great. But when the Sultan insisted, Ahmed grew more and more frightened, and began beating his forehead with a frenzied hand and blurting out his terror.

"Are you the offspring of some devil," the Sultan cried, "to fear the holy mosque? You shall go, and you shall go at once!"

Ahmed protested and wept and struggled, but the Sultan's guards picked him up and carried him off. As soon as he was inside the door of the mosque, Ahmed saw the angel again.

"Mercy, I beg of you!" cried Ahmed, on his knees.

"Allah is merciful," the angel said. "Pray to Him."

So Ahmed Hatab, who had tried to cheat death, did not die without saying his final prayers. Then, as he finished praying, he slumped down where he knelt, and the soul departed from the wretched little body of Ahmed the wood-seller.

So do men learn the futility of resisting the commands of Allah, the Compassionate, the Merciful.

CHAPTER FOURTEEN

The Imperialists

O UT OF THE tin trunks and the mothballs came the dress uniforms, brass-buttoned up to the chin. Out came the ladies' broad-brimmed hats, the flowered chiffon frocks in shades of forget-me-not or muted primrose – nothing ostentatious, purchased at Harrod's on the last leave and cherished like health. Medals and shoes were polished as never before, and in a score of bungalows the stewardboys brandished charcoal irons like battle-shields as the chosen garments were pressed and put in readiness. The great occasion was at hand, the English monarch's official birthday celebrated in the outposts of empire with pomp and with tumult, with *durbars* and with flags.

The morning was cool and fine. The sun by mid-day would draw the sweat of even the chilliest memsahibs, but for a while, for at least an hour or so, they were the daughters of Jerusalem, roses of Sharon and lilies of the valley, sweet-smelling and garbed in perfection, and their men were kingly as Solomons.

Outside the town, at the parade grounds, we punctually gathered. Somali men and women thronged indecisively around the edges of the square, pointing and snickering. But they had not been able to resist the occasion, either. Their cotton robes were bright and stiff with newness. Here was the Qadi of Hargeisa, lean and hawk-nosed, resplendent in white burnoose and a black robe embroidered with spider-webs of gold. Here were the local elders with their beards freshly trimmed, arrayed in robes of scarlet, turquoise, royal blue. The meek-eyed wives of Indian merchants were wearing their best saris of apricot or fuchsia silk, and their silver bangles tinkled and clashed softly on their languid wrists. Their husbands were speckless in white linen suits, and they sported those small topees known as Bombay bowlers. Through and around the crowds the Somali children skipped and butted like hordes of young goats.

The English were apart. They sat primly at one side, ourselves among them, behind a fence. Gloved and straw-hatted mothers hissed at their giggling young – *Behave yourself!* We all had to behave ourselves. It was a solemn event, sedately joyful. The top officials emerged in the white uniform of the Colonial Service, and all the military men of any rank had medals sprouting like corsages from their out-puffed chests.

His Excellency the Governor arrived. People leapt respectfully to their feet, but none of us was sure when to sit down again. Everyone looked enquiringly at everyone else. Finally we were settled, and the inspection of the troops began. The Somaliland Scouts and the police, long ranks of tall rangy Somalis, marched past in admirable precision. His Excellency wore a snowy uniform and the colonial governor's hat, which was the most distinctive piece of headgear I had ever seen. It resembled a London policeman's helmet, except that it was white, and from the top of it there flourished animatedly a great many red and white ostrich plumes. His Excellency was well over six feet, and was a fine-looking man, so he carried the uniform and the hat with ease and splendour. We had been told that all colonial governors were over six feet tall. This height, supposedly, was insisted upon in order to impress local populations. Personally, I did not believe this was the reason at all. It seemed to me that the British would simply be too sporting to ask a short man to wear those lofty plumes.

The Somali bandsmen bleeped out a tune that was recognizable as *God Save The Queen*, although there was about it a weird melancholy strongly suggestive of Arabic music. They played it five times, and each time the Royal Standard was run up, then down again, while the troops presented arms. The occasions were when the Governor arrived, when the monarch (symbolically) arrived, when the Royal Salute was given, when the monarch (symbolically) departed, and when His Excellency departed. What with the national anthem, the raising and lowering of flags, and the troops slapping rifles up and down, the spectators of all races found themselves confused. The English enclosure in particular was a scene of well-intentioned but uncoordinated action. People sat down hopefully, then bobbed up again when they noticed that no one else was sitting down. Men fumbled in weary desperation with hats which seemed never to be in the right position at the right time.

The Somalis, watching from a slight distance, did not appear surprised. They had always known that the *Ingrese* were demented.

And of course, a good many of them really were demented, and not in the harmless and rather touching musical-comedy manner of the Birthday Parade, either. I found the sahib-type English so detestable that I always imagined that if I ever wrote a book about Somaliland, it would give me tremendous joy to deliver a withering blast of invective in their direction. Strangely, I now find I cannot do so. What holds me back is not pity for them, although they were certainly pitiable, but rather the feeling that in thoroughly exposing such of their sores as I saw, there would be something obscene and pointless, like mutilating a corpse. For these people are dead, actually, although some of them will continue to lumber around Africa for a few more years, like lost dinosaurs. They bear no relation to most parts of Africa today, and however much Africans may have suffered at their hands, it is to be hoped that one day Africans may be able to see them for what they really were – not people who were motivated by a brutally strong belief in their own superiority, but people who were so desperately uncertain of their own worth and their ability to cope within their own societies that they were forced to seek some kind of mastery in a place where all the cards were stacked in their favour and where they could live in a self-generated glory by transferring all evils, all weaknesses, on to another people. As long as they could be scornful or fearful of Africa or Africans, they could avoid the possibility of being scornful or fearful of anything within themselves.

To this group belonged the sahib who referred to Somalis as "black bastards" except when he facetiously called them "our black brethren"; the memsahib who twittered interminably about the appalling cheekiness of the Somalis; the thin pallid lady who was haunted by the fear (or perhaps hope) that all Somali men over the age of twelve were constantly eyeing her with extreme lewdness; the timid memsahib who lived within the four walls of her bungalow as within a tissue-paper fortress which the slightest breath of Africa might cause to crumple around her. To this group, also, belonged the memsahib who one morning at the Hargeisa Club gave the steward a tongue-lashing that would have done credit to a termagant of Hogarth's day, because he had placed a salt shaker on the table instead of a salt cellar –"Don't you know that no lady ever sprinkles salt over her food?" Another of this ilk was the sahib who, when he was presiding over a district court once, shrilled at each Somali witness in turn – "You're lying!" – as perhaps they were, but whether they were or not, they could not risk replying in a tone like his. To this clan belonged the sahib who once ordered the Somali steward at the Hargeisa Club to bring back the magazine which the sahib had been reading and which the steward had put away while the Englishman was out at the bar; the Somali could not read and did not know one magazine from another, but the sahib would not walk across the room and find his own magazine – the steward was made to trot back and forth until by a process of elimination the right publication was fetched. To this sad company belonged the memsahibs who told gruesome stories over the mid-morning tea – the Englishwoman whose husband was away on trek and who was wakened one night by an invading shadow which proved to be an African bent on raping her; managing to reach under her pillow, she drew out the revolver she kept there and shot him – he staggered off into the night, and when the servants searched the compound, the man turned out to be the trusted night-watch-man whom the family had employed for years. I had no reason to disbelieve this tale at the time, but some years later the identical story was told to me in West Africa as having happened there. Dark myths germinated and flourished in the stagnant pool of boredom that was the greatest threat to the memsahibs.

Every last one of these people purported to hate Africa, and yet they all clung to an exile that was infinitely preferable to its alternative – nonentity in England. I have never in my life felt such antipathy towards people anywhere as I felt towards these pompous or whining sahibs and memsahibs, and yet I do not feel the same anger now. Their distortions have been presented in detail often enough, both fictionally and journalistically, in almost every tale of colonial life. As I see it, whatever incurable illness they may have had, they are archaic now and at least in the countries where they no longer have power they ought to be permitted to pass into history without too much further commentary. R.I.P.

But there were others for whom I was quite unprepared when I stepped ashore at Berbera, expecting all the English abroad to be fullblown imperialists, whatever I fancied that word meant. If I had ever read about them, it had been with scepticism. I had not really believed such people existed. Yet here they were, confounding every preconceived notion of old colonials or pukka sahibs, and defying any neat labelling. Each was unique, utterly unlike anyone else, and yet they had this in common – they were all intensely concerned with this land and with the work they were doing here, and they were all drawn to Africa, or some place far from home, deeply and irresistibly.

Who could ever forget *Libahh*, The Lion? This was the name given to him by the Somalis, but to the English he was known as The Baron. He was a major in the Somaliland Scouts, a short broad man with a balloon belly and a cheerful scarlet face. His eyes were large and keen, and when you looked beyond the rolls of fat around them, you saw that these eyes did not miss a thing. He played his role exactly as he wanted it; he was what he chose to be. In one eye he wore a monocle. His moustache curved ornately along both cheeks and tapered off towards his ears in a long fringe of wiry grey-black hair.

On the night of the Queen's Birthday dance at Government House, the Baron told me how he once shot crocodile with a twenty-two.

"Nothing to it," he said. "You simply aim for their eyes."

Now the time-honoured tales came out, the tales of the African bush and veld, the tales every old Africa hand keeps stowed away like treasured amulets, to bring out sometimes and touch – the elephants and buffalo tracked and slain, the Masai warriors who twisted the tail of a charging lion, the black leopards that used to live in the Sheikh hills. I would have believed anything this man told me, not because it was necessarily true, but for the same reason that one believes in first-rate fiction – within the framework of words, the story is absolutely convincing. Perhaps this was one reason the Baron got along so well with the Somalis. He could spin as good a tale as any of them.

He spoke boomingly, in a voice rich with underlying laughter. Only once did his mood turn serious, when he told of a gift some tribesmen had given him not long ago.

"Enormous great lion pelt with a black mane. Not many lion about, you know, these days. Thought it was jolly decent of them to give it to me. I've got it pegged up on my wall."

Abruptly, he swung back to his public self, his character of Baron. We chatted about the Parade that day, and he commented on the Governor's uniform and headgear.

"If he put these feathers on his bum," the Baron said, "he could fly."

Nearby, I heard the fluttering voice of a memsahib.

"He's so vulgar, that man – oh dear, he's so terribly common!"

The Baron might have been called many things, but common was certainly not one of them. He was one of the most uncommon men I had ever met. Suddenly he glared at me from behind his monocle and called me "bloody colonial." I told him there was only one thing worse than calling a Canadian an American, and that was to call one a colonial.

"No difference," snorted the Baron. "American came up to me once in a bar, and I said 'Who're you – a Yankee?' And he said, 'Suh, I'm a rebel.' So I told him, 'Hell, that's nothing – you're all bloody rebels to me!'"

The next morning we saw him at the Club. The waiter approached softly with the coffee, and the Baron let loose with a leonine roar.

"What's the matter, man? Quit stamping around like that, can't you?"

Then he grinned at us and at the Somali, who was well aware that *Libahh* did not mean to be taken seriously.

"Can't take my monocle out this morning," he said. "Need it to hold my eye in."

So he passed out of our life, and we heard no more about him until many years later, when we chanced to see a newspaper story from Auckland.

New Zealand's first television star has quit, and in doing so has shown up pitfalls in government operation of the service. Nicknamed the Baron in many out-of-the-way parts of the world, he was a natural as a T.V. personality, with his handlebar moustache, monocle and embroidered waistcoats. He has spent most of his life as a soldier, and has served in such legendary forces as the Arab legion, the King's African Rifles, and the Somaliland Scouts. But throughout his service as an announcer, he was classified as a class six clerk in the public service, on a salary less than some typists in his office were getting. "I loved the work," he said, "but I just couldn't afford it." The major has left to try his luck in Australia.

Godspeed him, wherever he may be, for there are few enough embroidered waistcoats in this world. But I have the feeling that however much his garb and manner may impress others, the Baron himself may value more a black-maned lion pelt that hangs upon his wall.

Chuck was a Canadian, the only fellow countryman we encountered in Somaliland, and the only unsponsored individual, for this was not tourist country and outsiders were normally here only as employees of some agency or government. Chuck lived in Ethiopia, and was visiting Hargeisa when we ran into him at the J.M.J. Hotel, a bizarre little place owned by one of the few Christian Somali families, the initials in the name standing for Jesus, Mary and Joseph. Chuck was in his thirties, almost bald, a toughly humorous man.

"I had some cash saved up after the war," he told us, "so I thought I'd come out to Africa. I'd always wanted to go big-game hunting. Just my luck, though – all my kit was lost on the way out. Guns, everything, all gone. Well, there I was, stuck in Ethiopia – I had to do something."

He soon noticed that the Juba River was full of crocodiles. He could not shoot them himself, having no equipment, but he saw dozens of rifle-carrying Ethiopian soldiers standing around doing nothing in particular. So he made a deal. They would shoot and skin the crocs, and he would make all the arrangements for selling the valuable skins.

"There's not as much useful skin on a croc as you might think. Only the underbelly is any good. But these soldiers were damn fine shots. We got dozens. It worked dandy for a while. The soldiers were happy to make a few extra bucks, and I was earning a tidy living. But – boy, I've really got problems now. The Ethiopian government has started bitching about it."

He had recently travelled from Harar, where he lived, to Addis Ababa, in the hope of placating Ethiopian officialdom, but he did not feel optimistic.

"Too many wheels within wheels," he said. "Too many rival factions. If you're friendly with one, you're liable to get yourself bumped off by another. I don't see why they had to go and kick up such a fuss. All I wanted to do was shoot a few lousy crocodiles."

If his present business folded up, he had another scheme in mind. He was positive he could make a fortune by getting a timber concession and selling ties to the Uganda Railways, and he had a marvellous plan worked out for transporting the ties by water. The next time we saw him, however, some months later, he had a new dream. He had found land in Ethiopia which would be perfect for growing cotton. He could buy the land cheaply – all it needed was irrigation.

"Here's the deal," he said to Jack. "You come in with me and look after the irrigation side. A couple of good seasons, and we'd be set for life. What do you say?"

Jack declined, although with a certain amount of reluctance. Chuck shrugged. Never mind. He would find a partner somewhere else. He went his way and we went ours. We never discovered what happened to him. I would be willing to bet that he has never gone home, though. If he is not still in the crocodile business on the Juba River, or growing cotton on the Ethiopian plains, more than likely he is rounding up the last of the reindeer in the Arctic tundras or catching South American bushmasters to sell to zoos.

Ernest, who was in charge of agriculture and veterinary services, was a man of phenomenal energy. He dashed around at top speed, always, accompanied by a gaunt and glossy-haired Irish setter which loped tiredly behind, suffering from the day's heat far more than its master ever did. Ernest had shaggy eyebrows and thick spectacles through which he peered with a keen blue-eyed look. He would not let you go, whoever you were, until he had finished explaining his latest scheme.

"Listen to this – I must just tell you about the garden at Bohotleh – the most astonishing results –"

This country grew practically nothing, but some food could be grown in the well areas if only the Somalis could be persuaded. Nothing ever discouraged Ernest, or if it did, he kept his discouragement to himself. If a jowari-growing scheme had failed – never mind. Maybe the date-growing scheme would succeed. Over the years he had studied and written extensively about the trees and plants of Somaliland, and had discovered which plants were believed by Somalis to possess medicinal properties. He had also done much research into livestock diseases, and was constantly attempting to introduce better methods of animal husbandry. It was slow going, for the tribesmen were highly suspicious of anything new. But the next effort, the next experiment – this was the one certain to succeed spectacularly.

He knew, of course, that it never would. Most of his work would not bear fruit that he would ever see. It was for other years, years that might be immensely distant. But he had the ability to travel hopefully, and here, where the earth was about as hard and unyielding as it is possible for earth to be, and where setbacks were not the exception but the norm, this ability was a great gift indeed.

Miles was a veterinary officer, a tall bony man with a reserved manner and a hesitant way of speech. He visited us when we were camped near Borama, and as he began to talk about his work he lost his shyness and was soon explaining the campaign to persuade tribesmen to bring their animals for vaccination.

"The cattle-owning Somalis of the west, you know, actually attempt to immunize their stock against rinderpest," he said earnestly, glancing up with brief uncertainty as though to make sure he was not boring us, but then forging ahead regardless, carried by the force of his own enthusiasm. "They make a brew of the urine, dung and milk of a sick animal and place a little of it in the nostrils of a healthy beast. Unfortunately, the disease is often spread in this way instead of being checked. But the really significant thing is that they do have some concept of immunization."

He was attempting to find out everything he could about the Somalis' traditional ways of caring for livestock and treating diseases, in the hope that some mental bridge could be provided which would enable the nomads to move from the old methods to the new.

Long afterwards, in West Africa, one day we saw a familiar figure on the streets of Accra. It was Miles, on a visit to the coastal city to get supplies. He was working in the northern part of Ghana, he told us, an area which resembled Somaliland. His work was needed there; he only hoped he would be allowed to go on doing it. He suspected he might be moved to the coast, and he did not want to be.

He was attracted – impelled, almost – towards the sparsely settled desert and the desert people. That is where he wanted to live and work. It was his kind of country. For those who have loved the desert, it can be difficult to be content anywhere else.

"I wish," Dexter said, "that they would not pinch the telephone wire. That's the third time this month that the phone line to Berbera has been cut."

The tribesmen in the Guban valued the government for this one thing if for nothing else – the quantity and quality of its copper wire, which was perfect for binding the head of a spear to the shaft. Dexter spoke of it plaintively, but without rancour. He no longer allowed himself to become unduly annoyed at these perpetual difficulties.

Dexter was in charge of the Public Works Department, and Jack was directly responsible to him. He was a quiet-spoken man who never interfered unless it was absolutely necessary, and then did so with diplomacy. When we were caught out on the Wadda Gumerad at the onset of the rains, and finally arrived back in Hargeisa in a depleted state, Dexter did not tell us, as he might well have done, that we were crazy to have gone out without food or water.

"Personally," he said casually, "I never go out even on a short trip without supplies. You'll probably find that's the soundest way."

Like almost everyone else here, he was hampered by a shortage of equipment and trained staff. But the main roads were kept open and each year a few more miles were added. Water continued to flow out of the taps; new bungalows were put up and old ones kept in repair. Things got done, somehow.

"When you've been out here for a while," he said, "you don't expect miracles any more. You just do what you can."

We found that this was the theme of many Englishmen's lives here. They did what they could. It was not everything, but it was something.

The Padre was the only Church of England clergyman in Somaliland. He had been sent out here many years ago, to serve the needs of the English community. Now he was an old man, and was supposed to be retired, but he was not the kind of person who could ever retire. He had gained permission from the government to stay on, for this was his home now.

Because the Somalis were strong Muslims, and because at the beginning of this century the Somalis waged against the British a war that was both nationalistic and religious in character, no missionaries were permitted here. This seemed an excellent policy to me, for I could never believe in anyone's right to foist his religious views upon others, and in any event, these desert people could not possibly have found a religion which would have sustained them better than the one they already had.

The Padre, naturally, did not regard the matter in this way. He had, I think, a sense of sorrow because he had not been able to proselytize here. He did not have that all-too-common missionary trait, the patronizing and basically scornful desire to enlighten people who are regarded as low savages. I think he would have liked to preach among Somalis merely because he was fond of them and would have wished to share with them the faith which was so close to his own heart.

He had spent years and years translating the Bible into Somali. Why would a man labour so pointlessly? For him, of course, it was not pointless. He really believed that his translation would be needed one day. He respected the Muslim religion, but his own belief so filled him that he could not help feeling that some day some Somalis would seek what he had found in the Man who to him was not merely a prophet but the Son of God. He was well aware that Muslims considered this concept to be at complete variance with monotheism. But he lived by faith, not logic, and in this way he was closer to the Somalis than we could ever be.

He was one of the frailest men I have ever seen, a man like thistledown, slight and fleshless, with a wispy white beard. He wore heavy boots several sizes too big for him, probably someone's castoffs, and a food-speckled black soutane. Accompanied only by his Somali "boy," who was nearly as old as he, he wandered around the country, sometimes living in Somali camps, sometimes giving church services in the European stations, marrying and baptizing and burying when English people needed these rites performed. He had no car. He walked across the desert, and the English in all the stations worried about him, thinking he would be found dead of thirst or sunstroke one day in the Haud or the Guban. But he never was.

Dexter told us of meeting the Padre out in the Haud. The old man was striding along through the dust, a tatty-looking topee on his head.

"You're miles from nowhere, Padre," Dexter said, half reproachfully. "What would you have done if I hadn't come along to give you a lift?"

The Padre was completely unperturbed.

"Ah, but you did come along, my dear boy, didn't you?" he replied. "Don't you see?"

The Padre's trust in divine bounty was apt to give those of lesser faith (which meant everyone else) many moments of concern. At the height of the *Jilal* – was he marching across the dry wastes of the Haud? Or when the rain came on – had he found shelter? And yet – how to explain it? – the Lord, or someone, always did provide for this incredible man.

The Somalis called him *wadaad*, a man of religion, and regarded him as a holy man. They understood his kind better than we did, and they fed him willingly whenever he stopped at their encampments. During the war, the Padre was ludicrously made a major. It is hard to imagine what he must have looked like, lean-shanked and fragile, swathed in a khaki uniform. He did not have much use for his officer's pay, which seemed a ridiculously large sum of money to him, so he used to give most of it away to urchins in the *magala*.

He had a fine disregard for any law which he considered to be silly. In Hargeisa immediately after the war there was a rule that all Europeans walking out at night must carry a hurricane lamp – in case of sudden attack, presumably, from the Somalis who were edgy and unsettled after the Italian occupation and their subsequent return to British jurisdiction. The Padre turned up at Government House one evening, gaily swinging his hurricane lamp - unlighted.

"They told me I must carry a lamp," he said mildly, "but they didn't specify that it should be a lighted one."

The true lantern he carried, of course, was always lighted – it would never go out until he died. Because his faith illuminated him so, it was tempting to see him simply as a saintly man, some gentler John the Baptist. But how intricate must be the forces which make life seem possible to some men only in the wilderness.

We travelled many miles over terrible roads to see the government geologist. His wife ushered us into the bungalow – would we like a cup of tea? Aubrey was working and could not be disturbed. Perhaps we would like to wait, or if not, could we return some other time? She spoke of him as though he were an artist whose inspiration must not be intruded upon. And in a sense, that is just what he was.

We waited for an hour or so, and finally Aubrey came stomping out of his study and beckoned to us, managing to look cordial and absent-minded at the same time.

"Come in, come in! Sorry to keep you waiting, but if I let people interrupt me, you know, I'd never get a blessed thing done."

His study was like a small natural history museum, crammed with maps, charts, rock specimens, animal skulls, collections of butterflies and insects.

"Rainfall records – that's what you wanted, wasn't it? Let's see, now –"

He ruffled through thousands of documents and emerged

triumphantly with the records Jack needed for his work. Aubrey was something of a legend in this country. He had done geological surveys, maps, charts of tribal migrations, rainfall records and heaven knows what-all. He was completely bound up in his work, and it seemed to him that there was never enough support for his projects. Only slowly were his reports and maps printed. He carried on a running battle with the Secretariat. He was on friendly enough terms with the administrative officers individually, but collectively he appeared to view them as a mammoth stone wall against which he was doomed forever to batter. He told us about it in gloomily ironic tones.

"No money, saith the government. It was ever thus. These things of mine have got to be printed, you know, but do you think they'll see that? Not they."

All the same, he knew his work was valued here. I only hope it will be valued as much in the independent Somali Republic.

The Colonel owned an infant ostrich and an exceedingly pregnant grey mare. The mare's condition was a source of anxiety to him.

"She's been pregnant for such a long time, I'm beginning to wonder if she'll ever foal. Or if she does, what on earth will come forth?"

Perhaps she mated with a camel by mistake, and at this very moment some exotic hybrid was being formed, some creature which required an unusually long period of gestation. The Colonel and Aul, his stable-boy, fussed over the swollen but placid mare like two worried physicians. When at last she dropped her foal, it was a little brown filly, perfectly formed, and the Colonel was almost disappointed.

The Colonel was retired from the Army and now served as an aide to the Governor. He was thoughtful and courteous, the gentlest of men, and his favourite pastime was telling ghastly battle stories. From him I learned more about the famous Mullah campaigns half a century ago, for he had read everything he could find on the subject, and he spoke almost as though he had been there.

"Now this shows you what sort of chaps the Somalis are when they're fighting – it was during the 1912 campaign, I believe, when a Somali dragged himself into the Berbera hospital one day with a bullet in his leg and a spear wound right through his body. The doctor started to take out the bullet, and the Somali gasped, 'No, no - never mind that. But for the love of Allah, do something about this spear wound – it hurts when I laugh.'"

And although this same anecdote had probably been told, with local variations, of warriors in every army since the days of Genghis Khan, the Colonel laughed delightedly.

"I can quite believe it, you know," he said. "We had some very good men in those campaigns, too. Corfield, who founded the Camel Corps – he was killed, of course. And Swayne – he led the Second Expedition. Along with Risaldar-Major Haji Musa Farah, he trekked across the Haud with five thousand tribesmen, to attack the Mullah's forts. Think of it – all that way. Water was the problem, and fever. The Mullah was holed up with all the water he needed. It wasn't a simple matter of spears, either – the Mullah's forces had rifles."

His face grew sombre as he recounted the series of campaigns that went on for twenty years. "When we got up the Third Expedition, we had regular forces of Sudanese and Sikhs as well as the Somalis. The worst battle was at Gumburu – our men were terribly outnumbered, holding out inside a *zareba* and entirely surrounded by the Mullah's men. After a while it looked as though the whole British force would be killed. And indeed they were, to a man. But first –"

The Colonel paused, for he was very much moved by this story, and hearing him tell it, so was I.

"Just before the Mullah's dervishes swept in," he finished, "Captain Johnson-Stewart broke up the Maxim guns so that they would never fire again."

We were silent, both of us, thinking of all the brave young men, the dead young men. But at least the gentle Colonel never doubted that they died for something worth while. And perhaps, after all, they did, if they believed they did. While on the other side, also believing, the Mullah's young Somali warriors died crying *Allah Akbar!*

Whether Mohamed Abdullah Hassan was a madman and a religious fanatic, as the British claimed, or an early nationalist and divinely inspired leader, as the Somalis claimed, was not a matter that could ever be settled. Perhaps he was both. Even the Somalis did not deny that he was a cruel man, but in their eyes this was not such an unusual thing for a sultan to be. He was a great *gabei* poet, and some of his poems survived to this day and were often recited by Somalis. The one I had heard showed skill and deep feeling and did not sound like the work of a madman.

"That may be," the Colonel said, "but we must remember that many of the tribesmen in the interior were not on the Mullah's side and were looking to us for protection against him."

Plain fact or wishful thinking? Again, probably both. One point, however, the Colonel conceded willingly.

"The Mullah was a courageous man," he said. "No one would deny that. Insane at times, no doubt. But he would never admit defeat, and that is something one has to admire, always."

Matthew had often been mentioned to us by the Somalis.

"Wait until you are meeting him," they told us. "There is a man."

Scarcely another Englishman in the country did they hold in this kind of esteem. We, however, were suspicious. Whenever I am told I will be certain to like someone, I become convinced that I will not like him at all. But when we finally met and got to know Matthew, we saw what the Somalis meant.

He was a District Commissioner, and as such he was entitled to one of the new large stone bungalows. But he could not be bothered with such fancy accommodation – it simply did not interest him. He lived in a small and almost shack-like bungalow, closer to the Somali *magala* than to the European settlement. His house was cluttered with files and papers, massive texts on Qoranic law, and every book that had ever been written about Somaliland. Matthew lived happily in the midst of this muddle, flicking the ash from his constant cigarette on the floor, for the ashtrays were always buried somewhere beneath the debris of paper.

There was about him a quickness, a kind of nervous energy. He did not belong to the "dinner-jackets-in-the-desert" set. He dressed in baggy khaki trousers, a bush jacket and an old Australian bush hat, and he took the formalities of colonial life as lightly as possible. He was the only Englishman in government service, as far as we could discover, who spoke really fluent Somali, and one of the few who understood the complexities of tribal organization and tribal law.

When fighting broke out between the Somalis of the Protectorate and the Ogaden Somalis on the other side of the border, or when a Protectorate tribe had a disagreement with the Ethiopians, Matthew was the person most often sent as government representative to the *shir*, the meeting between the opposing sides, where an attempt was made to reach a settlement of the trouble, for he was able to cope with the endlessly involved orations of a *shir* better than anyone else.

Like the Somalis themselves, Matthew was a skilled and rapid talker. Once he managed to quell a budding riot by cracking jokes in Somali – no mean feat, as the Somalis were hypercritical of any outsider attempting to speak their language, and their standards of wit and word jugglery were high. But sometimes his unorthodox methods went beyond speech. A friend told us why Matthew was awarded the M.B.E. The Desert Locust Control men in Somaliland set poisoned bait for the young hoppers, and at one time many Somalis believed that this locust poison would kill their camels which were grazing in the same places. One large section of a tribe in the Guban became so enraged that they were all prepared to take up their spears and massacre every locust officer in the area. When Matthew arrived on the scene, the tribesmen had gathered and were worked up to a fantastic pitch of anger and excitement. It was an isolated spot; there was no road, and the place was rarely visited by Europeans, so Matthew knew he could expect no help. The tribesmen threatened to kill him if he did not agree to stop the bait-laying. He refused, and at dusk they surrounded his camp. When darkness fell, Matthew somehow managed to escape, and made his way across the desert to a small tea shop on the Zeilah Road. He got away just in time, he later learned, for during the night the tribesmen made up their minds to kill him. They entered his camp, and furious at finding him gone, they burned the tents, slashed his clothes and even speared his bush hat. The next day they arrived at the Zeilah Road tea shop. If anything, they were angrier than before, having been cheated of a victim the previous night. It was too late for prolonged talk. Matthew said only one thing.

"If this locust poison doesn't kill a man, will you believe it won't kill your camels?"

The tribesmen murmured among themselves, and finally agreed – yes, they would believe it, in that case. But what was the use of such talk, when everyone knew the locust bait would certainly kill a man?

"No, it won't," Matthew said. "I'll prove it."

He then scooped up a handful of the poisoned bran and ate it himself. The tribesmen stared with considerable curiosity, and finally, when he did not drop dead, they dispersed.

A simple solution. But although he knew the locust bait did not poison camels, at the time when he ate it, he had no idea what effect it would have on a human. Camels, after all, are able to digest inch-long thorns, but men are not.

One evening we asked Matthew about this story. He was embarrassed. He laughed and shrugged.

"It was only that I couldn't think what else to do. Anyway, I thought I could probably get back to my bungalow in time, if necessary, and dose myself with a strong emetic. Never fear, I had no intention of dying for the cause or any nonsense like that."

I was relieved to hear it. I mistrusted martyrs, for I suspected that self-glorification was at the core of most self-sacrifice. There was nothing like that about Matthew. He would have performed such an act in the firm belief that he could pull it off. But he might not have pulled it off. What is bravery except the taking of a calculated risk, in the strong hope of winning but also in the realization that one may not win? This was the quality the Somalis perceived in Matthew when they said of him – "There is a man."

He explained to us, in other terms, the reason why he got along with the Somalis so well.

"I like them," he said quite frankly, "because they are so bloody-minded."

He valued in them the very qualities which many Englishmen abhorred – their argumentativeness, their passionate dramatization of events, the indestructible pride of these desert people.

He was delighted at one aftermath of the locust-bait crisis. The tribesmen, with that astonishing reversal so typical of Somalis, later came to him and told him that they now realized he was their friend and they would therefore like to offer him the full blood-compensation of a hundred camels for having once been determined to kill him.

Some months after we left Somaliland, we saw Matthew again in England, where he was on leave. He breezed into our flat in London, wearing an odd-looking suit of heavy hairy tweed.

"Damn silly, this suit," he said apologetically. "I had to buy something, you see, so I walked into a shop and when I was riffling through some off-the-peg suits, I saw one that had a most enticing label. It said *Thorn-proof*. Ah, I thought, just the job. So I bought it. It was only afterwards that I realized I wouldn't be likely to encounter many thorns along Oxford Street."

Matthew finally left Somaliland. We received a card – *Merry Christmas From Jerusalem*, with a picture of camels, and in his scrawled writing – "This reminds me of the Haud." He was working in the re-settlement of Arab refugees. Ultimately, he returned to Africa, as he was almost bound to do, and took a post with the Information Service in a country which has recently gained its independence. He was by turns elated and depressed.

"We've been doing a radio programme of contemporary negro poetry – terrific! Shall I send you the script?"

But in the next letter he wondered if it would not be better if all Europeans left Africa, for he was discouraged at the number of people who had political or religious motives for their work. If only Europeans could work there simply because various technical skills would be needed until African countries developed enough technically educated men of their own. But so many whites had axes to grind. The Africans saw this, and were not impressed.

He himself has no axe to grind. I believe he works for the work's sake, and because he loves Africa. Occasionally he has tried to settle down in England, but he never stays for long.

Perhaps for him, as for ourselves, Oxford Street is not entirely lacking in thorns after all.

The *Gu* rains were almost over when one day a tall thin grey-haired Englishman turned up at our bungalow and enquired politely if he might borrow Jack's Land-Rover and driver for a few days.

"My wife is at El Afweina," he explained. "She's become ill, so I must go and fetch her. I can't take my car – I don't think it would get through."

Jack readily agreed, and the Land-Rover set out with Abdi and the Englishman. Some days later, they returned. It had been a gruelling trip, through mud and *tugs*, over roads made non-existent by the rains. The Englishman was exhausted, but he thanked Jack courteously, and he answered our questions. Yes, his wife would be all right. He had taken her straight to the hospital and the doctor said she would soon be recovering nicely.

The man who had gone over the flooded desert to rescue his wife was the top administrative officer in the country, the Governor's second-in-command. His wife had been at El

Afweina because she was working in the *miskiin* camp there. *Miskiin* means "destitute." During the *Jilal*, the government had set up several of these camps in an effort to save some of the people who were dying of thirst and starvation. Allotments of water and jowari were sent to the camps, and after a while it was discovered that several of the Somali clerks who were in charge of distribution were selling the food and water instead of giving it to the *miskiin*. It was not easy to find government officers who could be spared from their jobs, so the Administrator's wife had gone to take charge of the El Afweina camp.

I could not think of any other Englishwoman in this country who could have or who would have done such a job. Most of the Englishwomen here, who had lived only in stations, did not even realize what it was that this woman had done. I realized it a little more clearly, perhaps, for I had lived out in the Haud during the *Jilal*. Even to meet these destitute ones face-to-face was an anguish and a horror which could not be conveyed in words – the gaunt bodies, the exposed ribs, the hands like dry twigs, the eyes that had ceased to hope. But to work among them day after day, to portion out the careful rations to their clamouring desperation – this took courage. Such courage I knew I did not possess.

Towards the end of our tour, I was forced to settle down in Hargeisa. To my great joy, I became pregnant, but after a near-miscarriage I felt it would be too risky to remain in camp, so I stayed in our bungalow and Jack came home on week-ends. I was still working on the Somali translations, but this was not enough now that I was alone for most of the time, so when an opportunity occurred for a job, I decided to take it. I went to work at the Secretariat, as the Administrator's secretary.

"Secretariat" is an important-sounding word, suggestive of marble halls and thick carpets. But the officers of government enjoyed no such grandeur here. The buildings were like small barracks, low and long and whitewashed. The offices were stifling, for the narrow windows with their thief-netting succeeded in keeping out every vestige of breeze. On the walls, the bulge-eyed geckos clung and stared. Outside, the pepper trees waved their feathery branches and the Somali messenger boys gathered in gossiping knots on the stoeps. The drowsy air was filled with a clacking of typewriters.

I had never before seen the inner workings of government. What the administration was doing now might be of future value, as a groundwork, or it might not. How could anyone really know? The Somalis might decide to take an entirely different course, and that would be up to them. But I could not see, in a general way, that the administration could do other than what they appeared to be trying to do at the moment, which was to prepare for the country's independence by a gradual transfer of power, beginning at the grassroots level, through the local authority system and the councils of elders, and by the extension of education in the hope that a large enough group of Somali leaders might have the opportunity for some political experience before independence.

The Administrator wrote his meticulously phrased reports to the Colonial Office, conferred with delegations of sheikhs and elders, talked with district officers. He never appeared hurried or impatient. He had worked here for many years and had a wider knowledge of the Somalis, their way of life and their history, than almost any other Englishman. But he was very much unlike them. He did not have, in dealing with them, the quick advantage of any ready-made mutuality of temperament. They were emotional and dramatic. He was restrained. They spoke with a thousand intricacies and embroideries. He spoke with a plain lucidity. They were capable of guile, when it served them, and could shift their expressed viewpoint in a flash, for effect. He spoke consistently what he believed to be true, and would not dissemble.

Crises flowed in and out of his office like perpetual tides. Verbal attacks, flattery, gratitude, the pleas of real need and the petitions of hopeful skulduggery – he received all these from the Somalis, and had to steer his way among them.

What he felt in his heart, only he knew. To outward observation, he discounted both laurels and barbs. If he became the object of the Somalis' anger, for some action the government had taken, he was not moved from his course – he never tried to buy their approval cheaply, nor did he look for an easy refuge in speaking scornfully of them, as many English did. If, on the other hand, he received their praise for some other action, he took it with a grain of salt.

"One shouldn't be too quick either to love or to hate," he said. "Both can be dangerous."

At first, he seemed to be a very cold man. I imagined he was able to act dispassionately towards the Somalis because his own feelings were not involved – it was a job to him, no more. But I discovered one day that this was not true at all. Another aspect of him was revealed through the Somali translations. I showed the manuscript to him, and he decided it should be published by the government. Discussing it, all at once he pointed to one page and spoke with an unexpected intensity.

"It would be worth while for this one passage in your introduction," he said, "even if there were nothing else in the book."

The passage was a description of the Somali tribesmen's harrowing and precarious life in the dry *Jilal*. I realized then how deep was his attachment to this land and these people, and how carefully he must keep his own feelings in check, if he was to do his work at all. As I talked about the country with him, I also realized how little I knew of it, how impossible it was to blow in from the sea and size up a land's centuries in a few months.

When the time came for us to leave Somaliland, the manuscript was left with the Administrator. He was trying to get an allocation of money from the government for the purpose of publication. Several years later, when we were in West Africa, I received one day a parcel and a letter.

"It took us a while," the Administrator's note said, "but we have managed it at last."

And here was the book. I was well aware that it would never be read by many people. Nevertheless, it was the first collection of Somali poems and folk-tales to appear in Eng-

lish. For me, the doing of it was a labour of love, and I could
not help feeling that for the Administrator, taking the time
and trouble to get it published, it had been much the same
sort of thing.

We saw him and his wife once more, when we were on leave
from West Africa. They had retired to England by this time,
and we went to visit them for a day. They had a big and
pleasantly rambling house in the country, and they were content to be there, they said. But they missed Somaliland. They
would always miss it – it had been home for a long time.

When we left, the Administrator drove us to the station.
He was not, of course, the Administrator any more. For the
first time I was seeing him only as himself. And yet he was
just the same. He was not altered or diminished now by the
lack of an official title, for what he had been before did not
depend upon titles. Looking at him as he sat behind the
wheel of his little Austin, in his trench-coat and old felt hat, I
knew somehow that I would not be seeing him again and I
wished that at this last moment I could tell him how greatly I
valued him. But I could not. Perhaps he knew – I hope so.

Opposite me, on the way back to London, Jack sat reading. Beside him, our daughter bent her marigold head over a
picture book, in three-year-old imitation of her father. Next
to me on the train seat, our small son slept in his Karri-Kot.
Everything was all right. But I looked out the window at the
countryside, a grey-brown winter colour in the rain, and I felt
that nothing was all right. I was thinking of all the people I
had known who had loved Africa and now must leave it.

The plane journey back to Ghana was filled with discom-
forts and delays. After a sleepless night, we finally got the
children settled. Jack beckoned me to the window.

"Look – we're coming over the desert. We're just in time to
see the dawn."

Above the Sahara, the night flowed away like water over
the precipice of the horizon. The faint and early light was
changing the sky to a milky gold. Far below, the ripples of
the great dunes were gilded and shone like the golden coffins

of the pharaohs. Then the sun mounted the sky and blazed in pure fire.

And then I saw that my sadness had been partly for myself, and my fascination with the reasons for others being drawn to Africa had been in some way a veiled attempt to discover my own. It seemed to me that my feeling of regret arose from unwisely loving a land where I must always remain a stranger. But it was also possible that my real reason for loving it was simply because I was an outsider here. One can never be a stranger in one's own land – it is precisely this fact which makes it so difficult to live there.

James Thomson, the famous explorer who journeyed so widely in East Africa, was subject to moods of intense depression, and in one of them, looking into himself, he wrote: "I am not an empire builder, I am not a missionary, I am not truly a scientist. I merely want to return to Africa and continue my wanderings."

In a book about the early and legendary white settlers in Kenya, the white hunter John Hunter, himself a legend, says in explanation of some of these pioneers: "Deep within every man is the desire to get away from it all – to drop everything and go and live on a desert island where the manifold complications of civilization can be forgotten."[1]

To Graham Greene, "Africa will always be the Africa of the Victorian atlas, the blank unexplored continent the shape of the human heart."[2]

Among the most perceptive and undeniable insights are those of Mannoni, in whose study of the psychology of colonization every European who has ever lived in Africa cannot fail to see something of himself, often much more than he would prefer to see.

[1] J.A. Hunter and Daniel P. Mannix, *Tales of the African Frontier*, Harper, 1954, p. 158.

[2] Graham Greene, *In Search of a Character. Two African Journals*, The Bodley Head, 1961, p. 123.

The typical colonial is compelled to live out Prospero's drama, for Prospero is in his unconscious as he was in Shakespeare's. . . . What the colonial in common with Prospero lacks, is awareness of the world of Others, a world in which Others have to be respected. This is the world from which the colonial has fled because he cannot accept men as they are. Rejection of that world is combined with an urge to dominate, an urge which is infantile in origin and which social adaptation has failed to discipline. The reason the colonial himself gives for his flight – whether he says it was the desire to travel, or the desire to escape from the cradle or from the 'ancient parapets', or whether he says that he simply wanted a freer life – is of no consequence, for whatever the variant offered, the real reason is still what I have called very loosely the colonial vocation. It is always a question of compromising with the desire for a world without men.[3]

Here, clearly, is the sahib who seeks a facile superiority in racialism. But here, too, in different degree, perhaps, and in different form, are many of those who believe they feel only sympathy towards the people of another land, and whose "sympathy" may lead them to see these people not as they really are but as the beholder feels they ought to be. Whether it is Ariel or Caliban who is chosen to populate Prospero's world, there is no basic difference, for both are equally unreal. What sort of world is it, then, Prospero's?

We waver between the desire for a society, quite different from our own, in which the attachments will be preserved with the maximum of emotional comfort and stability, and the desire for complete individuation where the individual is radically independent and relies wholly on his courage, technical skill and inventive powers. When the child suffers because he feels that the ties between himself and his parents are threatened and at the same time feels guilty because after all it is he who wants to break them, he reacts to the situation by dreaming of a world which is entirely his and into which he can project the images of his unconscious, to which he is attached in the way which is to him

[3] O. Mannoni, *Prospero and Caliban: A Study of the Psychology of Colonisation*, Methuen, 1956, p. 108.

the most satisfying. Now, it is this imaginary world which is, strictly speaking, the only 'primitive' world. . . . It is this 'primitive' image of the world which we have in mind when we become explorers, ethnographers, or colonials and go amongst societies which seem to us to be less real than our own.[4]

This was something of an irony for me, to have started out in righteous disapproval of the empire-builders, and to have been forced at last to recognize that I, too, had been of that company. For we had all been imperialists, in a sense, but the empire we unknowingly sought was that of Prester John, a mythical kingdom and a private world. I recall how apt I considered Hersi's description of the Haud – *this island place* – more apt, even, than I realized at the time.

Yet something of the real world did impinge upon our consciousness, and portions of the secret empire of the heart had to be discarded, one by one. In the Haud people died of thirst, people as actual as ourselves and with as much will to live. The magic potion of a five-grain aspirin very quickly proved inadequate, and the game of healer had to be abandoned. The unreal relationship with Abdi as a faithful retainer was shattered by the reality of him as a man – a man with outlooks far different from our own, but valid for him. Jack discovered the real world in his work, finding that an attempt had to be made, however imperfectly, to see the Somalis in terms of themselves and their own inheritance, not ours. How many other things there may have been which we perceived not as they were but as we wanted them to be – this we have no means of knowing.

Undoubtedly many Europeans have recognized or sensed in themselves the need for a fine and private place this side of the grave, and have sought to control it, to prevent it from distorting the outer world. Certain words return to me – do I merely read meanings into them, or do they in fact express such a recognition? *One should not be too quick either to love or to hate. You don't expect miracles – you just do what you can. If only Europeans could work here without an axe to*

[4] *Ibid.*, p. 207.

grind. It seems to me that these men went to Africa, as we all do, partly out of an inner need, but they managed to come to terms with it. They went on to do what work they could, not as crusaders in a desperate darkness and not as godlings in a solitary Eden, but as people in a world of people both different and similar to themselves.

To Africans, their land has never been "the Africa of the Victorian atlas," and they will not willingly allow it to be so to us now, either. Those who cannot bring themselves to relinquish the desert islands, the separate worlds fashioned to their own pattern and inhabited by creatures of their own design, must seek them elsewhere now, for they are no longer to be found in Africa.

CHAPTER FIFTEEN

Nabad Gelyo

No CONSTRUCTION job could ever be simple and straightforward in Somaliland – the people were too unpredictable and the land itself too full of unexpected snags. As the second *Jilal* went on, however, work on the *ballehs* did take on some kind of pattern. Each *balleh* took roughly four weeks to build, so Jack had to move camp only once a month. He drove in to Hargeisa most week-ends, and then I would get news of the week's work.

"You should see Isman Shirreh now. He's the best Cat operator I've got – he's certainly come a long way. Arabetto wants to learn how to drive a Cat, but I can't spare him all that often from the Bedford. I let him take Omar's shift this week, though, and he managed fine. Omar was off for a day – his wife just had a son. We had meat yesterday. The Illalo corporal shot a *gerenuk*, God knows how – I haven't seen any game around for weeks. The soil's like rock where we are now. The ripper teeth are wearing out again – I've got to go to P.W.D. today and see what can be done. Still, we'll have this *balleh* finished almost a week sooner than the last one."

In Jack's engineering phrase, everything was proceeding according to plan. But this relative harmony within the *balleh* job did not mean that all was harmonious as far as the Haud tribesmen were concerned. The poisoned water rumours had passed away, to be replaced by other rumours. One in particular worried Jack.

"There's something I've heard too often lately, and from

too many tribesmen – it can't be only idle talk. They're saying in the Haud that Sultan Shabel Esa plans to raise a force
and take over the *ballehs* once they're finished. He wouldn't
withhold the water – he'd just sell it. That would be a hell of a
situation, wouldn't it? I think I'd better talk it over with
Matthew. It looks as though the *ballehs* will have to be
patrolled by Illaloes. Sultan Shabel's absolutely unscrupulous, or so I hear, and he's said to be smuggling in rifles from
Ethiopia. But the other tribes won't take it lying down."

As usual, it was not the technical problems that proved the
most difficult, but the human ones. In a country where water
was so scarce, the presence of new watering places could
easily trigger a tribal war. Jack conferred with Matthew and
other administrative officers, and it was agreed that the *ballehs* would indeed have to be patrolled, at first by government
Illaloes and later, it was hoped, by some system of local
authorities to be set up by the various tribes concerned.

I missed the life in camp, but I was managing quite well in
Hargeisa. Alone in the bungalow, I found I could deal successfully with any scorpions that put in an appearance in the
evenings, by the simple method of impaling them upon the
spear which had belonged to the thieves of Selahleh. These
scorpions were large but they were not swift. Generally, they
obligingly stood still, and I became an expert scorpion-
spearer.

Domestically, life was quiet but never dull. Mohamed was
determined that I would have fresh milk to drink during my
pregnancy, but the obtaining of milk during the *Jilal* was
almost impossible. He searched the Somali town, and one
day came back carrying an old beer bottle filled with foamy
white liquid.

"This one woman, she my tribe, she say every day she sell
milk for you, small-small. I think I get lucky, for finding she.
Must be you drink it now."

I took a mouthful and immediately spat it out. It tasted
like chalk, saccharine and woodsmoke.

"Mohamed, for heaven's sake what kind of milk is it?"

"You drink it," he said, hurt. "It is good milk."

It was, I learned, a mixture of camel milk, sheep milk and goat milk, and it had been smoked, in the traditional way, for Somalis maintain that if milk is smoked it will not go sour so quickly. For a week I choked it down, with Mohamed standing beside me to make certain I did not cheat and pour it down the sink. Then I decided I could endure it no longer, and to Mohamed's disgust I went on to powdered milk, which he did not believe was real milk at all.

Several girls from Mohamed's tribe used to drop in sometimes in the afternoons and have tea with me, and occasionally, if I could get a lift to the Somali town, I visited their *aqals* there. Dahab was tall and rather heavy-boned. She was quiet and slightly withdrawn, always aware, I think, that her girl friend was more beautiful than she. Fadima was truly beautiful, slim and very vivacious, with dark expressive eyes. Neither girl was married yet. My grasp of Somali was not good, but it was good enough now to enable me to talk with them without the inhibiting presence of an interpreter. Mohamed used to serve tea, then tactfully disappear, although probably to listen from the kitchen.

"Your husband must be very glad you are having a child at last," Fadima said feelingly, one day.

"Yes, of course he is. I'm very glad, too."

"Ah yes," sighed Fadima, "but your husband – he must be really glad. You have been married five years – a long time. If you did not bear him a child soon, he would have had to divorce you."

She glanced at me smilingly. She never hesitated to ask any kind of question, but she did so with innate courtesy, always.

"How old are you?"

Twenty-five, I told her, almost twenty-six. She gasped a little, then turned away so I would not see the amused astonishment in her face.

"Why are you surprised?" I asked.

"Oh –" momentarily, she was covered with confusion, "you see – I had thought you were young."

It was through Fadima that I met Said the Midgan. Fadima, whose father was fairly well-off, possessed a wonderful collection of leather sandals – cheetah skin, camel hide finely tooled with intricate patterns, red leather set with glass gems. Every time I saw her, she wore a different pair. I asked her, finally, where she got them, for I had not seen such sandals in the marketplace. Said the Midgan made them, she told me. She promised to ask him if he would come to my bungalow. He was the best sandal-maker in Hargeisa, but he was somewhat temperamental and worked only when he felt like it. He did not need to work all the time, for his wife was such a good basket-weaver that she could support the family.

Said turned up one day, a short wiry man with an unruly crop of untrimmed hair and a ferocious moustache. All right, he agreed, as though bored by the whole thing, he would make some sandals for me, but he would not promise to have them done by any definite time. Nevertheless, they were completed a week later. They were made out of cheetah skin, yellow and brown, and they fitted perfectly. After that, Said made many pairs of sandals for me, and sometimes he would sit and talk under the *galol* tree in our yard, telling me about the old days when the Midgan people used to hunt with packs of dogs and how skilled the Midgans still were with their bows and poisoned arrows. One afternoon he brought around a Midgan bow and let me examine it.

"Look – I show you –" he snatched up the bow and an arrow, and whirling around, he aimed straight at Mohamed, who was standing some distance away, fortunately not looking in Said's direction. For a second I stood paralysed.

"Said! For God's sake, be careful!"

Zing! The arrow landed in a tree trunk, not more than an inch or so from Mohamed's head, just as Said had known it would. Mohamed leapt and let out a roar of rage and terror, and Said threw the bow down and bent double with laughter.

I made new acquaintances among English people as well as Somalis. I was asked to help out with a group of Somali girls who were learning to make crocheted table-mats and lace edging with the idea that this skill could develop into some sort of cottage industry. I did not know a crochet hook from

a knitting needle, but I agreed to help sort out the girls' work
and iron the finished mats. When the first of these sessions
was over, I began to talk with the Englishwoman who was in
charge of the class. To my surprise, I found that she, too, was
a writer and, like myself, she was extremely interested in the
translation of African poetry and folk-tales and had done this
kind of work herself some years ago when she was living in
Kenya. I had long ago given up the hope of ever talking to
anyone here about writing in general, and even the Europeans who were interested in Somali literature were exceedingly few and far between. I was delighted to have discovered
one other person who shared my interests, and when we had
been talking enthusiastically for an hour or so, I was about to
suggest that she drop over to my bungalow the following day
for a beer and a continuation of the discussion. I recalled in
time, however, that this was not possible. One does not ask
the Governor's wife to drop over for a beer. This kind of
formality, which prevents people from talking with one
another, seemed idiotic to me then, and it still does.

Towards the end of our tour, it became obvious that all the
ballehs would not be finished by the time we were due to go on
leave. Jack was in a quandary – to return or not? The scheme
was going well now, the remaining sites had been selected, the
staff was trained. The rest of the *ballehs* would be essentially a
repetition of those that had been already done. Furthermore,
the first Somali to graduate in engineering had recently
returned from England, and could take over the project. Jack
wanted to see the scheme finished; and yet he was reluctant to
stay when he felt he really was not needed here any more. In
many ways, it would be just as well if the scheme were completed by a Somali engineer. The tribesmen might accept it
better that way. He finally decided not to come back. But even
after the decision had been made, he felt torn two ways.

"Ali can handle the rest of the work just as well as I can – I
know that. But I'd like to have seen the *ballehs* after the
rains. I'd like to know if they're really going to work all
right."

If the *Jilal* went on much longer, or the *Gu* rains failed, we would have to leave the country without ever seeing the *ballehs* filled with water.

"*In sha' Allah*," the Somalis said, and we echoed the words.

Miraculously, the *Gu* rains fell early that year, and we were elated. We waited impatiently in Hargeisa, for the Haud was impassable during the weeks of downpour. Finally, when the rains had dwindled and were almost over, we went out with Hersi and Arabetto to Balleh Gehli, the Balleh of the Camels. It would be our last trip out into the Haud.

And there, among the thorn trees, in the place we knew so well, was the *balleh*. It looked enormous now, like a brown lake in the middle of the desert. Jack examined it minutely, and nodded, speaking almost brusquely in order not to show how pleased he was.

"Seems satisfactory. The wing walls have held, thank God. Not too much scouring, either. It's drained as large an area as I'd hoped, apparently – it's completely filled, anyway. Well, I expected it would be, but it's good to see it. I wonder what the Somalis think of it, now that it's full of water?"

We knew the tribesmen too well now to expect any great manifestations of joy from them. All we hoped was that there would not be too much disagreement over the use of the water, and that their suspicions about the *ballehs* would not arise once more.

At the far side of Balleh Gehli, sitting on the embankment with their rifles beside them, were half a dozen Illaloes. They were here to ensure that the water was used by anyone who needed it, and not sold to the ignorant or fearful by any bold and unscrupulous strongman who might see in the watering places an opportunity for himself.

Around the edges of the *balleh*, the camels milled and drank, led by tribesmen whose faces expressed nothing except the desire to get their beasts watered and back to the encampment. Somali women and girls hitched up their robes around their knees and waded into the *balleh* to fill their water vessels, which they then placed upon their heads and sauntered off with barely a glance in our direction.

Hersi, snorting with angry laughter, came back from a consultation with a group of the tribesmen. He threw up his hands in mock despair.

"I am not knowing what kind of people these bush people. They saying – what is these *Ingrese* doing here, beside our *balleh*?"

It was their *balleh* now. They had assimilated it; it belonged here. Jack grinned.

"It's okay. Tell them we're going now, and we won't be coming back."

As we climbed into the Land-Rover, an old Somali with a face seamed and hardened by the sun of many *Jilals*, passed by with his string of camels.

"*Ma nabad ba?*" he spoke the traditional greeting. "Is it peace?"

"*Wa nabad,*" we replied. "It is peace."

And then we drove away.

When the time came, we packed everything in our bungalow, the few possessions we brought here and the things we had accumulated, the skin of the cheetah that Abdi shot, the magical ostrich egg, the spear that the thieves had dropped, the camel bell that Ahmed Abdillahi gave to us. We had accumulated a great many other things as well, but these took up no space in our luggage, for they were memories – of Sheikh, of the Haud, of Zeilah and Hargeisa, of all the people we had known here.

Outside the small stone bungalow, a flock of birds with golden breastfeathers and electric-blue wings had gathered in the thorn tree. I had never known what their proper name was, but I thought of them as firebirds, for they always screeched distinctly the Somali word for fire – *Dab – dab – dab*. Their raucous voices followed us as we left.

Past the pepper trees waving sedately outside the Club,

down the dusty thorn-fringed road, through the streets swarming with children and camels. Past the strolling Somali girls with their silk headscarves, past women in ragged brown robes, past the hobbling beggars with their outstretched hands. Past the mudbrick tea shops where young men in white shirts and bright robes were having tea and politics in the shade. Finally the airport, and then goodbye. Almost before we knew it, we were flying over the Gulf of Aden, and although we could not quite believe it, Somaliland was already in the past.

And yet the voyage which began when we set out for Somaliland could never really be over, for it had turned out to be so much more than a geographical journey.

Whenever we think of Somaliland, we think of the line of watering places that stretches out across the Haud, and we think of the songs and tales that have been for generations a shelter to nomads on the dry red plateau and on the burnt plains of the coast, for these were the things through which we briefly touched the country and it, too, touched our lives, altering them in some way forever.

Out in the Haud, we felt we had heard the Prophet's camel bell. We had come to know something of these desert people, their pain and their faith, their anger, their ability to endure. The most prophetic note of that bell, however, was one we scarcely heard at all, although the sound was there, if we had had ears for it. In less than ten years, the two Somalilands that had been under British and Italian administration had joined and gained their independence as the Somali Republic. What will happen there now, no one knows, but whatever course they take will not be an easy one in a land that has so few resources except human ones.

The best we can wish them, and the most difficult, is expressed in their own words of farewell.

Nabad gelyo – May you enter peace.

THE END

Glossary of Somali Words

A S YET there is no official orthography for the Somali language. I have therefore used an anglicized version of Somali words, which will give the reader some idea of pronunciation. I have also, in this glossary, included in brackets the spellings recommended in 1961 by the Linguistic Committee of the Somali Ministry of Education, under the chairmanship of Musa Haji Ismail Galaal.

abor: mound-building termite (*aboor*)
amiin: Amen (*amiin*)
aul: Soemmering's gazelle (*cawl*)

balleh: natural pond or manmade excavation for holding rainwater (*balli*)
belwo: short lyric poem (*balwo*)
balanballis: butterfly or moth (*ballanbaallis*)
biyu: water (*biyo*)
beris: rice (*bariis*)

dadabgal: night spent together by an engaged couple (*dadabgal*)
dero: Speke's gazelle (*deero*)

dibad: dowry (*dhibaad*)
Dhair: the autumn rains (*Dayr*)
dab: fire (*dab*)

faal: a way of telling the future (*faal*)

Guban: the coastal plain; lit. "burnt" (*Guban*)
Gu: the spring rains (*Gu*)
gabei: long narrative poem (*gabay*)
gerenuk: Waller's gazelle (*garanuug*)
gabbati: token payment made to bride's parents (*gabbaati*)
galol: type of acacia tree (*galool*)
ghelow: a night bird (*galow*)

gedhamar: an aromatic herb (*geedchamar*)

gorayo: ostrich (*gorayo*)

harimaad: cheetah (*harimacad*)

helleyoy: refrain used with songs (*helleyoy*)

In sha' Allah: if God wills it (*In shaa' Alla*)

is ka warran: give news of yourself (*is ka warran*)

Jilal: the winter drought (*Jiilaal*)

jes: one family travelling alone (*jees*)

jinna: species of ant (*jinac*)

kharif: the summer monsoon. An Arabic word

khat: a leaf with narcotic properties (*qaad*)

Kitab: the Book, i.e. the Qoran (*Kitaab*)

libahh: lion (*libaach*)

lunghi: a length of cloth used as a man's robe. An East Indian word

magala: town (*magalo*)

miskiin: destitute (*miskiin*)

marooro: a plant (*marooro*)

mas: snake (*mas*)

meher: percentage of man's estate made over to his wife (*meher*)

ma nabad ba?: is it peace? – Somali greeting (*ma nabad baa*)

madow: black (*madow*)

Nasa Hablod: two hills near Hargeisa; lit. "The girl's breasts" (*Nasso Hablood*)

nabad gelyo: may you enter peace – Somali farewell (*nabad gelyo*)

nabad diino: the peace of faith – response to "nabad gelyo" (*nabad diino*)

nin: man (*nin*)

odei: old man, elder (*oday*)

Qadi: Muslim judge (*qaaddi*)

qaraami: a love poem; lit. "passionate" (*qaraami*)

rer: Somali tribal unit; section of a tribe (*reer*)

rob: rain (*roob*)

shabel: leopard (*shabeel*)

saymo: a dangerous situation (*saymo*)

shir: a meeting (*shir*)

shimbir: bird (*shimbir*)

shaitan: devil (*shaydaan*)

tusbahh: Muslim prayer beads (*tusbach*)

torri: a knife or dagger (*toorri*)

tug: a river-bed (*tog*)

wadda: road (*waddo*)

Wallahi: by God (*Wallaahi*)

wadaad: a man of religion, a holy man (*wadaad*)

wahharawallis: a type of flower (*wacharawaalis*)

warya: hey! (*waariya* or *waarya*)

wein: big (*weyn*)

warabe: hyena (*waraabe*)

wa fulley: he is a coward (*waa fulle*)

yarad: bride-price (*yarad*)

yerki: a small boy (*yarkii*)

Acknowledgements

I AM VERY GRATEFUL TO Dr. B.W. Andrzejewski, of the London School of Oriental and African Studies, for the information and advice he has given me about the spelling of Somali words.

I should also like to thank Messrs. Martin Secker & Warburg, Ltd., for their permission to use four lines from "The Gates of Damascus," by James Elroy Flecker, as the motto.

M.L.

Bibliography

Sir Richard Burton, *First Footsteps in East Africa*, J.M. Dent, London, 1856.

R.D. Drake-Brockman, *British Somaliland*, Hurst & Blackett, 1912.

J.A. Hunt, *A General Survey of the Somaliland Protectorate, 1944–50*, H.M. Stationers.

Douglas Jardine, *The Mad Mullah of Somaliland*, Herbert Jenkins, London, 1923.

J.W.C. Kirk, *A Grammar of the Somali Language*, Cambridge, 1905.

M. Laurence, *A Tree For Poverty, Somali poetry and prose*, Eagle Press, Nairobi, 1954.

R.G. Mares, "Animal Husbandry in Somaliland," *British Veterinary Journal*, Vol. 110, Nos. 10 and 11.

O. Mannoni, *Prospero and Caliban: A Study of the Psychology of Colonisation*, Methuen, 1956.

Afterword

. . . For the first time I was myself a stranger in a strange land, and was sometimes given hostile words and was also given, once, food and shelter in a time of actual need, by tribesmen who had little enough for themselves – *Thou shalt not oppress a stranger, for ye know the heart of a stranger, seeing ye were strangers in the land of Egypt.*

When Margaret Laurence reminisced with me about her African years, it was almost always about the books that had issued from them and her admiration for African people and their ancient tribal cultures. There were snatches of life memories – sometimes the early years of her children Jocelyn and David would surface, or the stint of baby-sitting she willingly did for a British officer in Ghana, not because she was fond of him, but because he had a complete set of the writings of Sir Richard Burton which she read avidly, or, most surprisingly, the fact that, while in Ghana, she typed for Barbara Ward the manuscript of her landmark work on African nations, *Faith and Freedom*. Often we talked of the African writers she admired so much, particularly the Nigerians, Chinua Achebe and Wole Soyinka, to whom, with others, she had paid tribute in *Long Drums and Cannons*. Achebe she met only three times, the last time in 1984 when she was already deliberating on the memoirs she would write and when he was struggling to finish his novel, *Anthills of the*

Savannah. I was present at all of their meetings and watched, deeply moved, as an empathetic, brotherly-sisterly bonding sprang up from their first moments together.

Two years in Somaliland and five in Ghana had been a powerful catalyst to Margaret's talent, issuing in *A Tree for Poverty*, her translation of Somali folk-tales and poems, the novel, *This Side Jordan*, the stories collected in *The Tomorrow-Tamer*, and culminating in *The Prophet's Camel Bell*, the book in which she closed the door on her African years, her apprentice years, and prepared the way for Manawaka. Many times she said that, once in Canada again, she knew beyond doubt that literature's themes were universal and that now she had to write of her own place and her own people. Ten years away from Somaliland she wrote *The Prophet's Camel Bell*, reflecting on her diaries and reconstructing her younger self from their notations and her memories. The book was "the most difficult thing I ever wrote," she said. Fiction she always considered her true *métier*. The first draft of *The Stone Angel* was already complete. Hagar in her wilderness had been growing in Margaret's mind and imagination for years, ever since her desert encounter with the Somali woman and her dying child. Then Hagar found her voice and began to tell her story. "It all came out complete. I did scarcely any revision."

She had found her themes in Africa, though – exile, the journey towards wholeness, personhood, knowing "the heart of a stranger," the unique dignity of every individual, the drive to freedom, faith, and the recognition of grace. It was during one of our frequent telephone conversations, she at "the Shack" on the Otonabee River near Peterborough, I in Toronto, that she lighted upon "Heart of a Stranger" as the title of her essay collection. We were both sorting through our heads for possibilities and that one, the absolutely right one, surfaced – to our enduring delight. Margaret honed her techniques in the African works, too. Undoubtedly her ear for tones of speech and shades of meaning was naturally acute, but it was certainly sharpened by her hours of listening to the Somalis tell their stories at their campfires and then working with the translations of her interpreter. She was fond of saying that she wrote *This Side Jordan* in episodes, then spread them all out on the dining-room table and thought, "Now what'll I do?" What she did was to achieve a compelling novel, playing many levels of variation on the themes of love and loss, exile, despair, and the finding of faith as she juxtaposed her African characters moving pell-mell into a new day and beset by its manifold terrors, and the anxious, exiled British, former masters and now, speedily, deposed and homeless, strangers to both Africa and England. At the same time she bore witness to her love of Ghana, the deep understanding she had developed for its past and its people, and the hope she shared with them for its future. The same themes permeate the nine *Tomorrow-Tamer* stories, written between 1954 and 1962 and first published separately, though begun while she was still in Ghana.

The Prophet's Camel Bell is Margaret's corresponding tribute to the Somalis and her Somaliland years, 1950–1952. Written in 1962 at a time of great stress, when she knew once and for all time that to be a committed writer was her fate, both joy and doom, and when she and her husband Jack were forcing themselves to realize that their marriage was shattering, the book is also a tribute to their early, happy days of adventuring together. She had been allowed to accompany Jack on his dam-building assignment in Somaliland only because he had described her to the reluctant officials as "an accomplished woodswoman." "Canadian peoples different," as the Somalis often said.

Librarians may well catalogue *The Prophet's Camel Bell* as travel literature; true, it is the story of a journey into a desert land whose nomadic people's lives had been unchanging since biblical times and whose Mohammedan faith was to them "as necessary as life, as inevitable as death." They looked up at the crescent moon in the sky and "knew that the Word had been made visible." But it is also a journey into awareness and understanding of the Somalis across a cultural chasm that might well, and excusably, have seemed unbridgeable. Most of all, though, it is the record of the maturing, the coming-of-age of Margaret Laurence herself. As she marvelled at the acceptance and endurance of the Somalis, she learned those qualities for herself.

Margaret had always been impatiently busy – she learned calm and quiet from Somaliland and its people. She watched them helplessly dying of thirst and she learned humility from the recognition that she and her medical kit could do little or nothing for them. Looking back on her diaries she recognized as "bosh" her early, facile statements about the easiness of becoming "popular" with the Somalis. Their story-telling inspired the story-teller in her, and she added immeasurably to the care, patience, and discipline that every professional writer must have as she listened and wondered at the retelling and repolishing of age-old stories around the campfires.

As she looked back on her younger self and wrote, she acknowledged and assimilated her own life's experiences. She had already known much love and much loss – the early deaths of her parents and Grandfather Simpson, whom she had fought and resented, but who "proclaimed himself in her veins." She had deeply loved her stepmother, always "mother" to her, her brother Robert, her husband Jack, and the enduring friends of her girlhood. She had known deep and continuing joy in her children and her work.

The *persona* who developed through the pages of *The Prophet's Camel Bell* is the same Margaret Laurence who became the most beloved woman in Canada. The qualities are all there. When you turn the last page you are not alone. Margaret is with you, saying "yes" to life, laughing, loving, kind, understanding and, always, with enduring faith and hope.

BY MARGARET LAURENCE

AUTOBIOGRAPHY
The Prophet's Camel Bell (1963)
Dance on the Earth (1989)

ESSAYS
Long Drums and Cannons:
Nigerian Dramatists and Novelists 1952–1966 (1968)
Heart of a Stranger (1976)

FICTION
This Side Jordan (1960)
The Tomorrow-Tamer (1963)
The Stone Angel (1964)
A Jest of God (1966)
The Fire-Dwellers (1969)
A Bird in the House (1970)
The Diviners (1974)

FICTION FOR YOUNG ADULTS
Jason's Quest (1970)
Six Darn Cows (1979)
The Olden Days Coat (1979)
The Christmas Birthday Story (1980)